I0613410

David Henry Montgomery

Heroic Ballads with Poems of War and Patriotism

David Henry Montgomery

Heroic Ballads with Poems of War and Patriotism

ISBN/EAN: 9783744771092

Printed in Europe, USA, Canada, Australia, Japan

Cover: Foto ©Andreas Hilbeck / pixelio.de

More available books at **www.hansebooks.com**

HEROIC BALLADS

WITH

OEMS OF WAR AND PATRIOTISM

EDITED WITH NOTES

BY

D. H. M&

————

BOSTON, U.S.A.:

PUBLISHED BY GINN & COMPANY.

1890.

Entered, according to Act of Congress, in the year 1890, by

GINN & COMPANY,

in the Office of the Librarian of Congress, at Washington.

———————

ALL RIGHTS RESERVED.

TYPOGRAPHY BY J. S. CUSHING & CO., BOSTON, U.S.A.

PRESSWORK BY GINN & CO., BOSTON, U.S.A.

PREFATORY NOTE.

THE following selections are given, in all but a very few instances, without abridgment. Where omissions have been made, it has been done with the view of better adapting the work to school use.

It is believed that all notes required for the full understanding of the poems have been subjoined.

D. H. M.

TABLE OF CONTENTS.

HEROIC BALLADS.

——⟶⚬⟨⚬⟩⚬⟵——

HORATIUS.

A Lay made about the Year of the City CCCLX.[1]

I.

Lars Porsena[2] of Clusium
  By the Nine Gods[3] he swore
That the great house of Tarquin[4]
  Should suffer wrong no more.
By the Nine Gods he swore it,
  And named a trysting[5] day,

[1] About three hundred and sixty years after the founding of Rome, or 393 B.C. The scene of the lay is chiefly in Etruria and in Rome.

[2] **Lars Porsena** (Por-sē'na or Por'se-na) : *Lars* was an Etruscan title of honor and office corresponding to *chief* or *lord*. The Etruscans were an ancient people occupying Etruria, a territory in Italy north and west of Rome, the river Tiber being the eastern and southern boundary. Lars Porsena was the most powerful chief or king of the twelve Etruscan tribes. His capital was Clu'si-um, about ninety miles northwest of Rome.

[3] **Nine Gods**: little is known respecting the Etruscan deities. The Romans supposed them to have nine chief gods, who, like Jupiter, had the power of hurling thunderbolts.

[4] **Tarquin**: Tarquin the Proud was the last king of Rome, 505 B.C. He robbed the people of their liberty, and his son, Sextus, committed an outrage which caused a revolution by which the monarchy was overthrown and Tarquin banished. Tarquin applied to Lars Porsena for aid, and that chief raised an army to compel the Romans to reinstate the exiled despot.

[5] **Trysting day** (trȳst'ing) : an appointed day of meeting; here, a day agreed on for the meeting of troops.

And bade his messengers ride forth,
East and west and south and north,
  To summon his array.[1]

II.

East and west and south and north
  The messengers ride fast,
And tower and town and cottage
  Have heard the trumpet's blast.
Shame on the false Etruscan [2]
  Who lingers in his home
When Porsena of Clusium
  Is on the march for Rome.

III.

The horsemen and the footmen
  Are pouring in amain,[3]
From many a stately market-place;
  From many a fruitful plain;
From many a lonely hamlet,
  Which, hid by beech and pine,
Like an eagle's nest, hangs on the crest
  Of purple Apennine;

IV.

From lordly Volaterræ,[4]
  Where scowls the far-famed hold

---

[1] **Array**: the whole body of fighting-men bound to follow a chief.
[2] **Etruscan**: an inhabitant of Etruria.   [3] **Amain**: at full speed.
[4] **Volater'ræ**: a famous city of Etruria, standing on a commanding height. Its citadel, or "hold," was built, like its walls, of massive uncemented stones.

Piled by the hands of giants
   For godlike kings of old;
From sea-girt Populonia,[1]
   Whose sentinels descry
Sardinia's snowy mountain-tops
   Fringing the southern sky;

V.

From the proud mart of Pisæ,[1]
   Queen of the western waves,
Where ride Massilia's triremes [2]
   Heavy with fair-haired slaves;
From where sweet Clanis [3] **wanders**
   Through corn and vines and flowers;
From where Cortona [1] lifts to heaven
   Her diadem **of towers.**

VI.

Tall are the oaks whose acorns
   Drop in dark Auser's [4] rill;
Fat are the stags that champ [5] the boughs
   Of the Ciminian [6] hill;
Beyond **all streams** Clitumnus [7]
   Is to the herdsman dear;

---

[1] **Populo'nia, Pi'sæ, Corto'na** : cities of Etruria.

[2] **Massil'ia** : a Greek colony in Gaul, the modern Marseille, **France.** The tri'remes were vessels propelled by three banks of oars on each side, one **bank or row above the** other. The "fair-haired slaves" were natives of Gaul obtained from the interior of the country.

[3] **Clăn'is** : a river of Etruria emptying into the Tiber.

[4] **Au'ser** : a stream of Northern Etruria.   [5] **Champ** : chew.

[6] **Cimin'ian hill** : a hill in Etruria.

[7] **Clitum'nus** : a river of Umbria, a district joining Etruria on the east. The meadows of the **river** were famous for their milk-white herds of cattle.

Best of all pools the fowler loves
  The great Volsinian mere.[1]

VII.

But now no stroke of woodman
  Is heard by Auser's rill;
No hunter tracks the stag's green path
  Up the Ciminian hill;
Unwatched along Clitumnus
  Grazes the milk-white steer;
Unharmed the water fowl may dip
  In the Volsinian mere.

VIII.

The harvests of Arretium,[2]
  This year, old men shall reap,
This year, young boys in Umbro[3]
  Shall plunge the struggling sheep;
And in the vats of Luna,[2]
  This year, the must[4] shall foam
Round the white feet of laughing girls
  Whose sires have marched to Rome.

IX.

There be thirty chosen prophets,[5]
  The wisest of the land,

---

[1] **Volsinian mere**: a lake or sheet of stagnant water in Etruria.

[2] **Arre'ti-um** and **Lu'na**: cities of Etruria.

[3] **Um'bro**: probably the river of that name in Etruria; as the men would all be engaged in the war against Rome, the boys would be left to wash the sheep at shearing time.

[4] **Must**: the juice of grapes for wine. The grapes are thrown into a vat, and the juice pressed out by men or girls treading them with bare feet.

[5] **Prophets**: these so-called " prophets " were sorcerers, who undertook

Who alway by Lars Porsena
  Both morn and evening stand:
Evening and morn the Thirty
  Have turned the verses [1] o'er,
Traced from the right on linen white [2]
  By mighty seers of yore.

X.

And with one voice the Thirty
  Have their glad answer given;
"Go forth, go forth, Lars Porsena;
  Go forth, beloved of Heaven;
Go, and return in glory
  To Clusium's royal dome;
And hang round Nurscia's [3] altars
  The golden shields of Rome."

XI.

And now hath every city
  Sent up her tale [4] of men;
The foot are fourscore thousand,
  The horse are thousands ten.
Before the gates of Sutrium [5]
  Is met the great array.

to discover the will of the gods by examining the entrails of victims offered in sacrifice, by the flight of birds, and other signs.

[1] **Verses**: these were probably similar to those of the famous Sibylline books which a sibyl or prophetess sold to Tarquin, king of Rome, and which professed to foretell the future of the nation. They were consulted in all emergencies concerning the city. So Lars Porsena now consults his books of prophecy, to learn whether his expedition will prove successful.

[2] The Etruscans wrote from right to left.

[3] **Nur'scia**: perhaps the guardian deity of Clusium.

[4] **Tale**: number or quota.　　　　[5] Su'trium: a town of Etruria.

A proud man was Lars Porsena
   Upon the trysting day.

XII.

For all the Etruscan armies
   Were ranged beneath his eye,
And many a banished Roman,
   And many a stout ally;
And with a mighty following
   To join the muster came
The Tusculan Mamilius,[1]
   Prince of the Latian name.[2]

XIII.

But by the yellow Tiber
   Was tumult and affright:
From all the spacious champaign[3]
   To Rome men took their flight.
A mile around the city,
   The throng stopped up the ways;
A fearful sight it was to see
   Through two long nights and days.

XIV.

For droves of mules and asses
   Laden with skins[4] of wine,
And endless flocks of goats and sheep,
   And endless herds of kine,

---

[1] Mamil'ius: of Tusculum, a town of La'tium, a country south of Rome. Mamilius was son-in-law to Tarquin, the banished king.

[2] Latian: relating to Latium, an ancient district of Italy; Latin.

[3] Champaign: a flat, open country; here, the great plain around Rome.

[4] Skins of wine: bags made of goat or other skins, for carrying or holding wine.

And endless trains of wagons
    That creaked beneath the weight
Of corn-sacks and of household goods,
    Choked every roaring **gate**.[1]

XV.

Now, from the rock Tarpeian,[2]
    Could the wan burghers[3] spy
The line of blazing villages
    Red in the midnight sky.
The Fathers of the City,[4]
    They sat all night and day,
For every hour some horseman came
    With tidings of dismay.

XVI.

To eastward and to westward
    Have spread the Tuscan **bands**;[5]
Nor house, **nor** fence, nor **dovecot**
    In Crustumerium[6] stands.
Verbenna[7] **down** to Ostia[8]
    Hath wasted all the plain;
Astur[9] hath stormed Janiculum,[10]
    And the stout guards **are** slain.

[1] **Gate**: **Rome was** protected by walls and gates.
[2] **Rock Tarpe'ian**: a high, precipitous rock in Rome; criminals were frequently thrown from it.   [3] **Burghers**: citizens.
[4] **Fathers of the City**: the senators or governing body of the city.
[5] **Tuscan bands**: Tuscan is another name for Etruscan or Etrurian.
[6] **Crustume'rium**: a town of the Sabine country not far from Rome, and belonging to it.
[7] **Verben'na**: one of the Etruscan leaders under Lars Porsena.
[8] **Os'tia**: the port of Rome, at the mouth of the Tiber.
[9] **As'tur**: an Etruscan leader.
[10] **Janic'ulum**: a fortified hill west of Rome, beyond the Tiber. It was

XVII.

I wis,[1] in all the Senate,
    There was no heart so bold,
But sore it ached, and fast it beat,
    When that ill news was told.
Forthwith up rose the Consul,[2]
    Up rose the Fathers all;
In haste they girded up their gowns,[3]
    And hied[4] them to the wall.

XVIII.

They held a council standing
    Before the River-Gate;
Short time was there, ye well may guess,
    For musing or debate.
Out spake the Consul roundly:
    "The bridge must straight go down;
For, since Janiculum is lost,
    Nought else can save the town."

XIX.

Just then a scout came flying,
    All wild with haste and fear:
"To arms! to arms! Sir Consul:[5]
    Lars Porsena is here."

connected with the city by the only bridge then existing on the river,—a wooden structure built on piles (the Pons Sublicius). If the enemy succeeded in getting possession of the bridge, they would probably soon effect an entrance into Rome. [1] **I wis**: an adverb, meaning *certainly*.

[2] **Consul**: one of the two chief magistrates or governors of Rome who took the place of the expelled kings.

[3] **Gowns**: the toga or gown, a loose, shawl-like garment, was the national dress of the Romans.

[4] **Hied**: hastened. [5] **Sir Consul**: Sir, a title of respect.

On the low hills to westward
  The Consul fixed his eye,
And saw the swarthy storm of dust
  Rise fast along the sky.

XX.

And nearer fast and nearer
  Doth the red whirlwind come;
And louder still and still more loud,
From underneath that rolling cloud,
Is heard the trumpet's war-note proud,
  The trampling and the hum.
And plainly and more plainly
  Now through the gloom appears,
Far to left and far to right,
In broken gleams of dark-blue light,
The long array of helmets bright,
  The long array of spears.

XXI.

And plainly and more plainly,
  Above that glimmering line,
Now might ye see the banners
  Of twelve fair cities [1] shine;
But the banner of proud Clusium
  Was highest of them all,
The terror of the Umbrian,[2]
  The terror of the Gaul.[3]

---

[1] Twelve fair cities: the twelve chief cities of Etruria.
[2] Umbrian: the people of Umbria east of Etruria.
[3] Gaul: a barbarous people that had conquered part of Northern Italy.

XXII.

And plainly and more plainly
　　Now might the burghers know,
By port[1] and vest,[2] by horse and crest,[3]
　　Each warlike Lucumo.[4]
There Cilnius[5] of Arretium
　　On his fleet roan was seen ;
And Astur[6] of the fourfold shield,[7]
Girt with the brand[8] none else may wield,
Tolumnius[9] with the belt of gold,
And dark Verbenna from the hold
　　By reedy Thrasymene.[10]

XXIII.

Fast by the royal standard,
　　O'erlooking all the war,
Lars Porsena of Clusium
　　Sat in his ivory car.[11]
By the right wheel rode Mamilius,
　　Prince of the Latian name ;
And by the left false Sextus,[12]
　　That wrought the deed of shame.

[1] **Port** : mien or bearing.　　　[2] **Vest** : an outer garment or vestment.
[3] **Crest** : a plume or ornament surmounting a helmet.
[4] **Lŭ'cumo** : the Etruscan name for a ruler or chief.
[5] **Cil'nius.**
[6] **As'tur** : who had stormed Janiculum ; see p. 7.
[7] **Fourfold shield** : a shield made of hide of four thicknesses.
[8] **Brand** a sword.　　　　　　　　　　　　[9] **Tolum'nius.**
[10] **Thrasyme'ne** : but here pronounced Thras-i-meen'; it is a lake of Etruria ; on its shores there was the fortification or stronghold of the chief Verbenna.
[11] **Ivory car** : a war-chariot ornamented with ivory ; it was usually drawn by four horses abreast.
[12] **Sextus** : the son of Tarquin the Proud ; see note 3, p. 1. He caused

XXIV.

But when the face of Sextus
  Was seen among the foes,
A yell that rent the firmament
  From all the town arose.
On the house-tops was no woman
  But spat towards him and hissed,
No child but screamed out curses,
  And shook its little fist.

XXV.

But the Consul's brow was sad,
  And the Consul's speech was low,
And darkly looked he at the wall,
  And darkly at the foe.

the death of Lucrece, a noble Roman matron. Macaulay thus refers to
Sextus in his "Battle of Lake Regillus" : —

  "Their leader was false Sextus,
      That wrought the deed of shame ;
    With restless pace and haggard face
        To his last field he came.
    Men said he had strange visions,
        Which none beside might see ;
  And that strange sounds were in his ears
      Which none might hear but he.
    A woman fair and stately,
        But pale as are the dead,
    Oft through the watches of the night
        Sat spinning by his bed.
    And as she plied the distaff,
        In a sweet voice and low,
    She sang of great old houses,
        And fights fought long ago.
    So spun she, and so sang she,
        Until the east was gray,
    Then pointed to her bleeding heart,
        And shrieked, and fled away."

        — " Battle of Lake Regillus," XII. (*Lays of Ancient Rome*).

" Their van [1] will be upon us
    Before the bridge goes down ;
And if they once may win the bridge,
    What hope to save the town ? "

XXVI.

Then out spake brave Horatius,
    The Captain of the Gate : [2]
" To every **man** upon this earth
    Death cometh soon or late.
And how can man die better
    Than facing fearful odds,
For the ashes of his fathers,
    And the temples of his Gods,

XXVII.

" And for the tender mother
    Who dandled him to rest,
And for the wife who nurses
    His baby at her breast,
And for the holy maidens [3]
    Who feed the eternal flame,
To save them from false Sextus
    That wrought the deed of shame ?

---

[1] **Van** : the advance **guard** of an army.

[2] **The Captain of the Gate** : Horatius had **charge** of the city gate at the entrance of the bridge leading to Janiculum.

[3] **The holy maidens**. six maiden priestesses of Vesta, the goddess of the hearth and home. On her **altar**, representing **not** only the domestic hearth, **but also the city** of Rome **as** the common home, a perpetual fire — the **emblem of** love and of patriotism — was kept burning. It **was** the duty **of these** " maidens " to feed and watch this sacred fire.

XXVIII.

" Hew down the bridge, Sir Consul,
  With all the speed ye may ;
I, with two more to help me,
  Will hold the foe in play.[1]
In yon strait [2] path a thousand
  May well be stopped by three.
Now who will stand on either hand,
  And keep the bridge with me ? "

XXIX.

Then out spake Spurius Lartius ; [3]
  A Ramnian [4] proud was he :
" Lo, I will stand at thy right hand,
  And keep the bridge with thee."
And out spake strong Herminius ; [5]
  Of Titian [6] blood was he :
" I will abide on thy left side,
  And keep the bridge with thee."

XXX.

" Horatius," quoth [7] the Consul,
  " As thou sayest, so let it be."
And straight against that great array
  Forth went the dauntless Three.

---

[1] **Hold the foe in play** : keep them occupied.

[2] **Strait** : narrow.   [3] Spu'rius Lar'tius.

[4] **Ramnian** : one of the three ancient patrician or ruling classes of Rome dating from its foundation by Romulus.

[5] Hermin'ius.

[6] **Titian** : one of the three ancient tribes of which the Ramnian was the first.   [7] **Quoth** : said.

For Romans in Rome's quarrel
  Spared neither land nor gold,
Nor son nor wife, nor limb nor life,
  In the brave days of old.

XXXI.

Then none was for a party;
  Then all were for the state;
Then the great man helped the poor,
  And the poor man loved the great:
Then lands were fairly portioned;[1]
  Then spoils were fairly sold:[1]
The Romans were like brothers
  In the brave days of old.

XXXII.

Now Roman is to Roman
  More hateful than a foe,
And the Tribunes[2] beard the high,
  And the Fathers[3] grind the low.
As we wax hot in faction,[4]
  In battle we wax cold:
Wherefore men fight not as they fought
  In the brave days of old.

XXXIII.

Now while the Three were tightening
  Their harness[5] on their backs,

---

[1] **Lands, spoils**: the lands and plunder taken in war.
[2] **Tribunes**: officers appointed to protect the interests of the common people of Rome. They could veto any measure they thought harmful.
[3] **Fathers**: see note 4, p. 7.
[4] **Faction**: here, political dissension or discord.   [5] **Harness**: armor.

The Consul was the foremost man
  To take in hand an axe :
And Fathers mixed with Commons,[1]
  Seized hatchet, bar, and crow,[2]
And smote upon the planks above,
  And loosed the props[3] below.

XXXIV.

Meanwhile the Tuscan army,
  Right glorious to behold,
Came flashing back the noonday light,
Rank behind rank, like surges bright
  Of a broad sea of gold.
Four hundred trumpets sounded
  A peal of warlike glee,
As that great host, with measured tread,
And spears advanced, and ensigns[4] spread,
Rolled slowly towards the bridge's head,
  Where stood the dauntless Three.

XXXV.

The Three stood calm and silent,
  And looked upon the foes,
And a great shout of laughter
  From all the vanguard[5] rose :
And forth three chiefs came spurring
  Before that deep array ;

---

[1] **Commons** : the common people. [2] **Crow** : crowbar.
[3] **Props** : it was a wooden bridge. See note 10, " Janiculum," p. 7.
[4] **Ensigns** : banners.   [5] **Vanguard** : the advance guard.

To earth they sprang, their swords they drew
And lifted high their shields, and flew
　　To win the narrow way;

XXXVI.

Aunus[1] from green Tifernum,[2]
　　Lord of the Hill of Vines;
And Seius,[3] whose eight hundred slaves
　　Sicken in Ilva's[4] mines;
And Picus,[5] long to Clusium
　　Vassal[6] in peace and war,
Who led to fight his Umbrian powers
From that gray crag where, girt with towers,
The fortress of Nequinum[7] lowers[8]
　　O'er the pale waves of Nar.[9]

XXXVII.

Stout Lartius hurled down Aunus
　　Into the stream beneath:
Herminius struck at Seius,
　　And clove him to the teeth:
At Picus brave Horatius
　　Darted one fiery thrust;
And the proud Umbrian's gilded arms
　　Clashed in the bloody dust.

---

[1] Au'nus.
[2] Tifer'num: a town of Umbria, on the Tiber.　　[3] Seius (Se'yus).
[4] Il'va: an island (the modern Elba) off the coast of Etruria, once noted for its iron mines.　　[5] Pi'cus.
[6] Vassal: a dependent.　　[7] Nequi'num: a town of Umbria.
[8] Lowers: having a gloomy or threatening look.
[9] Nar: a river of Umbria.

XXXVIII.

Then Ocnus[1] of Falerii[2]
   Rushed on the Roman Three;
And Lausulus[3] of Urgo,[4]
   The Rover[5] of the sea;
And Aruns[6] of Volsinium,[7]
   Who slew the great wild boar,
The great wild boar that had his den
Amidst the reeds of Cosa's[8] fen,[9]
And wasted fields, and slaughtered men,
   Along Albinia's shore.[10]

XXXIX.

Herminius smote down Aruns:
   Lartius laid Ocnus low:
Right to the heart of Lausulus
   Horatius sent a blow.
"Lie there," he cried, "fell[11] pirate:
   No more, aghast and pale,
From Ostia's walls the crowd shall mark
The track of thy destroying bark.
No more Campania's[12] hinds[13] shall fly
To woods and caverns when they spy
   Thy thrice accursed sail."

[1] Oc′nus.   [2] Fa-le′ri-i : a town of Etruria.
[3] Lausu′lus.   [4] Ur′go: an island off the coast of Etruria.
[5] Rover : here used in the sense of pirate and kidnapper.
[6] A′runs.   [7] Volsin′ium : a city of Etruria.
[8] Co′sa: a town of Etruria.   [9] Fen : a marsh.
[10] Albi′nia: a river of Etruria.   [11] Fell: cruel.
[12] Campa′nia : a very fertile district of Italy, south of Rome, having Naples as its chief port.
[13] Hinds : farm-laborers, peasants.

XL.

But now no sound of laughter
  Was heard among the foes.
A wild and wrathful clamor
  From all the vanguard rose.
Six spears' length from the entrance
  Halted that deep array,
And for a space no man came forth
  To win the narrow way.

XLI.

But hark! the cry is Astur:
  And lo! the ranks divide;
And the great Lord of Luna
  Comes with his stately stride.
Upon his ample shoulders
  Clangs loud the fourfold shield,
And in his hand he shakes the brand
  Which none but he can wield.

XLII.

He smiled on those bold Romans
  A smile serene and high;
He eyed the flinching Tuscans,
  And scorn was in his eye.
Quoth he, "The she-wolf's litter[1]
  Stand savagely at bay:
But will ye dare to follow,
  If Astur clears the way?"

----

[1] The she-wolf's litter: the Romans. The legend was that Romulus and Remus, founders of the Roman people, were suckled by a she-wolf.

XLIII.

Then, whirling up his broadsword
  With both hands to the height,
He rushed against Horatius,
  And smote with all his might.
With shield and blade Horatius
  Right deftly[1] turned the blow.
The blow, though turned, came yet too nigh;
It missed his helm,[2] but gashed his thigh:
The Tuscans raised a joyful cry
  To see the red blood flow.

XLIV.

He reeled, and on Herminius
  He leaned one breathing-space;
Then, like a wild cat mad with wounds,
  Sprang right at Astur's face.
Through teeth, and skull, and helmet
  So fierce a thrust he sped,
The good sword stood a hand-breadth out
  Behind the Tuscan's head.

XLV.

And the great Lord of Luna
  Fell at that deadly stroke
As falls on Mount Alvernus[3]
  A thunder-smitten oak.
Far o'er the crashing forest

---

[1] **Deftly**: dexterously.

[2] **Helm**: helmet (here put for head).

[3] **Mount Alver'nus**: probably a poetic form of the name of some mountain near Rome.

The giant arms lie spread ;
And the pale augurs,[1] muttering low,
Gaze on the blasted head.

XLVI.

On Astur's throat Horatius
Right firmly pressed his heel,
And thrice and four times tugged amain [2]
Ere he wrenched out the steel.
" And see," he cried, " the welcome,
Fair guests, that waits you here !
What noble Lucumo comes next
To taste our Roman cheer?"

XLVII..

But at this haughty challenge
A sullen murmur ran,
Mingled of wrath, and shame, and dread,
Along that glittering van.
There lacked not men of prowess,
Nor men of lordly race ;
For all Etruria's noblest
Were round the fatal place.

XLVIII.

But all Etruria's noblest
Felt their hearts sink to see
On the earth the bloody corpses,
In the path the dauntless Three :

[1] Augurs . a class of priests whose duty it was to foretell the future
from various signs — especially from the flight of birds; these were
Etrurian augurs who had probably predicted the success of the expedition
against Rome.   [2] Amain · violently, with all his might.

And, from the ghastly entrance
  Where those bold Romans stood,
All shrank, like boys who unaware,
Ranging the woods to start a hare,
Come to the mouth of the dark lair
Where, growling low, a fierce old bear
  Lies amidst bones and blood.

XLIX.

Was none who would be foremost
  To lead such dire attack :
But those behind cried " Forward ! "
  And those before cried " Back ! "
And backward now and forward
  Wavers the deep array ;
And on the tossing sea of steel,
To and fro the standards [1] reel ;
And the victorious trumpet-peal
  Dies fitfully [2] away.

L.

Yet one man for one moment
  Stood out before the crowd ;
Well known was he to all the Three,
  And they gave him greeting loud,
" Now welcome, welcome, Sextus !
  Now welcome to thy home !
Why dost thou stay, and turn away ?
Here lies the road to Rome."

---

[1] **Standards :** each division of the army had its banner or some figure, as
a horse, eagle, etc., surmounting a tall staff, to designate it ; these were
called standards, and it was a matter of military honor to keep them erect
and not let them fall into the hands of the enemy.   [2] **Fitfully :** unsteadily.

LI.

Thrice looked he at the city;
  Thrice looked he at the dead;
And thrice came on in fury,
  And thrice turned back in dread:
And, white with fear and hatred,
  Scowled at the narrow way
Where, wallowing in a pool of blood,
  The bravest Tuscans lay.

LII.

But meanwhile axe and lever
  Have manfully been plied;
And now the bridge hangs tottering
  Above the boiling tide.
"Come back, come back, Horatius!"
  Loud cried the Fathers all.
"Back, Lartius! back, Herminius!
  Back, ere the ruin fall!"

LIII.

Back darted Spurius Lartius;
  Herminius darted back:
And, as they passed, beneath their feet
  They felt the timbers crack.
But when they turned their faces,
  And on the farther shore
Saw brave Horatius stand alone,
  They would have crossed once more.

LIV.

But with a crash like thunder
  Fell every loosened beam,

And, like a dam, the mighty wreck
    Lay right athwart[1] the stream:
And a long shout of triumph
    Rose from the walls of Rome,
As to the highest turret-tops[2]
    Was splashed the yellow foam.

LV.

And, like a horse unbroken
    When first he feels the rein,
The furious river struggled hard,
    And tossed his tawny mane,
And burst the curb, and bounded,
    Rejoicing to be free,
And whirling down, in fierce career,
Battlement, and plank, and pier,
    Rushed headlong to the sea.

LVI.

Alone stood brave Horatius,
    But constant still in mind;
Thrice thirty thousand foes before,
    And the broad flood behind.
" Down with him ! " cried false Sextus,
    With a smile on his pale face.
" Now yield thee," cried Lars Porsena,
    " Now yield thee to our grace."

LVII.

Round turned he, as not deigning
    Those craven[3] ranks to see;
Nought spake he to Lars Porsena,

---

[1] Athwart: across.   [2] Turret-tops: tower-tops.   [3] Craven: coward.

To Sextus nought spake **he**;
But he saw on Palatinus [1]
   The white porch of his home;
And he spake to the noble river
   That rolls by the towers of Rome.

LVIII.

"O Tiber! **father Tiber!** [2]
   To whom **the** Romans pray,
A Roman**'s life, a** Roman's **arms,**
   Take thou **in** charge **this** day!"
So he spake, and speaking sheathed
   The good sword by his side,
And with **his** harness on his back,
   Plunged **headlong** in the tide.

LIX.

No sound **of** joy **or sorrow**
   Was heard from either **bank**;
But friends and **foes** in dumb **surprise,**
With parted lips **and** straining **eyes,**
   Stood gazing where he sank;
And when above **the** surges
   They saw his crest appear,
All Rome **sent forth a** rapturous cry,
And even the ranks of Tuscany
   Could scarce **forbear to** cheer.

---

[1] **Palati'nus**: one of the seven hills on **which** Rome was built.

[2] **Father Tiber**: the Romans believed that every hill, wood, and stream had its guardian spirit or deity. Father Tiber ("father" **is here** an appellation of **honor**) **was** represented as a venerable man reclining on a couch. **He holds** an urn, **from** which issue the waters of the river bearing his name.

LX.

But fiercely ran the current,
  Swollen high by months of rain:
And fast his blood was flowing;
  And he was sore in pain,
And heavy with his armor,
  And spent[1] with changing blows:
And oft they thought him sinking,
  But still again he rose.

LXI.

Never, I **ween,**[2] did swimmer,
  In such **an evil case,**[3]
Struggle through such a raging flood
  Safe to the landing place:
But his limbs were borne up bravely
  By the brave heart within,
And our good father Tiber
  Bore bravely up his chin.*

LXII.

"Curse on him!" quoth false Sextus;
  "Will not the villain drown?
But for this stay,[4] ere close **of day**

---

* "Our ladye bare upp her chinne."
                    — *Ballad of Childe* **Waters.**

" Never heavier man and horse
    Stemmed a midnight torrent's force;
      *   *   *   *   *   *   *
    Yet, through good heart and our **Lady's grace,**
    At length he gained the landing place."
                    — *Lay of the Last Minstrel,* I.

[1] **Spent**: exhausted with exchanging blows.
[2] **Ween**: think or imagine. [3] **Case**: condition or plight. [4] **Stay**: check.

We should have sacked[1] the town!"
"Heaven help him!" quoth Lars Porsena,
"And bring him safe to shore;
For such a gallant feat of arms
Was never seen before."

LXIII.

And now he feels the bottom;
Now on dry earth he stands;
Now round him throng the Fathers
To press his gory hands;
And now, with shouts and clapping,
And noise of weeping loud,
He enters through the River-Gate,
Borne by the joyous crowd.

LXIV.

They gave him of the corn-land,[2]
That was of public right,
As much as two strong oxen
Could plough from morn till night;
And they made a molten image,
And set it up on high,
And there it stands unto this day
To witness if I lie.

LXV.

It stands in the Comitium,[3]
Plain for all folk to see;

[1] **Sacked**: plundered.

[2] **Corn-land**: the common land owned by all the inhabitants of the city.

[3] **Comi'tium**: a part of the Forum, or great public square of Rome, where elections and other assemblies of the people were held.

Horatius in his harness,
  Halting upon one knee:
And underneath is written,
  In letters all of gold,
How valiantly he kept the bridge
  In the brave days of old.

LXVI.

And still his name sounds stirring
  Unto the men of Rome,
As the trumpet-blast that cries to them
  To charge the Volscian[1] home;
And wives still pray to Juno[2]
  For boys with hearts as bold
As his who kept the bridge so well
  In the brave days of old.

LXVII.

And in the nights of winter,
  When the cold north winds blow,
And the long howling of the wolves
  Is heard amidst the snow;
When round the lonely cottage
  Roars loud the tempest's din,
And the good logs of Algidus[3]
  Roar louder yet within;

---

[1] **Volscian**: a hostile people of Latium, a district adjoining Rome on the south.

[2] **Juno**: the wife of Jupiter, and "Queen of heaven."

[3] **Al'gidus**: a wooded mountain-range of Latium, about twelve miles southeast of Rome.

LXVIII.

When the oldest cask [1] is opened,
  And the largest lamp is lit;
When the chestnuts glow in the embers,
  And the kid turns on the spit;
When young and old in circle
  Around the firebrands close;
When the girls are weaving baskets,
  And the lads are shaping bows;

LXIX.

When the goodman mends his armor,
  And trims his helmet's plume;
When the goodwife's shuttle merrily
  Goes flashing through the loom;
With weeping and with laughter
  Still is the story told,
How well Horatius kept the bridge
  In the brave days of old.

LORD MACAULAY.

[1] **Cask** : cask of wine.

VIRGINIA.

FRAGMENTS OF A LAY SUNG IN THE FORUM[1] ON THE DAY WHEREON LUCIUS SEXTIUS SEXTINUS LATERANUS AND CAIUS LICINIUS CALVUS STOLO WERE ELECTED TRIBUNES OF THE COMMONS THE FIFTH TIME, IN THE YEAR OF THE CITY CCCLXXXII.

YE good men of the Commons, with loving hearts and
    true,
Who stand by the bold Tribunes[2] that still have stood
    by you,
Come, make a circle round me, and mark my tale with
    care,
A tale of what Rome once hath borne, of what Rome
    yet may bear.
This is no Grecian fable, of fountains running wine,
Of maids with snaky tresses,[3] or sailors turned to swine.[4]
Here, in this very Forum, under the noonday sun,
In sight of all the people, the bloody deed was done.
Old men still creep among us who saw that fearful day,
Just seventy years and seven ago, when the wicked
    Ten[5] bare sway.

[1] **Fo′rum**: a large square in Rome where public meetings were held, and judicial and commercial business transacted. It was surrounded by courts of justice, temples, and many other magnificent public buildings.

[2] See *Horatius*, p. 14.

[3] **Furies; goddesses** with snakes for hair. They took vengeance on those who shed blood without a cause.

[4] Circe, the daughter of the Sun, was said to have the power by her magic of turning men into swine. See Homer's "Odyssey."

[5] **Ten**: the ten magistrates who were chosen to rule the city of Rome, and to draw up a body of laws in 450. They behaved in the most tyrannical manner, and refused to resign when their term of office had expired.

Of all the wicked Ten still the names are held ac-
    cursed,
And of all the wicked Ten Appius Claudius [1] was the
    worst.
He stalked along the Forum like King Tarquin [2] in his
    pride :
Twelve axes [3] waited on him, six marching on a side ;
The townsmen shrank to right and left, and eyed
    askance [4] with fear
His lowering brow, his curling mouth, which always
    seemed to sneer :
That brow of hate, that mouth of scorn, marks all the
    kindred still ;
For never was there Claudius yet but wished the Com-
    mons ill :
Nor lacks he fit attendance ; for close behind his
    heels,
With outstretched chin and crouching pace, the client [5]
    Marcus steals,
His loins girt up to run with speed, be the errand what
    it may,
And the smile flickering on his cheek, for aught [6] his
    lord may say.
Such varlets [7] pimp [8] and jest for hire among the lying
    Greeks :
Such varlets still are paid to hoot when brave Licinius [9]
    speaks.

---

[1] Ap'pius Clau'dius.   [2] Tarquin : see *Horatius*, p. 1.

[3] Each of the Ten was attended by twelve men (" lictors ") armed with
rods and axes.   [4] Askance : sideways.

[5] Client : a dependent.   [6] Aught : anything.   [7] Varlets : menials.

[8] Pimp : to minister to the base passions of another.

[9] Licin'ius : one of the tribunes of the people.

Where'er ye shed the honey, the buzzing flies will
 crowd;
Where'er ye fling the carrion, the raven's croak is
 loud;
Where'er down Tiber garbage floats, the greedy pike ye
 see;
And wheresoe'er such lord is found, such client still
 will be.

Just then, as through one cloudless chink in a black
 stormy sky,
Shines out the dewy morning-star, a fair young girl
 came by.
With her small tablets[1] in her hand, and her satchel on
 her arm,
Home she went bounding from the school, nor dreamed
 of shame or harm;
And past those dreaded axes she innocently ran,
With bright, frank brow that had not learned to blush
 at gaze of man;
And up the Sacred Street[2] she turned, and, as she
 danced along,
She warbled gayly to herself lines of the good old song.
How for a sport the princes came spurring from the
 camp,
And found Lucrece,[3] combing the fleece, under the mid-
 night lamp.

[1] **Tablets**: small boards covered with a coat of wax, on which Roman
school children wrote or ciphered with a pointed instrument.

[2] **Sacred Street**: a celebrated street in Rome, on which stood the Temple
of Peace. The Sacred Street led to the Forum.

[3] **Lucrece**: a noble Roman matron who was foully wronged by Sextus,
and who stabbed herself to the heart in consequence.

The maiden sang **as** sings the lark, when up he darts
    his flight,
From his nest in the green April corn, to meet the
    morning light;
And Appius heard her sweet young voice, and saw her
    sweet young face,
And loved her with the accursed love of his accursed
    race,[1]
And all along the Forum, and up the Sacred Street,
His vulture eye pursued the trip of those small glancing
    feet.

     *   *   *   *   *   *

    Over the Alban mountains[2] the **light** of morning
    broke;
From **all the roofs of the** Seven **Hills**[3] curled the thin
    wreaths of smoke:
The city gates were opened; the Forum all alive
With buyers and with sellers was humming like a hive:
Blithely on brass and timber the craftsman's[4] stroke was
    ringing,
And blithely o'er her panniers[5] the market-girl was
    singing,
And blithely young Virginia came smiling from her
    home:
Ah! woe for **young** Virginia, the sweetest **maid** in
    Rome!
With her small **tablets** in her **hand,** and her satchel on
    her arm,

---

[1] The Claudian family was noted for its oppression of the people.

[2] **Alban mountains**: the mountains southeast of Rome; usually spoken of in the singular as Mount Alban.

[3] Rome was built on seven hills.   [4] **Craftsman**: artisan or mechanic.

[5] **Panniers**: large, **open** baskets for vegetables and fruit.

Forth she went bounding to the school, nor dreamed of
  shame or harm.
She crossed the Forum shining with stalls[1] in alleys
  gay,
And just had reached the very spot whereon I stand
  this day,
When up the varlet Marcus came; not such as when
  erewhile[2]
He crouched behind his patron's heels with the true
  client smile:
He came with lowering forehead, swollen features, and
  clenched fist,
And strode across Virginia's path, and caught her by
  the wrist.
Hard strove the frightened maiden, and screamed with
  look aghast;
And at her scream from right and left the folk came
  running fast;
The money-changer Crispus, with his thin silver hairs,
And Hanno from the stately booth glittering with
  Punic[3] wares,
And the strong smith Muræna,[4] grasping a half-forged
  brand,
And Volero[5] the flesher,[6] his cleaver in his hand.
All came in wrath and wonder; for all knew that fair
  child;
And, as she passed them twice a day, all kissed their
  hands and smiled;
And the strong smith Muræna gave Marcus such a blow,

---

[1] **Stalls: for** the **sale** of market produce or merchandise.
[2] **Erewhile:** a little while before.   [4] **Muræ na.**   [5] **Vo'lero.**
[3] **Pu'nic wares:** goods from Carthage.   [6] **Flesher:** a butcher.

The caitiff [1] reeled three paces back, and let the maiden
    go.
Yet glared he fiercely round him, and growled in harsh
    fell tone,
" She's mine, and I will have her: I seek but for mine
    own:
She is my slave, born in my house, and stolen away
    and sold,
The year of the sore sickness, ere she was twelve hours
    old.
'Twas in the sad September, the month **of** wail and
    fright,
Two augurs [2] were borne forth that morn ; the Consul
    died **ere** night.
I wait on Appius Claudius, I waited on his sire :
Let him who **works** the client wrong beware the patron's
    ire ! "

  So spake the varlet Marcus ; and dread and silence
    came
On all the people at the **sound** of the great Claudian
    name.
For then there **was** no Tribune to speak the word of
    might,
Which makes **the** rich man tremble, and guards the
    poor **man's** right.
There was no brave Licinius, no honest Sextius [3] then ;
But all **the** city, in great **fear,** obeyed the wicked
    Ten.

[1] **Caitiff** : a mean, cowardly fellow.
[2] **Augurs** : seers; see *Horatius*, p. 20.
[3] **Sex'tius** : he, like Licinius, was a tribune.

Yet ere the varlet Marcus again might seize the maid,
Who clung tight to Muræna's skirt, and sobbed, and
    shrieked for aid,
Forth through the throng of gazers the young Icilius [1]
    pressed,
And stamped his foot, and rent his gown, and smote
    upon his breast,
And sprang upon that column, by many a minstrel
    sung,
Whereon three mouldering helmets, three rusting swords,
    are hung.
And beckoned to the people, and in bold voice and clear
Poured thick and fast the burning words which tyrants
    quake to hear,

" Now, by your children's cradles, now by your fathers'
    graves,
Be men to-day, Quirites,[2] or be forever slaves!
For this did Servius [3] give us laws? For this did ·
    Lucrece bleed?
For this was the great vengeance [4] wrought on Tar-
    quin's evil seed?
For this did those false sons [5] make red the axes of their
    sire?

[1] Virginia was betrothed to Icil'ius.

[2] Qui-ri'tēs: a word used to designate the whole Roman people, both Patricians and Plebeians.

[3] Ser'vius: a just king, whose laws were highly esteemed.

[4] Great vengeance: referring to the assassination of Sextus Tarquinius (see "Sextus," *Horatius*, p. 10), on account of his acts of bloodshed and rapine. With his death the whole line of tyrants of that family practically came to an end.

[5] Bru'tus, the consul, ordered his two sons to be beheaded for conspiring to restore the tyrant Tarquin the Proud (see *Horatius*, p. 1) to power.

For this did Sçævola's[1] right hand hiss in the Tuscan
    fire?

Shall the vile fox-earth[2] awe the race that stormed the
    lion's den?

Shall we, who could not brook one lord, crouch to the
    wicked Ten?

Oh for that ancient spirit which curbed the Senate's
    will!

Oh for the tents which in old time whitened the Sacred
    Hill![3]

In those brave days our fathers stood firmly side by side;

They faced the Marcian fury;[4] they tamed the Fabian[5]
    pride:

They drove the fiercest Quinctius[6] an outcast forth
    from Rome;

They sent the haughtiest Claudius[7] with shivered
    fasces[8] home.

But what their care bequeathed us our madness flung
    away:

[1] **Sçævola** (Seev'o-la) attempted to assassinate Porsena of Clusium
(see *Horatius*, p. 1); when arrested he defied the magistrates, and thrusting
his hand into a pan of burning coals held it there to show how he disdained
the torture that awaited him.

[2] **Fox-earth**: a fox-hole — a term of contempt for the cunning but
cowardly Claudius.

[3] **Sacred Hill**: a hill near Rome where the people gathered at the time
when they revolted against the tyranny of their rulers.

[4] **Marcian fury**: referring to the banishment of Marcius Coriolanus by
the people on account of his disdain of their power.

[5] **Fabian**: the soldiers of the general Cæso Fabius deprived him of a
triumph by refusing to obey his orders and storm the enemy's camp.

[6] **Quinctius**: the people banished him from Rome on account of his
opposition to their cause.

[7] **Claudius**: in a riot which happened many years before, the haughty
head of the Claudian house was mobbed by the people.

[8] **Fasces**: the rods and axes of the lictors or guard of Claudius.

All the ripe fruit of threescore years was blighted in **a
  day**.
Exult, ye proud Patricians![1] The hard-fought fight
  is **o'er**.
We strove for honors — 'twas in vain: for freedom —
  'tis no more.
No crier to the polling[2] summons the eager throng;
No Tribune breathes the word of might that guards the
  weak from wrong.
Our very hearts, that were so high, sink down beneath
  your will.
Riches, **and** lands, and power, and state — ye have
  them: — keep them still.
Still keep the holy fillets;[3] still keep the purple gown,[4]
The axes,[5] and the curule chair,[6] the car,[7] and laurel
  crown.[8]
Still press[9] us for your cohorts,[10] and, when **the fight
  is done,**
Still fill your garners[11] from the soil which our good
  swords have won.
Still, like a spreading ulcer, which leech-craft[12] may not
  cure,

---

[1] **Patricians**: the aristocratic and governing class.

[2] **Polling**: the place where votes were cast by the people at elections.

[3] **Holy fillets**: bands for the hair worn by the priesthood, all of whom
were Patricians.

[4] **Purple gown**: this was worn by the consuls and Patricians on solemn
occasions.   [5] **Axes**: the axes of the lictors (see p. 30).

[6] **Curule chair**: the chair of state, originally an emblem of royalty.

[7] **The car**: or chariot was an indication of rank; it was also used by the
consuls as a triumphal car after a victory.

[8] **Laurel crown**: this was worn by the consuls on occasion of celebrating
a triumph over an enemy.

[9] **Press**: to force into military service.   [11] **Garners**: granaries.

[10] **Cohorts**: divisions of the army.   [12] **Leech-craft**: medical skill.

Let your foul usuance [1] eat away the substance of the
  poor.
Still let your haggard debtors bear all their fathers bore ;
Still **let your** dens of torment be noisome [2] as of yore ;
No fire when Tiber freezes ; no air in dog-star [3] heat;
And store of rods for free-born backs, and holes [4] for
  free-born feet.
Heap heavier still the fetters ; bar closer still the grate ;
Patient as sheep we yield **us** up unto your cruel hate.
But, by the Shades [5] **beneath** us, and by the Gods above,
Add not **unto** your cruel hate your yet **more** cruel
  love !
Have ye not graceful ladies, whose spotless lineage
  springs
From Consuls and High Pontiffs,[6] **and** ancient Alban
  kings ? [7]
Ladies, who deign not on our paths to set their tender
  feet,
Who from their cars [8] look down with scorn upon the
  wondering street,
Who in Corinthian mirrors [9] their own proud smiles
  behold,

---

[1] **Usuance**: usury. The usury laws were so severe that the person who
borrowed money was practically entirely at the mercy of the lender, who
not infrequently imprisoned him or even sold him into slavery.

[2] **Noisome**: disgusting, destructive to health.

[3] **Dog-star**: the same as dog-day.

[4] **Holes,** etc.: stocks into which the feet of debtors were thrust and
confined.   [5] **Shades**: the spirits of the departed.

[6] **High Pontiffs**: High Priests.

[7] **Alban kings**: the earliest of **the** Italian kings, who reigned according
to tradition at Alba Longa, the mother-city of Rome.   [8] **Cars**: chariots.

[9] **Corinthian mirrors**: Corinth was noted for its costly ornaments and
works of art and luxury.

And breathe of Capuan odors,[1] and shine with **Spanish
gold?** [2]
Then leave the poor Plebeian [3] his single tie to life —
The sweet, sweet love of daughter, of sister and of
wife,
The gentle speech, the balm for all that his vexed soul
endures,
The kiss, in which he half forgets even such a yoke as
yours.
Still let the maiden's beauty swell the father's breast
with pride;
Still let the bridegroom's arms infold **an** unpolluted
bride.
Spare us the inexpiable wrong, the unutterable shame,
That **turns the** coward's **heart to** steel, the sluggard's
blood to flame,
Lest, when our latest hope **is fled,** ye taste of our **de-**
spair,
And learn by proof, **in some wild hour,** how much the
wretched dare."

＊　　　＊　　　＊　　　＊　　　＊　　　＊

Straightway Virginius [4] led the maid a little space aside,
To where the reeking **shambles** [5] **stood,** piled up **with**
horn and hide,
Close to yon low dark **archway, where, in a crimson**
flood,
Leaps down to the great sewer the gurgling stream of
blood.

---

[1] **Capuan odors**: Capua, a city a short distance from Naples; it was celebrated for its riches and luxury.

[2] **Spanish gold**: Spain was famous for its mines of precious metals.

[3] **Plebe'ian**: a man without rank, one of the common people.

[4] **Virginius**: the father of Virginia.　　[5] **Shambles**: a butcher's shop.

Hard by, a flesher on a block had laid his whittle [1]
　　down;

Virginius caught the whittle up, and hid it in his gown.

And then his eyes grew very dim, and his throat began
　　to swell,

And in a hoarse, changed voice he spake, " Farewell,
　　sweet child!　Farewell!

Oh! how I loved my darling!　Though stern I some-
　　times be,

To thee, thou know'st I was not so.　Who could be so
　　to thee?

And how my darling loved me!　How glad she was to
　　hear

My footstep on the threshold when I came back last
　　year!

And how she danced with pleasure to see my civic
　　crown,[2]

And took my sword, and hung it up, and brought me
　　forth my gown![3]

Now all those things are over — yes, all thy pretty ways,

Thy needlework, thy prattle, thy snatches of old lays;[4]

And none will grieve when I go forth, or smile when I
　　return,

Or watch beside the old man's bed, or weep upon his
　　urn.[5]

---

[1] **Whittle**: a knife; here, a butcher-knife.

[2] **Civic crown**: a crown composed of oak leaves, and given to a Roman soldier who had saved the life of another Roman in battle by killing his antagonist.

[3] **Gown**: the toga, a white gown, the ordinary and distinctive dress of the Romans.

[4] **Lays**: songs.

[5] **Urn**: the Romans burned the bodies of their dead and enclosed the ashes in a funeral urn.

The house that was the happiest within **the Roman
walls,**
The house that envied not the wealth of Capua's mar-
ble halls,
Now, for the brightness of thy smile, must have eternal
gloom,
And for the music of thy voice, the silence of the tomb.
The time is come. See how he points his eager hand
this way!
See how his eyes gloat on thy grief, like a **kite's**[1] **upon**
the prey!
With all his **wit,**[2] **he little** deems,[3] that, spurned, be-
trayed, bereft,
Thy father hath in his despair **one** fearful refuge left.
He little deems that in this hand I clutch what still
can save
Thy gentle youth from taunts **and blows, the portion of**
the slave;
Yea, and from nameless evil, that **passeth** taunt and
blow —
Foul outrage which thou knowest not, which thou shalt
never know.
Then clasp me **round the neck** once more, **and give me**
one more kiss;
And now, mine own dear little **girl,** there **is no way**
but this."
With that he lifted high the steel, and smote her in the
side,
And in her blood she sank to earth, and with one sob
she died.

[1] **Kite** : a rapacious bird of the falcon family.
[2] **Wit:** intellect, sagacity.   [3] **Deems:** thinks.

Then, for a little moment, all people held their
    breath;
And through the crowded Forum was stillness as of
    death;
And in another moment brake forth from one and all
A cry as if the Volscians were coming o'er the wall.
Some with averted faces shrieking fled home amain;
Some ran to call a leech;[1] and some ran to lift the slain:
Some felt her lips and little wrist, if life might there be
    found;
And some tore up their garments fast, and strove to
    stanch the wound.
In vain they ran, and felt, and stanched; for never
    truer blow
That good right arm had dealt in fight against a Vols-
    cian foe.

When Appius Claudius saw that deed, he shuddered
    and sank down,
And hid his face some little space with the corner of
    his gown,
Till, with white lips and bloodshot eyes, Virginius
    tottered nigh,
And stood before the judgment-seat,[2] and held the knife
    on high.
"Oh! dwellers in the nether gloom,[3] avengers of the
    slain,[4]
By this dear blood I cry to you, do right between us
    twain;

[1] Leech: a physician.
[2] Judgment-seat: the seat of the judges or magistrates of the city.
[3] Nether gloom: the gloom of Hades, the lower world, or place of
departed spirits. [4] Avengers of the slain: the Furies; see p. 29.

And even as Appius Claudius hath dealt by **me** and
    mine,
Deal you by Appius Claudius and all the Claudian
    line!"
So spake the slayer of his child, and turned, and went
    his way;
But first he cast one haggard glance to where the body
    lay,
And writhed, and groaned a fearful groan, and then,
    with steadfast feet,
Strode right across **the** market-place **unto the Sacred**
    Street.

    Then up sprang Appius Claudius: "Stop him; alive
    or dead!
Ten thousand pounds of copper[1] to the **man who brings**
    his head."
He looked upon his clients; but none **would work his**
    will.
He looked upon his lictors; but they trembled, and
    stood still.
And, as Virginius through the press his way in silence
    cleft,
Ever the mighty multitude fell back to right and
    left.
And he hath passed in safety unto his woful home,
And there ta'en horse to tell the camp[2] what deeds are
    done in Rome.

[1] **Ten thousand pounds of copper: the** earliest Roman coin was the *as*
of copper, or copper and tin, and originally a pound Troy weight.

[2] Rome was then apparently at war with the inhabitants of Veii, a city
of Etruria about twelve miles distant.

By this the flood of people was swollen from every
　　side,
And streets and porches round were filled with that
　　o'erflowing tide ;
And close around the body gathered a little train
Of them that were the nearest and dearest to the slain.
They brought a bier, and hung it with many a cypress [1]
　　crown,
And gently they uplifted her, and gently laid her down.
The face of Appius **Claudius wore** the Claudian scowl
　　and sneer,
And in the Claudian note he cried, " What doth this
　　rabble **here** ?
Have they no crafts [2] to mind at home, that hitherward
　　they stray ?
Ho ! lictors, clear the market-place, and fetch the corpse
　　away ! "
The voice of grief and fury till then had not been loud ;
But a deep sullen murmur wandered among the crowd,
Like the moaning noise that goes before the whirlwind
　　on the deep,
Or the growl of a fierce watch-dog but half-aroused from
　　sleep.
But when the lictors at that word, tall yeomen [3] all and
　　strong,
Each with his axe and sheaf of twigs, went down into
　　the throng,
Those old **men say,** who **saw that** day of sorrow and
　　of sin,

[1] **Cypress**: an emblem of mourning for the dead.
[2] **Crafts**: occupations, especially mechanical occupations.
[3] **Yeomen**: countrymen ; here, equivalent to stalwart men.

That in the Roman Forum was never such a din.
The wailing, hooting, cursing, the howls of grief and
 hate,
Were heard beyond the Pincian Hill,[1] beyond the Latin
 Gate.[2]
But close around the body, where stood the little train
Of them that were the nearest and dearest to the slain,
No cries were there, but teeth set fast, low whispers
 and black frowns,
And breaking up of benches, and girding up of gowns.
'Twas well the lictors might not pierce to where the
 maiden lay,
Else surely had they been all twelve torn limb from
 limb that day.
Right glad they were to struggle back, blood streaming
 from their heads,
With axes all in splinters, and raiment all in shreds.
Then Appius Claudius gnawed his lip, and the blood
 left his cheek ;
And thrice he beckoned with his hand, and thrice he
 strove to speak ;
And thrice the tossing Forum set up a frightful yell ;
" See, see, thou dog ! what thou hast done ; and hide
 thy shame in hell !
Thou that wouldst make our maidens slaves must first
 make slaves of men.
Tribunes ! Hurrah for Tribunes ![3] Down with the
 wicked Ten ! "

[1] **Pincian Hill**: a hill on the extreme north of Rome.
[2] **Latin Gate**: a gate in the city wall on the southeast.
[3] See p. 34,
 " For then there was no Tribune to speak the word of might,
  Which makes the rich man tremble, and guards the poor man's right."

And straightway, thick as hailstones, came whizzing
    through the **air**
Pebbles, and bricks, **and** potsherds,[1] all **round the** curule
    chair :
And upon **Appius** Claudius great fear and trembling
    came ;
For never was a Claudius yet brave against aught but
    shame.
Though the great **houses**[2] love us not, we own, to do
    them right,
That the great houses, all save one, have borne them
    well **in** fight.
Still Caius of Corioli,[3] his triumphs and his wrongs,
His vengeance and his mercy, live in our camp-fire
    songs.
Beneath the yoke of Furius[4] oft have Gaul and Tus-
    can[5] bowed ;
And Rome may bear the pride of him of whom herself
    is proud.
But evermore a Claudius shrinks from a stricken
    field,
And changes color **like a maid** at sight of sword and
    shield.

---

[1] **Potsherds** : fragments of pottery.

[2] **The great houses** : the great or titled families.

[3] **Ca'ius of Cori'oli** : better known as Coriolanus. He was banished from
Rome on account of the disdain with which he treated the magistrates.
He then joined the enemies of Rome and marched to attack the city, but
yielding finally to the entreaties of his wife and his mother, he withdrew
without carrying out his design.

[4] **Fu'rius** : Furius Camillus delivered Rome from the attacks of the
Gauls.

[5] **Tuscan** : an inhabitant of Etruria, a country lying to the west and
north of the Tiber. Wars between the Tuscans and Romans were frequent.

The Claudian triumphs all were won within the city
  towers;
The Claudian yoke was never pressed on any necks but
  ours.
A Cossus,[1] like a wild cat, springs ever at the face;
A Fabius [2] rushes like a boar against the shouting
  chase;
But the vile Claudian litter, raging with currish spite,
Still yelps and snaps at those who run, still runs from
  those who smite.
So now 'twas seen of Appius. When stones began to
  fly,
He shook, and crouched, and wrung his hands, and
  smote upon his thigh.
" Kind clients, honest lictors, stand by me in this
  fray !
Must I be torn in pieces? Home, home, the nearest
  way !"
While yet he spake, and looked around with a bewil-
  dered stare,
Four sturdy lictors put their necks beneath the curule
  chair;
And fourscore clients on the left, and fourscore on the
  right,
Arrayed themselves with swords and staves,[3] and loins
  girt up for fight.
But, though without or staff or sword, so furious was
  the throng,

---

[1] **Cossus:** this was the surname of a family, one of whom, Cornelius
Cossus, had gained great renown in battle.
[2] **Fabius:** the Fabian family was noted for courage and devotion to
Rome.   [3] **Staves:** the plural of *staff*.

That scarce the train with might and main could bring
    their lord along.
Twelve times the crowd made at him; five times they
    seized his gown;
Small chance was his to rise again, if once they got him
    down:
And sharper came the pelting; and evermore the
    yell —
"Tribunes! we will have Tribunes!" — rose with a
    louder swell:
And the chair tossed as tosses a bark with tattered
    sail
When raves the Adriatic beneath an eastern gale,
When the Calabrian sea-marks [1] are lost in clouds of
    spume,[2]
And the great Thunder-Cape [3] has donned his veil of
    inky gloom.
One stone hit Appius in the mouth, and one beneath
    the ear;
And ere he reached Mount Palatine,[4] he swooned with
    pain and fear.
His cursed head, that he was wont to hold so high with
    pride,
Now, like a drunken man's, hung down, and swayed
    from side to side;
And when his stout retainers had brought him to his
    door,

---

[1] **Calabrian sea-marks**: rocky heights or other landmarks on the coast of Calabria, in Southeastern Italy.

[2] **Spume**: froth, or foam.

[3] **Thunder-Cape**: a rocky promontory on the coast of Greece, opposite Southeastern Italy.

[4] **Mount Palatine**: one of the seven hills of Rome.

His face and neck were all one cake of filth and clotted
     gore.

As Appius Claudius [1] was that day, so may his grandson
     be !

God send Rome one such other sight, and send me there
     to see !

LORD MACAULAY.

---

[1] **Appius Claudius:** The appeal of Virginius to the army (see **p. 43,**
note 2) led to the overthrow of the "Wicked Ten." The haughty Appius
was cast into prison, where rage and shame caused him to kill himself.

THE ARMADA.[1]

—◦—

Attend, all ye who list[2] to hear our noble England's
 praise;

[1] **Arma′da**: an armed fleet. Before it sailed it was boastfully styled by
the Spaniards the "Invincible **Armada.**"

The Armada was a fleet of 130 ships, carrying about 2500 cannon and
20,000 soldiers, which Philip II. of Spain sent to conquer England in the
reign of Queen Elizabeth.

The Armada entered the English Channel the last of July, 1588. The
ships were large, were all slow sailers, and were not easily managed.

The English vessels were small, but efficient, and were under the command of Lord Howard, Sir Francis Drake, and Lord Seymour. The Spanish fleet was first seen off Plymouth, where Lord Howard and Drake were
on the lookout for them. The fight began soon after the Armada passed
that point on the way to Holland to get re-enforcements of soldiers before
making the attempt to land on the English coast. The battle between the
unwieldy ships of Spain and the small, quick-moving vessels of England
was like a contest between a bear and a swarm of wasps. Followed in this
way, the Armada put into the friendly French port of Calais. Thence the
English drove them out by setting fire to several of their own vessels, and
letting them drift at night among the enemy's fleet. The Spaniards, in
alarm, cut their cables and put to sea. The English followed, and destroyed many vessels off the coast of Holland, and if their ammunition
had not given out, they would have utterly defeated the Armada in the
North Sea.

The dispirited Spaniards, finding the weather against them, determined
to give up the attack on England and retreat to Spain. The storm pre-
vented their going directly back, and they undertook to return by sailing
round the north of Scotland and Ireland. Many of the ships were wrecked,
with great loss of life, and only fifty-five out of the original one hundred
and thirty vessels succeeded in reaching Spain. In the defence of England
Catholics and Protestants had united, — it was a national triumph. In
commemoration of it Queen Elizabeth ordered a medal to be struck, bearing the motto, "God blew with his wind, and they were scattered."

[2] **List**: desire, wish.

I tell of the thrice famous deeds she wrought in ancient
    days,
When that great **fleet** invincible against her bore in vain
The richest spoils of Mexico,[1] the stoutest hearts of
    Spain.

It was about the lovely close of a warm summer
    day,
There came a gallant merchant-ship full sail to Plymouth
    Bay;[2]
Her crew hath seen Castile's[3] **black fleet,**[4] beyond
    Aurigny's isle,[5]
At earliest twilight, on the **waves lie** heaving many a
    mile.[6]
At sunrise she escaped their **van,**[7] **by God's especial**
    grace;
And the tall Pinta,[8] **till the noon had held her close in**
    chase.
Forthwith a guard at every gun was placed along the
    wall;[9]

---

1 **Spoils of Mexico**: perhaps because the plunder of Mexico had enabled
Spain to fit out the **Armada.**

2 **Plymouth Bay,** on the southwest coast of England. Here Lord Howard and Sir Francis Drake, with a small fleet, were stationed, **watching
for the** appearance of the Armada.

3 **Castile**: a political name for Spain, which was formed from the union
of the two kingdoms of Castile and Aragon.

4 **Black fleet**: black is the common color for ships of all classes.

6 **Aurigny's isle** (Ō-reen-ye'): Alderney, one of the English Channel
islands.

6 **Many a mile**: the Armada, when first seen, was said to be in the form
of a crescent, and to extend about seven miles from tip to tip.

7 **Van**: the foremost part of the fleet.

8 **Pinta**: one of the vessels of the **Armada.**

9 **The wall**: the sea-wall of Plymouth.

The beacon[1] blazed upon the roof of Edgecumbe's lofty
    hall;[2]

Many a light fishing bark put out to pry along the coast,

And with loose rein and bloody spur rode inland many
    a post.[3]

With his white hair unbonneted,[4] the stout old sheriff
    comes;

Behind him march the halberdiers;[5] before him sound
    the drums;

His yeomen[6] round the market-cross[7] make clear an
    ample space;

For there behooves him[8] to set up the standard[9] of Her
    Grace.[10]

And haughtily the trumpets peal, and gayly dance the
    bells,

As slow upon the laboring wind the royal blazon[11]
    swells.

---

[1] **Beacon**: here, a signal-fire.

[2] **Edgecumbe's lofty hall**: the residence of the Earl of Edgecumbe, on a **height about** seventeen miles northwest of Plymouth. Mount Edgecumbe **can be** seen from the "Hoe" (Height) in Plymouth, where, according **to tradition**, Sir Francis Drake **and Lord** Howard were playing a game of bowls (or ten pins), when news **of** the approach of the Armada was brought. See Kingsley's "Westward, Ho!"

[3] **Post**: here, a special messenger, one sent to ride with all haste through the country and give the alarm.

[4] **Unbonneted**: the **bonnet was** originally a cap worn by men.

[5] **Halberdiers**: guards armed with halberds, the halberd being a combined axe and **spear.**

[6] **Yeomen**: countrymen, but here equivalent to stout followers.

[7] **Market-cross**: it was customary in early times to erect a stone cross **in the** market-place of the chief towns. The remains of such crosses may still be seen in several cities (*e.g.* Chichester) on the south coast of England.   [8] **Behooves him**: it is his duty.

[9] **The standard**: the great royal flag, having the arms of England on it.

[10] **Her Grace**: **Queen** Elizabeth.

[11] **Blazon**. the arms **of** England emblazoned on the standard.

Look how the Lion[1] of the sea lifts up his ancient
    crown,

And underneath his deadly paw treads the gay lilies[2]
    down.

So stalked **he** when he turned to flight, on that famed
    Picard field,[3]

Bohemia's plume,[4] and Genoa's bow,[5] and Cæsar's eagle
    shield.[6]

So glared he when **at** Agincourt[7] in wrath he turned
    to bay,[8]

And crushed and torn beneath his claws the princely
    hunters lay.

Ho! strike the flagstaff deep, Sir Knight:[9] ho! scatter
    flowers, fair maids:

Ho! gunners, fire a loud salute: ho ! gallants,[10] draw
    your blades:

[1] **Lion**: the lion rampant in the arms of England.

[2] **The lilies**: **the** ancient arms of France, — fleur-de-lis , the English lion trampling down these lilies represents the early English conquests in France.

[3] **Picard field**: in 1346 the English gained a great and decisive victory over the French at Crécy, in the province of Picardy, Northwestern France.

[4] **Bohemia's plume**: the blind old king of Bohemia was an ally of the king of France, and fought in his behalf at Crécy.

[5] **Genoa's bow**: the French king had hired 15,000 Genoese cross-bowmen, in **the** hope that they would **be able to hold the English archers** in check.

[6] **Cæsar's eagle** shield: referring to the eagle on the shield of the king of the Romans, son of the king of Bohemia, and, like his father, an ally of France.

[7] **Agincourt** (Ah-zhan-koor'): a battle-field near Crécy, where, in 1415, the English gained another great victory over **the French**.

[8] **Turned to bay**: **turned** to face the enemy, as a stag pursued by dogs **turns** and faces them.

[9] **Sir Knight**: Sir, a **title** of honor given **to a** knight.

[10] **Gallants**: brave, high-spirited young men.

Thou sun, shine on her joyously; ye breezes, waft her
    wide;
Our glorious SEMPER EADEM,[1] the banner of our pride.

The freshening breeze of eve unfurled that banner's
    massy fold;
The parting gleam of sunshine kissed that haughty
    scroll of gold;[2]
Night sank upon the dusky beach, and on the purple
    sea,
Such night in England ne'er had been, nor e'er again
    shall be.
From Eddystone[3] to Berwick bounds,[4] from Lynn[5] to
    Milford Bay,[6]
That time of slumber was as bright and busy as the day;
For swift to east and swift to west the ghastly war-
    flame[7] spread,
High on St. Michael's Mount[8] it shone: it shone on
    Beachy Head.[9]

[1] **Semper Eadem**: always the same; perhaps conveying the idea here
of always victorious.

[2] **Scroll of gold**: the royal standard with its arms emblazoned in gold.

[3] **Eddystone**: a rock in the sea fourteen miles south of Plymouth. It is
submerged at high tide. On it stands the celebrated Eddystone lighthouse.

[4] **Berwick bounds**: the boundaries or limits of Berwick, on the south
coast of England (Sussex), nearly two hundred and **fifty miles** east of Plymouth.

[5] **Lynn**: King's Lynn or Lynn is on the eastern coast of England (Nor-
folk County).

[6] **Milford Bay**: on the southwestern coast of Wales. From Lynn to
Milford Bay; that is, across the country from one extremity to the other.

[7] **War-flame**: the beacon or signal of alarm kindled from height to
height and point to point.

[8] **St. Michael's Mount**: a high, rocky islet off the southern coast of
Cornwall, near Penzance, and between Lizard Head and Land's End.

[9] **Beachy Head**: a lofty promontory on the south coast of England
(Sussex), east of Brighton.

Far on the deep the Spaniard saw, along each southern
    shire,[1]
Cape beyond cape, in endless range those twinkling
    points of fire.
The fisher left his skiff to rock on Tamar's[2] glittering
    waves:
The rugged miners poured to war from Mendip's[3] sun-
    less caves:
O'er Longleat's towers,[4] o'er Cranbourne's oaks,[5] the
    fiery herald flew:
He roused the shepherds of Stonehenge,[6] the rangers[7]
    of Beaulieu.[8]
Right sharp and quick the bells all night rang out from
    Bristol town,[9]
And ere the day three hundred horse had met on Clif-
    ton[10] Down ;[11]

[1] **Shire**: county.

[2] **Tamar**: a river separating Devonshire from Cornwall. It empties into the English Channel just west of Plymouth.

[3] **Mendip's caves**: the Mendip Hills are a limestone range in Somersetshire, in the southwest of England. They abound in caves and old Roman mines.

[4] **Longleat's towers**: Longleat, the seat of the Marquis of Bath, Wiltshire, about midway between Bristol and Salisbury. It is said to be the finest Elizabethan mansion in England.

[5] **Cranbourne's oaks** referring to the oaks on the grounds of the Manor House of Lord Salisbury at Cranborne, or Cranbourne, Wiltshire, near the borders of Dorsetshire, in the south of England, or to the woodland near by called Cranborne Chase.

[6] **Stonehenge**: a famous ruin, supposed to be the remains of a temple built by the ancient Britons. It is about nine miles north of Salisbury, in Wiltshire, in the south of England.

[7] **Rangers**: officers having the charge of the royal forest or hunting grounds of the New Forest, Hampshire, in the south of England.

[8] **Beaulieu** (commonly pronounced Beuley, but here Bew-loo'): the ruins of an abbey on the borders of New Forest, on the coast near Southampton.

[9] **Bristol**: a city on the southwest coast of England, on Bristol Channel.

[10] **Clifton Down**: Clifton, a suburb of Bristol; for Down, see note 11.

[11] **Down**: a rounded, barren hill of chalk or limestone.

The sentinel on Whitehall gate [1] looked forth into the
    night,
And saw o'erhanging Richmond Hill [2] the streak of
    blood-red light.
Then bugle's note and cannon's roar the deathlike
    silence broke,
And with one start, and with one cry, the royal city [3]
    woke.
At once on all her stately gates [4] arose the answering
    fires;
At once the wild alarum clashed from all her reeling [5]
    spires;
From all the batteries of the Tower [6] pealed loud the
    voice of fear;
And all the thousand masts of Thames sent back a
    louder cheer;
And from the furthest wards **was heard the rush of**
    hurrying feet,
And the broad streams of pikes [7] and flags rushed down
    each roaring street;
And broader still became the blaze, and louder still the
    din,
As fast from every **village** round the horse came spur-
    ring in:

[1] **Whitehall** the palace of Whitehall, London; only a small portion of
it now exists.

[2] **Richmond Hill**: a hill a short distance southwest of London.

[3] **The royal city**: London; formerly the chief residence of the sovereign.

[4] **Gates**: London was formerly surrounded by a high wall pierced with
gates.

[5] **Reeling**: said of the church-spires, because they seem to sway or
rock from the swinging and clanging of the bells.

[6] **Tower**: the Tower of London; it was formerly used as a palace, fortress, and prison.   [7] **Pikes**: spears.

And eastward straight from wild Blackheath[1] the warlike errand went,
And roused in many an ancient hall[2] the gallant squires[3]
of Kent.[4]
Southward from Surrey's[5] pleasant hills flew those
bright couriers[6] forth;
High on bleak Hampstead's[7] swarthy moor they started
for the north;
And on, and on, without a pause, untired they bounded
still:
All night from tower to tower they sprang; they sprang
from hill to hill:
Till the proud Peak[8] unfurled the flag o'er Darwin's[9]
rocky dales,
Till like volcanoes flared to heaven the stormy hills of
Wales,
Till twelve fair counties saw the blaze on Malvern's[10]
lonely height,
Till streamed in crimson on the wind the Wrekin's[11]
crest of light,

[1] **Blackheath**: a heath or tract of land then uncultivated and unsettled, a short distance southeast of London.

[2] **Hall**: a country-seat; the residence of a man of rank or property.

[3] **Squires**: country gentlemen.

[4] **Kent**: a county in the southeast of England.

[5] **Surrey**: a county south of the Thames. It includes part of London.

[6] **Bright couriers**: the signals, or beacon lights.

[7] **Hampstead**: a northern suburb of London; it was then waste land.

[8] **The Peak**: a high point in the limestone hills of Derbyshire. It is about twenty-five miles southeast of Manchester. There was formerly a castle on the Peak.

[9] **Darwin's dales**: another name for the valleys of the river Derwent in Derbyshire.

[10] **Malvern's height**: the "Worcester Beacon," the highest of the Malvern Hills, in Worcestershire, in the west of England.

[11] **Wrekin**: a high hill in Shropshire, about twenty miles from the eastern boundary of Wales.

Till broad and fierce **the star** came forth on Ely's [1]
   stately fane,
And tower and hamlet [2] rose in arms o'er all the bound-
   less plain ;
Till Belvoir's [3] lordly terraces the sign [4] to Lincoln [5]
   sent,
And Lincoln sped the message on o'er the wide vale of
   Trent; [6]
Till Skiddaw [7] saw the fire that burned **on Gaunt's** em-
   battled pile, [8]
And the red glare on Skiddaw roused the burghers of
   Carlisle. [9]

*   *   *   *   *   *

LORD MACAULAY.

[1] **Ely's fane** : Ely Cathedral, in Cambridgeshire, in the east of England.

[2] **Tower and hamlet** : castle and cottage.

[3] **Belvoir's lordly terraces** : Belvoir Castle, on a height of that name in the east of England, about twenty-five miles southeast of Nottingham.

[4] **Sign** : the flame of the beacon-fire.

[5] **Lincoln** : a cathedral town in the east of England. It is situated on a commanding height.

[6] **Trent** : the valley of the river Trent, in central England.

[7] **Skiddaw** : a mountain in Cumberland, in the northwest of England.

[8] **Gaunt's** embattled pile : Lancaster Castle, a noble pile, standing on an eminence in Lancaster, Lancashire, in the northwest of England. In the fourteenth century the castle came into the possession of John of Gaunt, Duke of Lancaster, who built large additions to it.

[9] **Burghers of Carlisle** : the citizens of Carlisle. Carlisle is the county town of Cumberland.

IVRY.[1]

Now glory to the Lord of Hosts, **from whom all** glories
are!
And glory to our Sovereign Liege,[2] King Henry of
Navarre!
Now let there **be the merry sound of music** and of
dance,
Through thy corn-fields **green, and** sunny vines, O
pleasant land of France!
And thou, Rochelle,[3] our own Rochelle, proud city of
the **waters,**
Again let rapture light **the eyes of all thy mourning**
daughters.

[1] **Ivry** (Ē-vrĕ'): Henry III. ascended **the** throne of France in 1574 at a
time when the kingdom was rent by a terrible civil war.

The two factions in the contest were the Catholics, led by Henry of
Guise, and the Huguenots, or Protestants, under Henry of Navarre — so
called because his mother, the queen of Navarre, held a small kingdom
originally lying partly in Spain and partly in France.

Henry III. endeavored to reconcile the contending parties, but the Catholics distrusted his policy, and formed a league to defend the interests of their
faith. Henry was assassinated in 1589. He named Henry of Navarre as
his successor; but the Duke of Mayenne and the people of Paris disputed
his right to the throne. In 1590 Henry gained the decisive battle of Ivry
(a village about thirty miles west of Paris) over Mayenne.

Three **years** later he publicly embraced the Catholic faith. Henry
showed **himself a wise and** just ruler, and a true benefactor to his country.
No sovereign **in French history** stands so high in the estimation of all
parties, and he is justly entitled to be called "Henry the Great."

[2] **Liege**: lord.

[3] **Rochelle**: a city on the western **coast** of France; it was once the
stronghold of the Huguenot, or Protestant party.

As thou wert constant in our ills, be joyous in our joy,
For cold, and stiff, and still are they who wrought thy
 walls annoy.
Hurrah! Hurrah! a single field hath turned the chance
 of war,
Hurrah! Hurrah! for Ivry, and Henry of Navarre.

Oh! how our hearts were beating, when at the dawn
 of day
We saw the army of the League [1] drawn out in long
 array;
With all its priest-led citizens, and all its rebel peers, [2]
And Appenzel's [3] stout infantry, and Egmont's Flemish
 spears. [4]
There rode the brood of false Lorraine, [5] the curses of
 our land;
And dark Mayenne [6] was in the midst, a truncheon [7] in
 his hand:
And, as we looked on them, we thought of Seine's empurpled flood, [8]

[1] **The League:** the compact organized in defence of the Catholic faith.
See note 1, on *Ivry*, p. 59.

[2] "**Priest-led citizens**" and "**rebel peers**" (peers: lords): Macaulay
here puts in the mouth of a Huguenot warrior the strong partisan ex-
pressions characteristic of the period.

[3] **Appenzel:** the leader of the Swiss troops under Mayenne.

[4] **Egmont's Flemish spears:** Philip, Count of Egmont, led a body of
troops from Flanders to support the League.

[5] **Lorraine:** the Guise family, who were among the foremost supporters
of the League, were originally from Lorraine, on the east of France.

[6] **Mayenne:** the **Duke** of Mayenne, commander-in-chief of the army of
the League. **See note** 1, on *Ivry*, p. 59.

[7] **Truncheon: staff** of office.

[8] **Seine's** empurpled **flood:** during the massacre of St. Bartholomew in
Paris (1572), it is said that so many bodies of the slain were cast into the
river that the water was tinged with blood.

The massacre was an attempt of Catharine de Medici, the mother of
Charles IX., to destroy all the Huguenot leaders of France.

And good Coligni's [1] hoary hair all dabbled with his
    blood;
And we cried unto the living God, who rules the fate
    of war,
To fight for his own holy name, and Henry of Navarre.

  The King is come to marshal us, in all his armor
    drest,
And he has bound a snow-white plume upon his gallant
    crest.
He looked upon his people, and a tear was in his eye;
He looked upon the traitors, and his glance was stern
    and high.
Right graciously he smiled on us, as rolled from wing
    to wing,
Down all our line, a deafening shout, "God save our
    Lord the King!"
"And if my standard-bearer fall, as fall full well he may.
For never saw I promise yet of such a bloody fray,
Press where ye see my white plume shine, amidst the
    ranks of war,
And be your oriflamme [2] to-day the helmet of Navarre."

  Hurrah! the foes are moving. Hark to the mingled
    din
Of fife, and steed, and trump, and drum, and roaring
    culverin.[3]

---

[1] **Coligni** (Ko-leen-yĕ´): the chief of the Huguenot party. He was murdered in the St. Bartholomew massacre.

[2] **Oriflamme** (or'e-flăm): the ancient royal banner of France; it was purple, or red, with rays of gold.

[3] **Culverin**: a kind of cannon.

The fiery **Duke**[1] **is** pricking[2] fast across Saint André's[3]
    plain,
With all the hireling chivalry of Guelders[4] and Al-
    mayne.[5]
Now by the lips of those **ye love,** fair gentlemen of
    France,
Charge for the golden lilies,[6] — upon them with the
    lance.
A thousand spurs are striking deep, a thousand spears
    in **rest,**[7]
A thousand knights are pressing close behind **the** snow-
    white crest ;
And in they **burst,** and **on** they rushed, while, like a
    guiding star,
Amidst the thickest carnage blazed the helmet of
    Navarre.

    Now, God be praised, the day is ours. Mayenne
    hath turned his rein.
D'Aumale[8] hath cried for quarter. The Flemish count
    is slain.
Their ranks are breaking like thin clouds before a Bis-
    cay **gale ;**
The field is **heaped with** bleeding steeds, and flags, and
    cloven mail.[9]

---

[1] **Duke** : the Duke of Mayenne.
[2] **Pricking** : spurring, riding at **full speed.**
[8] **Saint André** (An-dray´).
[4] **Guelders** : a part of Flanders, or **the** Netherlands.
[5] **Almayne** : probably a poetical form for Allemagne, or Germany.
[6] **Golden lilies** : the lilies on the royal arms and standard of France.
[7] **In rest** : in attitude of attack.
[8] **D'Aumale** (Doh-mahl´) : the Duke D'Aumale, one of the chiefs of the
League.   [9] **Mail** : armor made of links, or rings.

And then we thought on vengeance, and, all along our
    van,[1]
" Remember St. Bartholomew,"[2] was passed from man
    to man.
But out spake gentle Henry, "No Frenchman is my
    foe :
Down, down with every foreigner, but let your brethren
    go."
Oh! was there ever such a knight, in friendship or in
    war,
As our Sovereign Lord, King Henry, the soldier of
    Navarre ?

Right well fought all the Frenchmen who fought for
    France to-day ;
And many a lordly banner God gave them for a prey.
But we of the religion [3] have borne us best in fight ;
And the good Lord of Rosny [4] hath ta'en the cornet [5]
    white.
Our own true Maximilian [6] the cornet white hath ta'en,
The cornet white with crosses black, the flag of false
    Lorraine.
Up with it high ; unfurl it wide ; that all the host may
    know
How God hath humbled the proud house which wrought
    his church such woe.

---

[1] **Van** : front of an army.
[2] **St. Bartholomew** : see note 8, p. 60.
[3] **The religion** : the Huguenot faith.
[4] **Rosny** : the Duke of Sully, Baron of Rosny, an eminent French states-
man. He was a firm Protestant ; but for the sake of ending the civil war,
he urged Henry of Navarre to join the Catholic Church.
[5] **Cornet** : the flag or standard of a troop of cavalry.
[6] **Maximilian** : the Christian name of Sully, Duke of Rosny.

Then on the ground, while trumpets sound their loud-
    est point of war,
Fling the red shreds, a footcloth neat for Henry of
    Navarre.

Ho! maidens of Vienna;[1] ho! matrons of Lucerne;[2]
Weep, weep, and rend your hair for those who never
    shall return.
Ho! Philip,[3] send, for charity, thy Mexican pistoles,[4]
That Antwerp monks may sing a mass for[6] thy poor
    spearmen's souls.
Ho! gallant nobles of the League, look that your arms
    be bright;
Ho! burghers[6] of Saint Geneviève,[7] keep watch and
    ward[8] to-night.
For our God hath crushed the tyrant, our God hath
    raised the slave,
And mocked the counsel of the wise, and the valor of
    the brave.
Then glory to his holy name, from whom all glories are;
And glory to our Sovereign Lord, King Henry of
    Navarre.

LORD MACAULAY.

[1] **Vienna**: alluding to the Austrian allies of the defeated Duke of Mayenne.

[2] **Lucerne**: Lucerne, Switzerland, also furnished troops to fight for Mayenne.

[3] **Philip**: Philip II. of Spain; he was an ally of the Duke of Mayenne.

[4] **Pistoles**: gold coins.

[6] **Mass: here, a** Roman Catholic service sung for the repose of the souls of the dead.

[6] **Burghers**: citizens.

[7] **Saint Geneviève** (Zhen-ve-āv'): the patron saint of Paris; here used as a name for the city itself.

[8] **Watch and ward**: watching and guarding night and day.

NASEBY.[1]

OH! wherefore come ye forth in triumph from the
    north,[2]
With your hands, and your feet, and your raiment
    all red?
And wherefore doth your rout[3] send forth a joyous
    shout?
  And whence be the grapes of the wine-press[4] that ye
    tread?

Oh! evil was the root, and bitter was the fruit,
  And crimson was the juice of the vintage that we
    trod;
For we trampled on the throng of the haughty and the
    strong,

[1] **Naseby**: the battle of Naseby was fought near the village of that name in Northamptonshire, Central England, in 1645.

It was one of the decisive battles of the great civil war between Parliament or the English people and King Charles I. and his supporters.

The Parliamentary forces were led by Cromwell, Fairfax, and Ireton; the king's army, by Prince Rupert and Sir Marmaduke Langdale. Charles did not engage in the battle, but took his position on a hill commanding a distant view of the field.

The contest **resulted** in the total defeat of the king. It was the last great battle fought by the Royalists. In less than a year Charles fled to the Scots, **who** gave him up a prisoner to **his enemies, by** whom he was tried and executed in 1649.

[2] **The north**: Northamptonshire; a shire north of London.

[3] **Rout**: concourse, multitude.

[4] **Wine-press** an allusion to **Rev. xiv.** 18-20.

Who sate in the high places and slew the saints of
God.[1]

It was about the noon of a glorious day of June,
That we saw their banners dance and their cuirasses[2]
shine,
And the man of blood[3] was there, with his long[4] es-
senced hair,
And Astley,[5] and Sir Marmaduke,[6] and Rupert[7] of
the Rhine.

Like a servant of the Lord, with his bible and his
sword,
The general rode along us to form us for the fight;
When a murmuring sound broke out, and swelled into
a shout
Among the godless horsemen upon the tyrant's
right.[8]

[1] **The saints of God**: a title arrogated to themselves by the Puritan
party, most of whom had by this time separated wholly from the Church
of England and were bitterly hostile to it. The poem represents an account
of the battle by one of this class, and is full of the intense feeling which so
often blinded each party to the merit possessed by the opposite side.

[2] **Cuirasses**: the cuirass is a piece of armor covering the body from the
neck to the girdle.

[3] **Man of blood**: a scriptural quotation from 2 Sam. xvi. 7. It was
applied by the Puritans as a term of opprobrium to Charles I., because he
made war against Parliament.

[4] **Long hair**: the Royalists, or Cavaliers, wore their hair in long curls.
The Puritans considered this fashion a sinful vanity, and cut their hair
off short; as this showed the shape of the head, the Cavaliers nicknamed
them "Round Heads."

[5] **Astley**: Lord Astley. He commanded the foot-soldiers of the Royalist
army at Naseby.   [6] **Marmaduke**: see note 1, p. 65.

[7] **Rupert**: his father was a prince on the Rhine.

[8] **Right**: the right wing of Charles's army under the command of Prince
Rupert, nephew of the king. He was a man of impetuous courage, but
lacking in judgment.

And hark! like the roar of the billows on the shore,
  The cry of battle rises along their charging line :
For God! for the Cause![1] for the Church! for the
    laws!
  For Charles, king **of** England, and Rupert of the
    Rhine![2]

The furious German comes, with his clarions[3] **and his**
    drums,
  His bravoes[4] of Alsatia[5] **and** pages[6] of Whitehall;[7]
They are bursting on our **flanks! Grasp your pikes!**
    Close your **ranks!**
  For Rupert never comes, but to conquer or to fall.

They are here — **they rush on** — we are broken — we
    are gone —
  Our left is borne before them like stubble **on the**
    blast.
O Lord, put forth thy might! O Lord, defend the
    right!
  Stand back to back, in God's name! and fight it to
    the last!

Stout Skippen[8] hath **a wound** — the centre hath given
    ground.

---

[1] **The Cause**: the Royal Cause.

[2] **Rupert of the Rhine**: historians speak of the "terror of Rupert's
name."

[3] **Clarions**: the clarion is a trumpet having a peculiarly shrill sound, and
hence used for giving signals.   [4] **Bravoes**: ruffians.

[5] **Alsatia**: then one of the lowest quarters of London. It was frequented
by fugitive debtors and desperate criminals.   [6] **Pages**: royal attendants.

[7] **Whitehall**: the royal palace of Whitehall, London.

[8] **Skippen**: Philip Skippen, or Skippon, major-general of the Parliamentary forces.

Hark! **hark!** what means the trampling of horsemen
    on our rear?
Whose banner do I see, boys? 'Tis **he!** thank God!
    'tis he, boys!
Bear up another minute! Brave Oliver [1] is here!

Their heads all stooping **low, their** points [2] all in a row:
    Like a whirlwind **on** the trees, like a deluge on the
        dikes,
Our cuirassiers have burst on the ranks **of** the accurst,
    And at a shock have scattered the forest of his pikes.

Fast, fast, the gallants ride, in some safe nook to hide
    Their coward heads, predestined to rot on Temple
        Bar; [3]
And he [4] — **he turns!** he **flies!** shame on those cruel
    eyes
    That bore **to** look **on** torture, **and dare not** look on
        war!

Ho, comrades! scour the **plain; and ere ye** strip the
    slain,
First give another stab **to** make your search secure;
Then shake from **sleeves** and pockets their broad-pieces [5]
    and lockets,
    The tokens of the wanton, [6] the plunder **of** the poor.

[1] **Oliver:** Oliver Cromwell.   [2] **Points:** spear-points.
[3] **Temple Bar:** an archway forming an entrance or gate to the city of
London, pulled down in 1878. It was customary then to place the heads
of traitors on this **arch** as a warning to others. In the civil war each faction regarded the **other** as guilty of **the** crime of trying to overthrow the
constitutional government of the realm.
[4] **He:** Charles I.   [5] **Broad-pieces:** gold pieces.
[6] **Wanton:** "tokens of the wanton," gifts or keepsakes of women of
low character.

Fools ! your doublets[1] shone with gold, and your hearts
    were gay and **bold,**
  When you kissed your lily hands **to** your lemans[2]
    to-day ;
And to-morrow shall **the** fox from **her chambers** in the
    rocks
  Lead forth her tawny **cubs** to howl above the prey.

Where be your tongues, that late mocked **at heaven,**
    and hell, and fate ?
  And the fingers **that once were so busy with your**
    blades ?
Your perfumed satin clothes, **your** catches[3] and your
    oaths ?
  Your stage plays and your sonnets, your diamonds
    and your spades ?[4]

Down ! down ! for ever down, with the **mitre**[5] **and the**
    crown !
  With the Belial[6] of the court, and the Mammon of
    the Pope ![7]
There is woe in Oxfor'' halls,[8] there is wail in Dur-
    ham's stalls ;[9]

---

[1] **Doublet:** a kind of jacket or short coat, usually of silk, then **worn by** men of fashion.   [2] **Lemans: the same as wantons.** See note 6, p. 68.

[3] **Catches** : rollicking songs.

[4] **Diamonds and spades** : playing-cards.

[5] **Mitre** : a tall, pointed, cleft cap **worn** by bishops and other Church dignitaries of high rank. Here the word is used for the Church of England.

[6] **Belial** : wickedness ; from Belial, Satan.

[7] **Mammon:** worldliness, love of wealth ; from Mammon, the Syrian god of riches.   [8] **Oxford:** Oxford sided with the king.

[9] **Durham's stalls:** stalls, seats in the choir ; here " Durham's stalls " is equivalent to Durham Cathedral, which was one of the leading cathedrals on the king's side.

The Jesuit[1] smites his bosom, the bishop rends his
　cope.[2]

And she of the seven hills[3] shall mourn her children's
　ills,
　And tremble when she thinks on the edge of Eng-
　　land's sword;
And the kings of earth in fear shall shudder when they
　hear
　What the hand of God hath wrought for the houses[4]
　and the word![5]

LORD MACAULAY.

[1] **Jesuit**: a member of the most celebrated of all the Roman Catholic
religious orders, founded for the purpose of resisting the spread of Protes-
tantism. Charles I. married a Catholic princess of France; the Parliamentary or Puritan Party in the Civil War believed that, through the queen's
influence, he was endeavoring to reinstate the Catholic religion in England,
and to restore the Jesuits, **who had been** driven **out of** the country in 1604.
But if the king had no sympathy for the Puritans, he certainly was not a
Catholic, although he endeavored, and with good reason, to mitigate the
severity of the English laws against the **Catholics.**

[2] **Cope**: a kind of cloak worn by bishops and other ecclesiastics.

[3] **She of the seven hills**: the Church of Rome.

[4] **Houses**: Houses of Parliament, especially the House of Commons.

[5] **The word**: the Puritan faith, which its adherents maintained was
based solely on the Bible, or Word of God.

BANNOCK-BURN.[1]

ROBERT BRUCE'S ADDRESS TO HIS ARMY.

SCOTS, wha [2] hae [3] wi' [4] Wallace [5] bled —
Scots, wham [6] Bruce has aften [7] led —
Welcome to your gory bed,
    Or to victorie!

Now's the day, and now's the hour;
See the front o' battle lower;
See approach proud Edward's power —
    Chains and slaverie!

Wha will be a traitor knave?
Wha can fill a coward's grave?
Wha sae [8] base as be a slave?
    Let him turn and flee!

Wha for Scotland's king and law
Freedom's sword will strongly draw,
Freeman stand or freeman fa' [9] —
    Let him follow me!

---

[1] **Bannock-Burn**, near Stirling, was in 1314, the scene of a desperate battle between Edward II. of England and Robert Bruce the Scottish hero. The English, although they had a far larger force, were utterly defeated, and Edward narrowly escaped capture.

[2] **Wha**: who.
[3] **Hae**: have.
[4] **Wi'**: with.
[5] **Wallace**: see note 3, p. 109.

[6] **Wham**: whom.
[7] **Aften**: often.
[8] **Sae**: so.
[9] **Fa'**: fall.

By oppression's **woes and pains**!
By your sons **in servile chains**!
We **will** drain **our dearest veins,**
        But they shall be **free**!

Lay the proud usurpers low!
Tyrants fall **in** every foe!
Liberty's in every blow!
        Let us do, or die!

ROBERT BURNS.

LEONIDAS.[1]

SHOUT for the mighty men
  Who died along this shore,
Who died within this mountain's glen!
For never nobler chieftain's head
Was laid on valor's crimson bed,
  Nor ever prouder gore
Sprang forth, than theirs who won the day
Upon thy strand, Thermopylæ!

Shout for the mighty men
  Who on the Persian tents,
Like lions from their midnight den
Bounding on the slumbering deer,
Rushed — a storm of sword and spear;
  Like the roused elements,
Let loose from an immortal hand
To chasten or to crush a land!

But there are none to hear —
  Greece is a hopeless slave.
Leonidas! no hand is near

---

[1] **Xerxes,** king of Persia, invaded Greece with an almost countless host, in 480 B.C. Leonidas, **king** of Sparta, with a small number of chosen men defended the rocky pass **of** Thermopylæ (Ther-mop'y-lē), until the last of his heroic band fell. **A monument** was erected in the pass by the Greeks, which bore this inscription: "Go, traveller, and tell at Lacedæmon (Lac-e-dĕ-mon) [or Sparta] that we fell here in obedience to her laws."

To lift thy fiery falchion [1] now;
No warrior makes the warrior's vow
    Upon thy sea-washed grave.
The voice that should be raised by men
Must now be given by wave and glen.

And it is given!   The surge,
    The tree, the rock, the sand
On freedom's kneeling spirit urge,
In sounds that speak but to the free,
The memory of thine and thee!
    The vision of thy band
Still gleams within the glorious dell
Where their gore hallowed as it fell!

And is thy grandeur done?
    Mother of men like these!
Has not thy outcry gone
Where justice has an ear to hear?
Be holy! God shall guide thy spear,
    Till in thy crimsoned seas
Are plunged the chain and scimitar.
Greece shall be a new-born star!

GEORGE CROLY.

---

[1] Falchion (fawl'chon): a short broadsword with a slightly curved point.

BOADICEA.[1]

WHEN the British warrior queen,
  Bleeding from the Roman rods,
Sought, with an indignant mien,
  Counsel of her country's gods,

Sage beneath the spreading oak
  Sat the Druid,[2] hoary chief;
Every **burning word he spoke**
  Full of rage and full of grief:

Princess! if our aged eyes
  Weep upon thy matchless wrongs,
'Tis because resentment ties
  All the terrors of our tongues.

Rome shall perish — write that word
  In the blood that she has spilt;
Perish, hopeless and abhorred,
  Deep in ruin as in guilt.

[1] **Boadicea** (Bo-ad-I-se'a): widow of a British chief, and queen of one of the tribes of the Britons. The Romans, who had conquered Britain, treated **her and her daughter with** atrocious cruelty and insult. Boadicea led a revolt against the conquerors of her country, and though at first successful was finally defeated, and, according to some accounts, killed at Battle Bridge, in what is now North London, **A.D. 62.**

[2] **Druid:** a name of uncertain origin, though sometimes derived from *drus*, an oak, given to **a priest of the ancient** Britons. The Druids were also the poets, teachers, and historians of the people.

Rome, **for empire** far renowned,
    Tramples on a thousand states;
Soon her pride shall kiss **the ground** —
    Hark! **the** Gaul[1] is at her gates!

Other Romans shall arise,
    Heedless of **a** soldier's name;
Sounds, not arms, shall win the prize,
    Harmony the path to fame.

Then the progeny that springs
    From the forests of our land,
Armed with thunder,[2] clad with wings,[3]
    Shall a wider world command.[4]

Regions Cæsar never knew
    Thy posterity shall sway;
Where his eagles[5] never flew,
    None invincible as they.

Such the bard's prophetic words,
    Pregnant with celestial fire,
Bending as he swept the chords
    Of his sweet but awful lyre.

---

[1] **Gaul**: the Gauls, **or** inhabitants of **France**, did not attack Rome or invade Roman territory in Italy after 284 B.C. The city finally fell through **the** invasion of the northern barbarians. Here, Gaul may **be** used in a general sense for any uncivilized people.

[2] **Thunder**: the thunder of firearms, especially cannon.

[3] **Wings**: alluding to the sails of ships.

[4] **Wider world command**: Britain became the greatest exploring, conquering, **and** colonizing nation on the globe; but as the ancient Britons **were in great** measure killed off or driven into Wales and Cornwall by the Saxons in the fifth century, they can hardly be said to have had much part in this movement.

[5] **Eagles**: alluding to the figure of the eagle on the Roman war-standards.

She, with **all** a monarch's pride,
  Felt them in her bosom glow:
Rushed to battle, fought, and died;
  Dying, hurled them at the foe.

Ruffians, pitiless as proud,
  Heaven awards the vengeance due;
Empire is on us bestowed,
  Shame and ruin wait for you.

WILLIAM COWPER.

MARMION[1] AND DOUGLAS.

THE train [2] from out the castle drew,
But Marmion stopp'd to bid adieu:
  " Though something I might plain," [3] he said,
" Of cold respect to stranger guest,
Sent thither by your king's behest,[4]
  While in Tantallon's [5] towers I stay'd,
Part we in friendship from your land,
And, noble Earl, receive my hand."

But Douglas round him drew his cloak,
Folded his arms, and thus he spoke:

[1] **Marmion**: the name of an imaginary English hero who died fighting in the great battle of Flodden, in the war between Scotland and England, 1513. See note 1, p. 98. Douglas was the name of a noble Scotch family of great wealth and influence. Marmion goes as an ambassador from the king of England to the Scottish sovereign. He makes his journey before hostilities break out between the two countries; his object being to learn —

" Why through all Scotland, near and far,
  Their king is mustering troops for war."
                                    (*Marmion*, Canto I. xx.)

At the request of King James of Scotland, Lord Douglas receives Marmion as his guest at Tantallon Castle. The extract represents the English knight on the point of bidding adieu to his host.

[2] **The train**: the troops of Marmion.

[3] **Plain**: complain.

[4] **Behest**: command.

[5] **Tantallon's towers**: Tantallon Castle, the principal stronghold of the Douglas family in the east of Scotland, was built on a rocky promontory overlooking the German Ocean, or North Sea. It was situated about two miles from North Berwick, just at the entrance of the Firth of Forth.

" My manors,[1] halls and bowers [2] shall still
Be open, at my sovereign's will,
To each one whom he lists,[3] howe'er
Unmeet [4] to be the owner's peer.[5]
My castles are my king's alone
From turret [6] to foundation-stone;
The hand of Douglas is his own,
And never shall in friendly grasp
The hand of such as Marmion clasp."

Burn'd Marmion's swarthy cheek like fire,
And shook his very frame for ire,
And, " This to me ! " he said;
" An 'twere not for thy hoary beard,
Such hand as Marmion's had not spared
   To cleave the Douglas' head!
And, first, I tell thee, haughty Peer,[5]
He who does England's message here,
Although the meanest in her State,
May well, proud Angus,[7] be thy mate :
And, Douglas, more I tell thee here
   Even in thy pitch of pride,[8]
Here in thy hold,[9] thy vassals near,
(Nay, never look upon your lord,
And lay your hands upon your sword,[10])

[1] Man'ors : the estates of a lord or person of rank.
[2] Bowers : chambers.   [4] Unmeet : unfit.
[3] Lists : chooses.   [5] Peer : equal; but in second instance, lord.
[6] Turret : a small tower, usually rising above a larger one as a look-out station ; hence, the topmost tower.
[7] Angus : Douglas was earl of Angus.
[8] Pitch of pride : here, apparently, equivalent to lofty castle.
[9] Hold : stronghold.
[10] This speech in parenthesis is addressed to the vassals or dependents of Douglas.

I tell thee, thou'rt defied!
And, if thou said'st I am not peer
To any lord in Scotland here,
Lowland or Highland, far or near,
    Lord Angus, thou hast lied!"

On the Earl's cheek the flush of rage
O'ercame the ashen hue of age;
Fierce he broke forth, "And darest thou then
To beard the lion in his den,
    The Douglas in his hall?
And hopest thou hence unscathed[1] to go?
No, by Saint Bride[2] of Bothwell, no!
Up drawbridge,[3] grooms,[4] — what, Warder, ho!
Let the portcullis[5] fall."
Lord Marmion turn'd, — well was his need! —
And dash'd the rowels[6] in his steed,
Like arrow through the archway sprung;
The ponderous gate[7] behind him rung:
To pass there was such scanty room,
The bars, descending, razed[8] his plume.

The steed along the drawbridge flies,
Just as it trembled on the rise;

---

[1] **Unscathed**: unharmed.

[2] **Saint Bride of Bothwell**: Bothwell is on the Clyde a short distance above Glasgow; here there is an old church which may have been dedicated to St. Bride (or Bridget) of Ireland, as many churches were throughout the British Isles.

[3] **Drawbridge**: a bridge over the moat or ditch in front of the main entrance of the castle. It was raised and lowered by chains.

[4] **Grooms**: servants.

[5] **Portcullis**: a strong, heavy grating sliding in a vertical groove. When let down, it barred entrance to the castle.

[6] **Rowels: spurs.**   [7] **Gate**: the portcullis.   [8] **Razed**: here, grazed.

Not lighter does the swallow skim
Along the smooth lake's level brim;
And, when Lord Marmion reach'd his band,
He halts, and turns with clenchèd hand,
And shout of loud defiance pours,
And shook his gauntlet[1] at the towers.

SIR WALTER SCOTT.

[1] **Gauntlet**: a glove plated with steel, and coming up so as to protect the lower arm.

SCOTLAND'S MAIDEN MARTYR.[1]

A TROOP of soldiers waited at **the door,**
A crowd of people gather'd in the street,
Aloof a little from them sabres gleam'd,
And flash'd into their faces. Then the **door**
Was open'd, and two women meekly stepp'd
Into the sunshine of the sweet May-noon,
Out of the prison. One was weak and **old,**
A woman full of tears and **full of** woes;

[1] In 1638 Charles I. endeavored to compel the Church of Scotland, which
was strongly Presbyterian, to use the service-book of the Episcopal Church
of England.

The people of all classes rose against those who were sent to enforce the
king's will, and signed a covenant or solemn oath to maintain their own
national church and furthermore to require others to accept it.

When Charles II. **came** to the throne he ordered the Covenant to be
burned, and an act was passed ordering **all persons to** refuse and condemn
it **as an** unlawful oath.

Those who persisted in maintaining the Covenant were now regarded
by the government as rebels and were treated with frightful severity. All
religious meetings of the Covenanters were denounced under pain of death.
These extreme measures provoked insurrection and **almost** civil war.

John Graham, better known as Claverhouse, was especially cruel in his
persecution of those who refused to renounce the Covenant.

In 1685 two women were tied to stakes and drowned in the rising tide
at Solway Firth, **in the** southwest of Scotland, for persisting in holding to
the Covenant. **One** was Margaret M'Lauchlan, who was advanced in years;
and the other Margaret Wilson, **a girl of** eighteen.

Burton in his History **of** Scotland (Vol. VII.) coolly remarks that "these
ferocities" were **limited** to a small corner of the southwest of Scotland,
and **that** "there was not much sympathy with the sufferers in other parts
of the country."

The other was a maiden in her morn ;
And they **were one** in name and one in faith,
Mother **and** daughter **in the bond of** Christ,
That bound them closer than the **ties** of blood.

The troop moved on ; and down the sunny street
The people follow'd, ever falling back
As in their faces flash'd the naked blades.
But **in** the midst the women simply went
As if they two were walking, side by side,
Up to God's **house** on some still Sabbath morn ;
Only they **were not** clad for Sabbath day,
But as they went about their daily tasks :
They went to prison and they went to death,
Upon their Master's service.

On the shore
The troopers halted ; all the shining **sands**
Lay bare and glistering ; [1] for the tide had
Drawn back to its farthest margin**'s** weedy mark ;
And each succeeding wave, with flash and curve,
That seem'd to mock the sabres on **the** shore,
Drew nearer by a hand-breadth. **" It** will be
A long day's work," murmur'd those murderous men,
As they slack'd rein. The leader of **the** troops
Dismounted, and the people **passing near**
Then heard the pardon proffer'd, with the **oath**
Renouncing and abjuring [2] part with all
The persecuted, **covenanted** folk.
But both refused the oath ; " because," they said,

---

[1] **Glistering** : glistening.
[2] **Abjuring** : swearing to give up or withdraw from.

" Unless with Christ's dear servants we have part,
We have no part with Him."

On this they took
The elder Margaret, and led her out
Over the sliding sands, the weedy sludge,[1]
The pebbly shoals, far out, and fasten'd her
Unto the farthest stake, already reach'd
By every rising wave, and left her there :
And as the waves crept round her feet, she pray'd
" That He would firm uphold her in their midst,
Who holds them in the hollow of His hand."

The tide flow'd in.   And up and down the shore
There paced the Provost[2] and the Laird[3] of Lag, —
Grim Grierson, — with Windram and with Graham ;[4]
And the rude soldiers, jesting with coarse oaths,
As in the midst the maiden meekly stood,
Waiting her doom, delay'd, said " she would
Turn before the tide, — seek refuge in their arms
From the chill waves."   But ever to her lips
There came the wondrous words of life and peace :
" If God be for us, who can be against ? "
" Who shall divide us from the love of Christ ? "
" Nor height, nor depth, nor any other creature."

From the crowd
A woman's voice cried a very bitter cry, —
"O Margaret ! my bonnie,[5] bonnie Margaret !

[1] **Sludge** : mud, mire.   [2] **Provost** : the magistrate or mayor.
[3] **Laird** . lord ; often used for a Scottish squire or country gentleman.
   [4] **Graham** : this was not John Graham of Claverhouse but his brother,
who was sheriff.   [5] **Bonnie** : pretty.

Gie [1] in, gie in, my bairnie,[2] dinna [3] ye drown,
Gie in, and tak' the oath."

      The tide flow'd in ;
And so wore on the sunny afternoon ;
And every fire went out upon the hearth,
And not a meal was tasted in the town [4] that day.
And still the tide was flowing in :
Her mother's voice yet sounding in her ear,
They turn'd young Margaret's face towards the sea,
Where something white was floating, — something
White as the sea-mew [5] that sits upon the wave :
But as she look'd it sank ; then show'd again ;
Then disappear'd ; and round the shore
And stake the tide stood ankle-deep.

       Then Grierson
With cursing vow'd that he would wait
No more ; and to the stake the soldier led her
Down, and tied her hands ; and round her
Slender waist too roughly cast the rope, for
Windram came and eased it while he whisper'd
In her ear, " Come, take the test [6] and ye are free " ;
And one cried, " Margaret, say but God save
The King !" " God save the King of his great grace,"
She answer'd, but the oath she would not take.

     And still the tide flow'd in,
And drove the people back and silenced them.

[1] Gie in : give in, submit. [2] Bairnie : child. [3] Dinna : do not, don't.
[4] The town : the town of Wigton, on Solway Firth, where this martyrdom occurred.
 [5] Sea-mew : a species of gull or sea-bird having white plumage.
 [6] Test : here meaning the oath of abjuration of the Covenant.

The tide flow'd in, and rising to her knees,
She sang the psalm, "To Thee I lift my soul"; [1]
The tide flow'd in, and rising to her waist,
"To Thee, my God, I lift my soul," she sang.
The tide flow'd in, and rising to her throat,
She sang no more, but lifted up her face,
And there was glory over all the sky,
And there was glory over all the sea, —
A flood of glory, — and the lifted face
Swam in it [2] till it bow'd beneath the flood,
And Scotland's Maiden Martyr went to God.

ANONYMOUS

[1] Psalm xxv.
[2] Compare Tennyson's "Two Voices," —

> "But looking upward, full of grace,
> He prayed, and from a happy place
> God's glory smote him on the face."

THE EXECUTION OF MONTROSE.[1]

I.

COME hither, Evan Cameron,
    Come, stand beside my knee —
I hear the river roaring down
    Towards the wintry sea.
There's shouting on the mountain-side,
    There's war within the blast —
Old faces look upon me,
    Old forms go trooping past ;
I hear the pibroch[2] wailing

[1] James Grahame, Marquis of Montrose, was born in Edinburgh in 1612.
During the English Civil War between King Charles I. of England and
Parliament, Montrose served at first on the side of the people, but eventually went over to the Royalists. Charles made him Marquis of Montrose
and commander-in-chief of the Scottish army.

He gained several victories for the crown, but was defeated by General
Leslie at Philiphaugh in 1645.

Montrose then went to the continent, but after the execution of Charles
I. by Parliament, he returned to Scotland in 1650, and led an insurrection
in behalf of Prince Charles (Charles II.). The effort failed, and the Marquis was taken prisoner and executed "with all the vindictive insult which
his hereditary enemy, the Marquis of Argyle," could heap upon him.

"Montrose," said an eminent French nobleman, "is the only man in
the world that has ever realized to me the ideas of certain heroes, whom
we now discover nowhere but in the lives of Plutarch." Professor Aytoun
states that in the historical incidents recorded in the following ballad there
is no element of fiction. "It may," he says, "be considered as a narrative
related by an aged Highlander who had followed Montrose through his
campaigns, to his grandson — Evan Cameron."

[2] Pibroch : the battle-music of the bagpipe.

Amidst the din of fight,
And my dim spirit wakes again
Upon the verge of night.

II.

'Twas I that led the Highland host [1]
Through wild Lochaber's [2] snows,
What time the plaided [3] clans [4] came down
To battle with Montrose.
I've told thee how the Southrons [5] fell
Beneath the broad claymore,[6]
And how we smote the Campbell clan,[7]
By Inverlochy's [8] shore.
I've told thee how we swept Dundee,[9]
And tamed the Lindsays' [10] pride ;

[1] **Highland host**: the Highlanders were, as a rule, on the side of the king.

[2] **Lochaber's snows**: Lochaber is a wild, mountainous district in Inverness, in the northeast of Scotland.

[3] **Plaided**: the plaid is a shawl-like garment formerly worn by all Highlanders.

[4] **Clans**: among the Highlands a clan consisted of all the common descendants of the same ancestor — hence a family or tribe. These battles between the Highland clans and Montrose occurred when Montrose was fighting against the king; later he espoused his cause, and then, of course, the Highlanders were on his side.

[5] **Southrons**: the English.

[6] **Claymore**: a heavy, two-edged sword.

[7] **Campbell clan**: the Marquis of Argyle (Archibald Campbell) with his clan fought against the king in the Civil War.

[8] **Inverlochy**: Inverlochy Castle stands on a height overlooking Loch (Lake) Eil in the southwestern part of Inverness, Central Scotland.

[9] **Dundee**: a city in the east of Scotland, on the river Tay. It was strongly opposed to the king. Montrose with his men took the place in 1645.

[10] **Lindsays' pride**: apparently referring to raids made by Montrose in Forfarshire, in the east of Scotland, where many of the Lindsay family resided.

But never have I told thee yet
How the great Marquis [1] died.

III.

A traitor sold **him** to his foes ;
O deed of deathless shame !
I charge thee, boy, if e'er thou meet
With one of Assynt's name [2] —
Be it upon **the mountain's side,**
Or yet **within** the **glen,**
Stand he in martial **gear alone,**
Or backed by **armèd men** —
Face him **as** thou **wouldst** face the man
Who wronged thy sire's renown ;
Remember of what blood thou art,
And strike the **caitiff** down **!**

IV.

They brought him to the **Watergate,**[3]
Hard bound with hempen span,[4]
As though they held **a lion** there,
And **not a fenceless**[5] **man.**
They set him **high upon a cart**[6] —

[1] **Marquis** : the Marquis of Montrose ; he was executed at Edinburgh.

[2] **Assynt** : Macleod of Assynt, a former adherent of Montrose, to whom the Marquis applied for food and shelter, basely betrayed him to his enemies.

[3] **Watergate** : a gate at the east of the city, near **Holyrood Palace, in** the old wall which formerly surrounded Edinburgh.

[4] **Span** : rope.   [5] **Fenceless** : defenceless.

[6] **Cart** : they placed Montrose high upon a cart, taking off his hat and binding his hands, in the hope that the people would stone him, and that he might not be able to save his face with his hands. But even those who had been hired to stone him were so moved by his noble bearing that they could not find heart to carry out **their purpose.**

The hangman rode below —
They drew his hands behind his back,
    And bared his noble **brow.**
Then, as a hound is **slipped** from leash,[1]
    They cheered, the common throng,
And blew the note with yell and shout,
    And bade him pass along.

V.

It would have **made a** brave man's **heart**
    Grow sad and sick that day,
To watch the keen, malignant eyes
    Bent down on that array.
There stood the Whig[2] west-country lords,
    In balcony and bow;[3]
There sat the gaunt and withered dames,
    And their daughters all a-row.
And every open window
    Was full as full might be
With black-robed Covenanting[4] carles,[5]
    That goodly sport to see!

VI.

But when he came, though pale and wan,
    He looked so great and high,
So noble was his manly front,
    So calm his steadfast eye; —

---

[1] **Leash** . a cord for holding a dog.

[2] **Whig**: the Whig party had its origin in Southwestern Scotland, and sprang from the clan that was opposed to Charles I. and to his son.

[3] **Bow**: a bow or bay-window.

[4] **Covenanting carles**: those who had bound themselves by the Covenant or oath to maintain the Scottish Church. During the Civil War they were opposed to the **king.**   [5] **Carles**: low, base fellows.

The rabble rout forebore to shout,
   And each man held his breath,
For well they knew the hero's soul
   Was face to face with death.
And then a mournful shudder
   Through all the people crept,
And some that came to scoff at him
   Now turned aside and wept.

VII.

But onwards — always onwards,
   In silence and in gloom,
The dreary pageant labored,[1]
   Till it reached the house of doom.[2]
Then first a woman's voice[3] was heard
   In jeer and laughter loud,
And an angry cry and a hiss arose
   From the heart of the tossing crowd:
Then as the Græme[4] looked upwards,
   He saw the ugly smile
Of him who sold his king for gold —
   The master-fiend Argyle![5]

[1] **Labored**: the procession was three hours passing from the Watergate to the Tolbooth, or city prison, though the distance was less than a mile.

[2] **House of doom**: the Tolbooth, or prison.

[3] **A woman's voice**: the only person who insulted Montrose was the Lady Jean Gordon, Countess of Haddington. She was the niece of Argyle, — Montrose's life-long enemy, — and is said to have been of infamous character.

[4] **The Græme**: the same as Grahame; the family name of Montrose.

[5] **Argyle**: Archibald Campbell, Earl and Marquis of Argyle. During the Civil War he fought on the side of the Covenanters against the king, and was particularly cruel toward Royalist prisoners. After the king's capture it was thought by some that Argyle and Cromwell plotted his execution. (See Burton's History of Scotland, VII. 245.) He suffered death, on a charge of treason, 1661.

VIII.

The Marquis gazed a moment,
  And nothing did he say,
But the cheek of Argyle grew ghastly pale
  And he turned his eyes away.
The painted harlot by his side,
  She shook through every limb,
For a roar like thunder swept the **street**,
  And hands were clenched at him;
And a Saxon[1] soldier cried aloud,
  " Back, coward, from thy place !
For seven long years thou hast **not** dared
  To look him in the face."

IX.

Had I been there with sword in hand,
  And fifty Camerons[2] by,
That day through high Dunedin's[3] streets
  Had pealed the slogan-cry.[4]
Not all their troops of trampling horse,
  Nor might of mailèd[5] men —
Not all the rebels in the south[6]
  Had borne us backwards then !
Once more his foot on highland heath[7]

---

[1] **Saxon** : English.

[2] **Camerons** : the clan of Cameron **was on the** side of the king, and hence friendly to Montrose.

[3] **Dunedin** : an ancient name of Edinburgh.   [4] **Slogan**-cry : war-cry.

[5] **Mailèd** (pronounced here in two syllables, *mail'ed*) ; wearing linked or mail armor.

[6] **The south** : England is usually meant by "the south," but here the south of Scotland, in distinction from the Highlands, appears to be referred to.   [7] **Heath** : waste land covered with heath or heather.

Had trod as free as air,
Or I, and all who bore my name,
Been laid around him there!

X.

It might not be.   They placed him next
Within the solemn hall,[1]
Where once the Scottish kings were throned
Amidst their nobles all.
But there was dust of vulgar feet
On that polluted floor,
And perjured traitors filled the place
Where good men sate before.
With savage glee came Warristoun,[2]
To read the murderous doom;
And then uprose the great Montrose
In the middle of the room.

XI.

"Now, by my faith, as belted knight,[3]
And by the name I bear,
And by the bright Saint Andrew's cross [4]
That waves above us there —
Yea, by a greater, mightier oath —
And oh, that such should be! —

---

[1] **Hall**   the Parliament House, Edinburgh.
[2] **Warristoun:** Archibald Johnston of Warristoun, an inveterate enemy of Montrose. He met the same fate as Montrose some years later, and died the death of a coward.
[3] **Belted knight:** the belt was a badge or sign of knighthood.
[4] **Saint Andrew's cross:** the cross of Scotland on the Scottish flag, Saint Andrew being the patron saint of Scotland.

By that dark stream of royal blood[1]
   That lies 'twixt you and me —
I have not sought in battle-field
   A wreath of such renown,
Nor dared I hope on my dying day
   To win the martyr's crown!

XII.

" There is a chamber far away
   Where sleep the good and brave,
But a better place ye have named for me
   Than by my father's grave.
For truth and right, 'gainst treason's might,
   This hand hath always striven,
And ye raise it up for a witness still
   In the eye of earth and heaven.
Then nail my head on yonder tower[2] —
   Give every town a limb[3] —
And God who made shall gather them:
   I go from you to Him!"

XIII.

The morning dawned full darkly,
   The rain came flashing down,
And the jagged streak of the levin-bolt[4]
   Lit up the gloomy town:

[1] **Royal blood**: an allusion to the belief that Argyle had been concerned in the execution of Charles I. See note 5, p. 91.

[2] **Tower**: a pinnacle of the prison on which, according to the sentence, his head was to be fastened on an iron pin.

[3] **A limb**: by the death sentence the body was to be quartered, and the limbs fastened up in public places in four of the principal towns of Scotland.

[4] **Levin-bolt**: lightning; the thunderbolt.

The thunder crashed across the heaven,
   The fatal hour was come;   ·
Yet aye [1] broke in with muffled beat,
   The 'larum [2] of the drum.
There was madness on the earth below
   And anger in the sky,
And young and old, and rich and poor,
   Came forth to see him die.

XIV.

Ah, God! that ghastly gibbet! [3]
   How dismal 'tis to see
The great, tall, spectral skeleton,
   The ladder and the tree! [4]
Hark! hark! it is the clash of arms —
   The bells begin to toll —
" He is coming! he is coming!
   God's mercy on his soul!"
One last, long peal of thunder —
   The clouds are cleared away,
And the glorious sun once more looks down
   Amidst the dazzling day.

XV.

" He is coming! he is coming!"
   Like a bridegroom [5] from his room

[1] **Aye**: ever, constantly.

[2] **'Larum** (alarm): here, the roll or beat of drums.

[3] **Gibbet**: the gibbet, or gallows, was erected in the Grassmarket, a large square near the castle in the old city of Edinburgh. In executions there the criminal was obliged to mount a high ladder placed at the side of the gallows; after the hangman, who accompanied him, had adjusted the halter, he pushed the victim off the ladder.

[4] **Tree**: another name for the gallows.

[5] **Bridegroom**: Montrose was richly dressed in scarlet overlaid with silver lace, so that he looked rather like a bridegroom going to his wedding than a criminal going to the gallows.

Came the hero from his prison
  To the scaffold and the doom.
There was glory on his forehead,
  There was lustre in his eye,
And he never walked to battle
  More proudly than to die;
There was color in his visage
  Though the cheeks of all were wan,
And they marvelled as they **saw him pass**,
  That great and goodly man!

XVI.

He mounted up the scaffold,
  And he turned him **to** the crowd;
But they dared not trust the people,
  So **he** might not speak aloud.
But he looked upon the heavens,
  And they were clear and blue,
And in the liquid ether
  The eye of God shone through.
Yet a black and murky battlement[1]
  Lay resting on the hill,
As though the thunder slept within —
  All else was **calm** and still.

XVII.

The grim Geneva ministers[2]
  With anxious scowl drew near,

---

[1] **Battlement**: **the** battlement **or wall of** the castle of Edinburgh. It overlooks the Grassmarket.

[2] **Geneva ministers**: the Presbyterian ministers — those opposed to the **Church of England and the** king. They are called "Geneva ministers" because **Calvin, the** Protestant Reformer, was originally their teacher at Geneva, Switzerland.

As you have seen the ravens flock
  Around the dying deer.
He would not deign them word nor sign,
  But alone he bent the knee;
And veiled his face for Christ's dear grace
  Beneath the gallows-tree.
Then radiant and serene he rose,
  And cast his cloak away:
For he had ta'en his latest look
  Of earth and sun and day.

XVIII.

A beam of light fell o'er him,
  Like a glory round the shriven,[1]
And he climbed the lofty ladder
  As it were the path to heaven.
Then came a flash[2] from out the cloud,
  And a stunning thunder-roll;
And no man dared to look aloft,
  For fear was on every soul.
There was another heavy sound,[3]
  A hush and then a groan;[4]
And darkness swept across the sky —
  The work of death was done!

                              PROFESSOR AYTOUN.

[1] **Shriven**: absolved, purified from guilt; said originally of one who had confessed his sins to a priest and received absolution.

[2] **Flash**: **the flash of** the cannon from the battlement giving the signal for the execution.

[3] Sound: **the fall of the body when it** was pushed off the ladder.

[4] **Groan**: the multitude present at the execution uttered "a general groan."

This ballad should be compared with **Sir** Walter Scott's "Legends of Montrose," which represent the Marquis in a different light.

EDINBURGH AFTER FLODDEN.[1]

——◆◇◆——

I.

NEWS of battle! — news of battle!
  Hark! 'tis ringing down the street:
And the archways and the pavement
  Bear the clang of hurrying feet.
News of battle! who hath brought it?
  News of triumph? Who should bring
Tidings from our noble army,
  Greetings from our gallant King?
All last night we watched the beacons

[1] Flodden: a hill in Northumberland in the northeast of England. It is but a few miles south of the Scottish border or boundary. Here in 1513 a desperate battle was fought between the Scotch and the English forces.

James IV. of Scotland thought to take advantage of the absence of Henry VIII. of England, who was then on the continent, to renew an alliance with France, England's old enemy.

The Scottish king easily found causes of complaint against Henry, and demanded satisfaction. That monarch returned a contemptuous answer, and James declared war, and invaded England.

The Earl of Surrey led the English. James commanded his own troops. The result of the battle was the defeat of the Scotch, though so valiantly did they fight that the English just barely gained an indecisive victory. The Scottish army, however, lost an enormous number, among whom was King James with all his chief men — in fact so terrible was the slaughter that it is said that "every noble house in Scotland left some of its name on the fatal field."

The news of the defeat at Flodden caused the wildest grief, especially in Edinburgh. Later the citizens of that place rallied and built a new wall round their city, but the English did not advance; there was no second battle, and peace was made between the combatants.

Blazing on the hills afar,
Each one bearing, as it kindled,
   Message of the opened war.
All night long the northern streamers [1]
   Shot across the trembling sky :
Fearful lights that never beckon
   Save when kings or heroes die.

II.

News of battle!   Who hath brought it ?
   All are thronging to the gate ;
" Warder [2] — warder ! open quickly ;
   Man — is this a time to wait ? "
And the heavy gates are opened :
   Then a murmur long and loud,
And a cry of fear and wonder
   Bursts from out the bending crowd.
For they see in battered harness [3]
   Only one hard-stricken man ;
And his weary steed is wounded,
   And his cheek is pale and wan :
Spearless hangs a bloody banner
   In his weak and drooping hand —
God ! can that be Randolph Murray,
   Captain of the city band ? [4]

III.

Round him crush the people, crying,
   " Tell us all ; oh, tell us true !

---

[1] **Northern streamers** : the Aurora Borealis or Northern Lights.

[2] **Warder** : a guard or sentinel ; one who kept the gate of the city, which was walled and fortified.

[3] **Harness** : armor.   [4] **City band** : the guard or militia of Edinburgh.

Where are they who went to battle,
  Randolph Murray, sworn to you?
Where are they, our brothers — children?
  Have they met the English foe?
Why art thou alone, unfollowed?
  Is it weal [1] or is it woe?"
Like a corpse the grisly warrior
  Looks from out his helm [2] of steel;
But no word he speaks in answer —
  Only with his armèd [3] heel
Chides his weary steed, and onward
  Up the city streets they ride —
Fathers, sisters, mothers, children,
  Shrieking, praying by his side.
" By the God that made thee, Randolph!
  Tell us what mischance hath come."
Then he lifts his riven [4] banner,
  And the asker's voice is dumb.

IV.

The elders of the city
  Have met within their hall —
The men whom good King James [5] had charged
  To watch the tower and wall.
" Your hands are weak with age," he said,
  " Your hearts are stout and true;
So bide ye in the Maiden Town, [6]

---

[1] **Weal**: welfare, prosperity, joy. [2] **Helm**: helmet.
[3] **Armèd**: pronounce in two syllables, *arm'ed.*
[4] **Riven**: rent, torn. [5] **King James**: James IV. of Scotland.
[6] **Maiden Town**: in the seventh century Edinburgh Castle was called
" Castrum Puellarum " or the Maidens' Castle, as the daughters of the
ancient kings were kept and educated there until they were married. This

While others fight for you.
My trumpet from the Border-side [1]
  Shall send a blast so clear
That all who wait within the gate
  That stirring sound may hear.
Or, if it be the will of Heaven
  That back I never come,
And if, instead of Scottish shouts,
  Ye hear the English drum, —
Then let the warning bells ring out,
  Then gird you to the fray,
Then man the walls like burghers stout,
  And fight while fight you may.
'Twere better that in fiery flame
  The roofs should thunder down,
Than that the foot of foreign foe
  Should trample in the town!"

V.

Then in came Randolph Murray, —
  His step was slow and weak,
And, as he doffed [2] his dinted helm,
  The tears ran down his cheek:
They fell upon his corslet [3]
  And on his mailèd [4] hand,
As he gazed around him wistfully,

may be the reason of the name "Maiden Town" or it may be an allusion to the well-known resemblance of Edinburgh to Athens, the sacred city of Athena or Minerva, goddess of wisdom.

[1] **Border-side**: the boundary between Scotland and England near which the battle of Flodden was fought.

[2] **Doffed**: took off.   [3] **Corslet**: armor for the trunk of the body.

[4] **Mailèd**: pronounce in two syllables, *mail'ed*.

Leaning sorely [1] on his brand.
And none who then beheld him
    But straight were smote with fear,
For a bolder and a sterner man
    Had never couched a spear.[2]
They knew so sad a messenger
    Some ghastly news must bring ;
And all of them were fathers,
    And their sons were with the King.

VI.

And up then rose the Provost [3] —
    A brave old man was he,
Of ancient name, and knightly fame,
    And chivalrous degree.[4]
He ruled our city like a Lord
    Who brooked [5] **no** equal here,
And ever for the **townsman's rights**
    Stood up 'gainst prince and peer.
And **he had** seen **the Scottish** host
    March from the Borough-muir,[6]
With music-storm and clamorous shout,
    And all **the din that** thunders out
        When youth's **of** victory sure.
But yet a dearer thought had he, —

---

[1] **Sorely** : grievously, heavily.

[2] **Couched a spear** : held a spear in attitude of attack; the butt-end of the spear rested in a socket of the armor so as to hold it firm.

[3] **Provost** : the **mayor** or governor of the city.

[4] **Degree** : descent, family.   [5] **Brooked** : endured.

[6] **Borough-muir** : a vacant tract of land or common just outside of Edinburgh on the south. Here James IV. reviewed his army before marching for the fatal field of Flodden.

For with a father's pride,
He saw his last remaining son
　Go forth by Randolph's side,
With casque [1] on head and spur on heel,
　All keen to do and dare ;
And proudly did that gallant boy
　Dunedin's banner bear.
Oh ! woful now was the old man's look,
　And he spake right heavily —
" Now, Randolph, tell thy tidings,
　However sharp they be !
Woe is written on thy visage,
　Death is looking from thy face,
Speak ! though it be of overthrow —
　It cannot be disgrace ! "

VII.

Right bitter was the agony
　That wrung that soldier proud :
Thrice did he strive to answer,
　And thrice he groaned aloud.
Then he gave the riven banner
　To the old man's shaking hand,
Saying — " That is all I bring ye
　From the bravest of the land.
Ay ! ye may look upon it —
　It was guarded well and long
By your brothers and your children,
　By the valiant and the strong.
One by one they fell around it,

---

[1] **Casque:** helmet.

As the archers [1] laid them low,
  Grimly dying, still unconquered,
    With their faces to the foe.
Ay! ye may well look upon it —
    There is more than honor there,
Else, be sure, I had not brought it
    From the field of dark despair.
Never yet was royal banner
    Steeped in such a costly dye;
It hath lain upon a bosom
    Where no other shroud shall lie.
Sirs! I charge you, keep it holy;
    Keep it as a sacred thing,
For the stain ye see upon it
    Was the life-blood of your King!"

VIII.

Woe, and woe, and lamentation!
    What a piteous cry was there!
Widows, maidens, mothers, children,
    Shrieking, sobbing in despair!
Through the streets the death-word rushes,
    Spreading terror, sweeping on —
" Jesu Christ! our King has fallen —
    O Great God, King James is gone!
Holy Mother Mary,[2] shield us,
    Thou who erst [3] didst lose thy Son!

---

[1] **Archers**: the skill of the English archers with the long-bow was proverbial; few troops, even those in armor, could stand against their volleys of well-aimed arrows.

[2] **Mother Mary**: the Virgin Mary; this was before the Reformation, and Scotland was then a Catholic nation.

[3] **Erst**: once, or long ago.

O the blackest day for Scotland
　That she ever knew before !
O our King — the good, the noble,
　Shall we see him never more ?
Woe to us, and woe to Scotland !
　O our sons, our sons and men !
Surely some have 'scaped the Southron,
　Surely some will come again !
Till the oak that fell last winter
　Shall uprear its shattered stem —
Wives and mothers of Dunedin —
　Ye may look in vain for them !

IX.

But within the Council Chamber
　All was silent as the grave,
Whilst the tempest of their sorrow
　Shook the bosoms of the brave.
Well indeed might they be shaken
　With the weight of such a blow :
He was gone — their prince, their idol,
　Whom they loved and worshipped so !
Like a knell of death and judgment
　Rung from heaven by angel hand,
Fell the words of desolation
　On the elders of the land.
Hoary heads were bowed and trembling,
　Withered hands were clasped and wrung ;
God had left the old and feeble,
　He had ta'en away the young.

X.

Then the Provost he uprose,
  And his lip was ashen white ;
But a flush was on his brow,
  And his eye was full of light.
" Thou hast spoken, Randolph Murray,
  Like a soldier stout and true ;
Thou hast done a deed of daring
  Had been perilled but by few.
For thou hast not shamed to face us,
  Nor to speak thy ghastly tale,
Standing — thou a knight and captain —
  Here, alive within thy mail ! [1]
Now, as my God shall judge me,
  I hold it braver done,
Than hadst thou tarried in thy place,
  And died above my son !
Thou need'st not tell it : he is dead.
  God help us all this day !
But speak — how fought the citizens
  Within the furious fray ?
For by the might of Mary !
  'Twere something still to tell
That no Scottish foot went backward
  When the Royal Lion [2] fell !"

XI.

" No one failed him !   He is keeping
  Royal state and semblance still ;

[1] **Mail :** linked or chain armor.
[2] **Royal Lion :** the Lion emblazoned on the Scottish banner.

Knight and noble lie around him,
　Cold on Flodden's fatal hill.
Of the brave and gallant-hearted,
　Whom you sent with prayers away,
Not a single man departed
　From his monarch yesterday.
Had you seen them, O my masters !
　When the night began to fall,
And the English spearmen gathered
　Round a grim and ghastly wall
As the wolves in winter circle
　Round the leaguer [1] on the heath,
So the greedy foe glared upward,
　Panting still for blood and death.
But a rampart rose before them,
　Which the boldest dared not scale ;
Every stone a Scottish body,
　Every step a corpse in mail !
And behind it lay our monarch,
　Clenching still his shivered sword ;
By his side Montrose and Athole,
　At his feet a Southron lord.
All so thick they lay together,
　When the stars lit up the sky,
That I knew not who were stricken,
　Or who yet remained to die.
Few there were when Surrey halted,
　And his wearied host withdrew ;
None but dying men around me,
　When the English trumpet blew,
Then I stooped, and took the banner,

[1] **Leaguer** : the camp of a besieging army.

As you see it, from his breast,
   And I closed our hero's eyelids,
      And I left him to his rest.
In the mountains growled the thunder,
      As I leaped the woful wall,
And the heavy clouds were settling
      Over Flodden, like a pall."

XII.

So he ended.   And the others
      Cared not any answer then;
Sitting silent, dumb with sorrow,
      Sitting anguish-struck, like men
Who have seen the roaring torrent
      Sweep their happy homes away,
And yet linger by the margin,
      Staring wildly on the spray.
But, without, the maddening tumult
      Waxes ever more and more,
And the crowd of wailing women
      Gather round the Council door.
Every dusky spire is ringing
      With a dull and hollow knell,
And the Miserere's [1] singing
      To the tolling of the bell.
Through the streets the burghers hurry,
      Spreading terror as they go;
And the rampart's thronged with watchers
      For the coming of the foe.

---

[1] **Miserere** (Mis-e-re're): the 57th Psalm — a Psalm of lamentation. In the Roman Catholic or Latin version of the Bible, it begins " Miserere mei, domine " — " Pity me, O Lord."

From each mountain-top a pillar [1]
   Streams into the torpid air,
Bearing token from the Border
   That the English host is there.
All without is flight and terror,
   All within is woe and fear —
God protect thee, Maiden City,
   For thy latest hour is near!

XIII.

No! not yet, thou high Dunedin!
   Shalt thou totter to thy fall;
Though thy bravest and thy strongest
   Are not here to man the wall.
No, not yet! the ancient spirit
   Of our fathers hath not gone;
Take it to thee as a buckler [2]
   Better far than steel or stone.
Oh, remember those who perished
   For thy birthright at the time
When to be a Scot was treason,
   And to side with Wallace [3] crime!
Have they not a voice among us,
   Whilst their hallowed dust is here?
Hear ye not a summons sounding
   From each buried warrior's bier?
Up! — they say — and keep the freedom
   Which we won you long ago:

---

[1] **Pillar**: a bonfire; a pillar of fire.   [2] **Buckler**: a shield.

[3] **Wallace**: a Scotch hero of the thirteenth century. He rose against the English when they invaded Scotland. Eventually he was betrayed to them, taken to London and executed as a traitor and rebel in 1305. See Burns's "Scots wha hae wi' Wallace bled," p. 71.

Up! and **keep our** graves unsullied
  From the insults of the foe!
Up! and if ye cannot save them,
  Come to us in blood and fire:
Midst the crash of falling turrets [1]
Let the last **of Scots** expire!

XIV.

Still the **bells** are tolling **fiercely,**
  And the cry comes louder in;
Mothers wailing for their children,
  Sisters for their slaughtered kin.
All is terror and disorder,
  Till the Provost rises up,
Calm, as though he had not tasted
  Of the fell [2] and bitter cup.
All so stately from **his** sorrow,
  Rose the old undaunted chief,
That you had not deemed, to see him,
  His was more than common grief.
" **Rouse ye,** Sirs!" **he** said; "we may not
  Longer mourn for what is done;
If our King be taken from us,
  We are left to guard his son.[3]
We have sworn to keep the city
  From the foe, whate'er they be,
And the oath that we have taken
  Never shall be broke by me.
Death is nearer to us, brethren,

---

[1] **Turrets**: towers or pinnacles.
[2] **Fell**: sharp, cruel, deadly.
[3] **His son**: James V. of Scotland.

Than it seemed to those who died,
Fighting yesterday at Flodden,
  By their lord and master's side.
Let us meet it then in patience,
  Not in terror or in fear;
Though our hearts are bleeding yonder,
  Let our souls be steadfast here.
Up, and rouse ye! Time is fleeting,
  And we yet have much to do;
Up! and haste ye through the city,
  Stir the burghers stout and true,
Gather all our scattered people,
  Fling the banner out once more, —
Randolph Murray! do thou bear it,
  As it erst was borne before:
Never Scottish heart will leave **it,**
  When they see their monarch's gore.

XV.

" Let them cease that dismal knelling;
  It is time enough to ring,
When the fortress-strength [1] of Scotland
  Stoops to ruin like its King.
Let the bells be kept for warning,
  Not for terrors or alarm;
When the next is heard to thunder,
  Let each man and stripling **arm.**
Bid the women leave their wailing —
  Do they think that woful strain,
From the bloody heaps of Flodden,

[1] **Fortress-strength** : referring to the castle and fortifications **of** Edinburgh.

Can redeem their dearest slain?
Bid them cease, — or rather hasten
  To the churches every one;
There to pray to Mary Mother,
  And to her anointed Son,
That the thunderbolt above us
  May not fall in ruin yet;
That in fire and blood and rapine
  Scotland's glory may not set.
Let them pray, — for never women
  Stood in need of such a prayer! —
England's yeomen shall not find them
  Clinging to the altars there.
No! if we are doomed to perish,
  Man and maiden, let us fall,
And a common gulf of ruin
  Open wide to whelm [1] us all!
Never shall the ruthless spoiler
  Lay his hot insulting hand
On the sisters of our heroes,
  Whilst we bear a torch or brand!
Up! and rouse ye, then, my brothers, —
  But when next ye hear the bell
Sounding forth the sullen summons
  That may be our funeral knell,
Once more let us meet together,
  Once more see each other's face;
Then, like men that need not tremble,
  Go to our appointed place.
God, our Father, will not fail us,
  In that last tremendous hour, —

[1] **Whelm**: overwhelm.

If all other bulwarks crumble,
    He will be our strength and tower:
Though the ramparts rock beneath us,
    And the walls go crashing down,
Though the roar of conflagration
    Bellow o'er the sinking town;
There is yet one place of shelter,[1]
    Where the foemen cannot come,
Where the summons never sounded
    Of the trumpet or the drum.
There again we'll meet our children,
    Who, on Flodden's trampled sod,
For their King and for their country
    Rendered up their souls to God.
There shall we find rest and refuge,
    With our dear departed brave
And the ashes of the city
    Be our universal grave!"

PROFESSOR AYTOUN.

[1] **One place of shelter** : the grave.

THE HEART OF THE BRUCE.[1]

I.

It was upon an April morn,
　While yet the frost lay hoar,[2]
We heard Lord James's[3] bugle horn
　Sound by the rocky shore.

II.

Then down we went, a hundred knights,
· All in our dark array,
And flung our armor in the ships
　That rode within the bay.

III.

We spoke not, as the shore grew less,
　But gazed in silence back,
Where the long billows swept away
　The foam behind our track.

---

[1] **Bruce**: Robert Bruce, "Scotland's **greatest king and** hero" joined William Wallace **in** resistance to the efforts **of** England to get and keep control of the country. He won the great victory of Bannockburn over Edward II. in 1314. Fourteen years later Edward was obliged to recognize the independence **of** Scotland. Bruce died the year following (1329), and according to the legend, Sir James Douglas was chosen to carry his heart **in a case of gold** to the Holy Land and bury it near the sepulchre of Christ. **The ballad narrates what** followed the attempt to **carry out** the hero's wishes.

[2] **Hoar**: white.　　　　　[3] **Lord James**: Sir James Douglas.

IV.

And aye the purple hues decayed
   Upon the fading hill,
And but one heart in all that ship
   Was tranquil, cold, and still.

V.

The good Lord Douglas paced the deck —
   Oh, but his face was wan!
Unlike the flush it used to wear
   When in the battle-van.[1]

VI.

"Come hither, I pray, my trusty knight,
   Sir Simon of the Lee;
There is a freit[2] lies near my soul
   I needs must tell to thee.

VII.

"Thou know'st the words King Robert spoke
   Upon his dying day:
How he bade me take his noble heart
   And carry it far away;

VIII.

"And lay it in the holy soil
   Where once the Saviour trod,
Since he might not bear the blessed Cross,
   Nor strike one blow for God.

[1] Battle-van: front of the battle.
[2] Freit: presentiment or superstition; notion or belief.

IX.

" Last night as in my bed I lay,
    I dreamed a dreary dream : —
Methought I saw a Pilgrim stand
    In the moonlight's quivering beam.

X.

" His robe was of the azure dye —
    Snow-white his scattered hairs —
And even such a cross he bore
    As good Saint Andrew bears.

XI.

" ' Why go ye forth, Lord James,' he said,
    ' With spear and belted brand ?
Why do you take its dearest pledge
    From this our Scottish land ?

XII.

" ' The sultry breeze of Galilee
    Creeps through its groves of palm,
The olives on the Holy Mount
    Stand glittering in the calm.

XIII.

" ' But 'tis not there that Scotland's heart
    Shall rest, by God's decree,
Till the great angel calls the dead
    To rise from earth and sea !

XIV.

" ' Lord James of Douglas, mark my rede ![1]
    That heart shall pass once more

[1] **Rede** : word.

In fiery fight against the foe,
　As it was wont of yore.

XV.

" ' And it shall pass beneath the cross,
　And save King Robert's vow ;
But other hands shall bear it back,
　Not, James of Douglas, thou ! '

XVI.

" Now, by thy knightly faith, I pray,
　Sir Simon of the Lee —
Nor truer friend had never man
　Than thou hast been to me —

XVII.

" If ne'er upon the Holy Land
　'Tis mine in life to tread,
Bear thou to Scotland's kindly earth
　The relics of her dead."

XVIII.

The tear was in Sir Simon's eye
　As he wrung the warrior's hand —
" Betide [1] me weal, betide me woe,
　I'll hold by thy command.

XIX.

" But if in battle-front, Lord James,
　'Tis ours once more to ride,
Nor force of man, nor craft of fiend,
　Shall cleave me from thy side ! "

[1] **Betide** : happen, befall.

XX.

And aye we sailed, and aye we sailed,
  Across the weary sea,
Until one morn the coast of Spain
  Rose grimly on our lee.[1]

XXI.

And as we rounded to the port,
  Beneath the watch-tower's wall,
We heard the clash of the atabals,[2]
  And the trumpet's wavering call.

XXII.

" Why sounds yon Eastern music here
  So wantonly[3] and long,
And whose the crowd of armèd[4] men
  That round yon standard throng ? "

XXIII.

" The Moors have come from Africa
  To spoil, and waste, and slay,
And King Alonzo of Castile
  Must fight with them to-day."

XXIV.

" Now shame it were," cried good Lord James,
  " Shall never be said of me
That I and mine have turned aside
  From the Cross in jeopardie ![5]

---

[1] **Lee**: the quarter toward which the wind blows.
[2] **Atabals** : Moorish drums.   [3] **Wantonly** : unrestrainedly, gayly.
[4] **Armèd (arm'ed).**   [5] **Jeopardie**: jeopardy, peril.

XXV.

" Have down, have **down,** my merry men **all** —
   Have down unto the plain ;
We'll let the Scottish lion loose [1]
   Within the fields of Spain ! "

XXVI.

" Now welcome to me, noble Lord,
   Thou and thy stalwart power ;
Dear is the sight of a Christian knight,
   Who **comes in** such an hour !

XXVII.

" Is **it for bond** [2] or faith you **come,**
   Or yet for golden fee ?
Or bring ye France's lilies [3] here,
   Or the flower [4] of Burgundie ? "

XXVIII.

" God greet thee well, thou **valiant king,**
   Thee and thy belted peers —
Sir James of Douglas am **I** called,
   And these are Scottish spears.

XXIX.

" We do not fight **for bond or plight,** [5]
   Nor yet for golden fee ;
But for the sake of our blessed Lord,
   Who died upon the tree. [6]

---

[1] **Scottish lion loose :** unfold the flag bearing the **Scottish** lion or arms of Scotland.

[2] **Bond :** meaning either in fulfilment of a vow or to liberate captives.

[3] **Lilies :** the lilies of **the arms** of France.

[4] **Flower :** arms of Burgundy.

[5] **Plight :** in fulfilment of a pledge or oath.   [6] **The tree :** the cross.

XXX.

" We bring our great King Robert's heart
    Across the weltering [1] wave
To lay it in the holy soil
    Hard by [2] the Saviour's grave.

XXXI.

" True pilgrims we, by land or sea,
    Where danger bars the way;
And therefore are we here, Lord King,
    To ride with thee this day! "

XXXII.

The King has bent his stately head,
    And the tears were in his eyne [3] —
" God's blessing on thee, noble knight,
    For this brave thought of thine!

XXXIII.

" I know thy name full well, Lord James,
    And honored may I be,
That those who fought beside the Bruce
    Should fight this day for me!

XXXIV.

" Take thou the leading of the van,
    And charge the Moors amain; [4]
There is not such a lance as thine
    In all the host of Spain! "

---

[1] **Weltering**: rising and **falling**.   [3] **Eyne**: eyes.
[2] **Hard by**: near by.   [4] **Amain**: furiously.

XXXV.

The Douglas turned towards us then,
    Oh, but his glance was high!
" There is not one of all my men
    But is as frank [1] as I.

XXXVI.

" There is not one of all my knights
    But bears as true a spear —
Then — onwards, Scottish gentlemen,
    And think, King Robert's here! "

XXXVII.

The trumpets blew, the cross-bolts [2] flew,
    The arrows flashed like flame,
As, spur in side, and spear in rest,[3]
    Against the foe we came.

XXXVIII.

And many a bearded Saracen [4]
    Went down both horse and man;
For through their ranks we rode like corn,
    So furiously we ran!

XXXIX.

But in behind our path they closed,
    Though fain [5] to let us through;
For they were forty thousand men,
    And we were wondrous few.

---

[1] **Frank**: sincere, true.

[2] **Cross-bolts**: arrows shot from cross-bows.

[3] **Spear in rest**: spear in attitude of attack. See note on *couched*, p. 102.

[4] **Saracen**: Mohammedan, Turk.

[5] **Fain**: glad, eager. The enemy let them through their ranks that they might close round them, and so utterly destroy them.

XL.

We might **not see** a lance's length,
   So dense was their array,[1]
But the long, fell sweep of the Scottish blade
   Still held them hard at bay.

XLI.

" Make in ! make in ! " Lord **Douglas** cried —
   " Make in, my brethren dear !
Sir William of St. Clair is down ;
   We **may** not leave him here ! "

XLII.

But thicker, thicker grew the swarm :
   And sharper shot the rain ;[2]
And the horses reared amid the press,[3]
   But they would not charge again.

XLIII.

" Now Jesu help thee," said Lord James,
   " Thou kind **and** true St. Clair !
An' if **I may not** bring thee off,
   I'll die **beside** thee there ! "

XLIV.

Then in the stirrups up he stood,
   So lion-like and bold,
And held the precious **heart** aloft
   All in its case of gold.

[1] **Array : line** of battle.
[2] **The rain :** the showers of arrows.
[3] **Press :** the multitude of troops.

XLV.

He flung it from him far ahead,
  And never spake he more,
But — "Pass thee first, thou dauntless heart,
  As thou wert wont of yore!"

XLVI.

The roar of fight rose fiercer yet,
  And heavier still the stour,[1]
Till the spears of Spain came shivering in,
  And swept away the Moor.

XLVII.

"Now praised be God the day is won!
  They fly o'er flood and fell [2] —
Why dost thou draw the rein so hard,
  Good knight, that fought so well?"

XLVIII.

"Oh, ride ye on, Lord King!" he said,
  "And leave the dead to me;
For I must keep the dreariest watch
  That ever I shall dree![3]

XLIX.

"There lies above his master's heart,
  The Douglas,[4] stark [5] and grim;
And woe that I am living man,
  Not lying there by him!

---

[1] **Stour**: battle; or the word may refer to the **dust** raised by the fight.
[2] **Fell**: stony, barren hills.   [4] **The Douglas**: Sir James Douglas.
[3] **Dree**: suffer or endure.   [5] **Stark**: stiff, rigid in death.

L.

" The world grows cold, **my** arm is old,
   And thin my lyart [1] hair,
And all that I loved best **on** earth
   Is stretched before me there.

LI.

" O Bothwell banks,[2] that bloom so bright
   Beneath the sun of May !
The heaviest cloud that ever blew
   Is bound for you this day.

LII.

" And, Scotland, thou may'st veil thy head
   In sorrow and in pain :
The sorest stroke upon thy brow
   Hath fallen this day in Spain !

LIII.

" We'll **bear** them back unto our ship,
   We'll bear them o'er **the** sea,
And lay them in the hallowed earth,
   Within our own countrie.

LIV.   .

" And be thou strong of heart, Lord King,
   For this I tell thee sure,
The sod that drank the Douglas' blood
   Shall never bear the Moor ! "

---

[1] **Lyart**: gray.
[2] **Bothwell banks** : Bothwell Castle, the **seat** of the Douglas family on the banks of the Clyde near Glasgow.

LV.

The King he lighted from his horse,
  He flung his brand away,
And took the Douglas by the hand,
  So stately as he lay.

LVI.

" God give thee rest, thou valiant soul !
  That fought so well for Spain;
I'd rather half my land were gone,
  So thou wert here again !"

LVII.

We lifted thence the good Lord James,
  And the priceless heart he bore;
And heavily we steered our ship
  Towards the Scottish shore.

LVIII.

No welcome greeted our return,
  Nor clang of martial tread,
But all were dumb and hushed as death,
  Before the mighty dead.

LIX.

We laid our chief in Douglas Kirk,[1]
  The heart in fair Melrose ;[2]
And woful men were we that day —
  God grant their souls repose !

PROFESSOR AYTOUN.

[1] **Kirk**: church; the church of Douglas Castle.
[2] **Melrose**: Melrose Abbey, the finest specimen of Gothic architecture in Scotland, is situated on the Tweed about forty miles southeast of Edinburgh. Here the heart of the Bruce is said to have been buried.

THE CHARGE OF THE LIGHT BRIGADE.[1]

HALF a league, half a league,
Half a league onward,
All in the valley of death
   Rode the six hundred.
Forward, the Light Brigade!
Charge for the guns, he said.
Into the valley of death
   Rode the six hundred.

Forward, the Light Brigade!
Was there a man dismay'd?
Not though the soldiers knew
   Some one had blundered.
Theirs not to make reply,
Theirs not to reason why,
Theirs but to do and die.
Into the valley of death
   Rode the six hundred.

[1] During the Crimean War between England, France, and Russia, Lord Lucan, who commanded the English Light Brigade of Cavalry, chose to interpret an order of attack to mean that he should attempt to take a Russian battery at the extreme end of a long, narrow valley. To accomplish it the Brigade had to run the gauntlet of two lines of infantry and artillery, besides meeting the full fire of the battery directly in the face. The movement was a terrible blunder. Out of six hundred and seventy-three that went into action, only one hundred and ninety-five came out unscathed. The rest were killed or wounded.

Cannon to right of them,
Cannon to left of them,
Cannon in front of them
    Volley'd and thunder'd ;
Storm'd at with shot and shell,
Boldly they rode and well.
Into the jaws of Death,
Into the mouth of Hell
    Rode the six hundred.

Flash'd all their sabres bare,
Flash'd as they turn'd in air,
Sabering the gunners there,
Charging an army, while
    All the world wonder'd :
Plunged in the battery-smoke,
Right through the line they broke ;
Cossack [1] and Russian
Reel'd from the sabre-stroke
    Shatter'd and sunder'd.
Then they rode back, but not,
    Not the six hundred.

Cannon to right of them,
Cannon to left of them
Cannon behind them
    Volley'd and thunder'd ;
Storm'd at with shot and shell,
While horse and hero fell,
They that had fought so well

---

[1] **Cossack**: one of a race of people inhabiting Southern Russia. On account of their great skill in horsemanship, they have long been largely employed in the Russian army as cavalry.

Came through the jaws of Death
Back from the mouth of Hell,
All that was left of them,
　Left of six hundred.

When can their glory fade?
O, the wild charge they made!
　All the world wondered.
Honor the charge they made!
Honor the Light Brigade,
　Noble six hundred!

ALFRED TENNYSON.

A LEGEND OF BREGENZ.

GIRT round with rugged mountains the fair Lake Con-
stance [1] lies;
In her blue heart reflected, shine back the starry skies;
And, watching each white cloudlet float silently and
slow,
You think a piece of heaven lies on our earth below!

Midnight is there; and silence, enthroned in heaven,
looks down
Upon her own calm mirror, upon a sleeping town:
For Bregenz [2], that quaint city upon the Tyrol [3] shore,
Has stood above Lake Constance a thousand years and
more.

Her battlements and towers, upon their rocky steep,
Have cast their trembling shadows for ages on the
deep;
Mountain and lake and valley, a sacred legend know,
Of how the town was saved one night, three hundred
years ago.

Far from her home and kindred a Tyrol maid had fled,
To serve in the Swiss valleys, and toil for daily bread;

---

[1] **Lake** Constance: a lake on the borders of Switzerland, Austria [the Tyrol], and Germany.　　[2] **Bregenz** (g hard).
[3] **Tyrol** (Tir'rol or Te-rōl'): a province of Austria.

And every year that fleeted so silently and fast
Seem'd to bear further from her the memory of the past.

She served kind, gentle masters, nor ask'd for rest or
        change ;
Her friends seem'd no more new ones, their speech
        seem'd no more strange ;
And, when she led her cattle to pasture every day,
She ceased to look and wonder on which side Bregenz
        lay.

She spoke no more of Bregenz, with longing and with
        tears ;
Her Tyrol home seem'd faded in a deep mist of years ;
She heeded not the rumors of Austrian war or strife ;
Each day she rose, contented, to the calm toils of life.

Yet, when her master's children would clustering round
        her stand,
She sang them the old ballads of her own native land ;
And, when at morn and evening she knelt before God's
        throne,
The accents of her childhood rose to her lips alone.

And so she dwelt: the valley more peaceful year by
        year ;
When suddenly strange portents[1] of some great deed
        seem'd near.
The golden corn was bending upon its fragile stalk,
While farmers, heedless of their fields, paced up and
        down in talk.   ˙

[1] **Portents:** signs of coming events, especially of evil or calamity.

The men seem'd stern and alter'd, with looks cast on
    the ground;
With anxious faces, one by one, the women gather'd
    round;
All talk of flax, or spinning, or work, was put away;
The very children seem'd afraid to go alone to play.

One day, out in the meadow with strangers from the
    town,
Some secret plan discussing, the men walk'd up and
    down.
Yet now and then seem'd watching a strange, uncertain
    gleam,
That look'd like lances 'mid the trees that stood below
    the stream.

At eve they all assembled, all care and doubt were
    fled;
With jovial laugh they feasted, the board was nobly
    spread.
The elder of the village rose up, his glass in hand,
And cried, " We drink the downfall of an accursed
    land!

"The night is growing darker; ere one more day is
    flown
Bregenz, our foeman's stronghold, Bregenz shall be our
    own!"
The women shrank in terror, (yet pride, too, had her
    part,)
But one poor Tyrol maiden felt death within her heart.

Before her stood fair Bregenz, once more her towers
    arose ;
What were the friends beside her?   Only her country's
    foes !
The faces of her kinsfolk, the days of childhood flown,
The echoes of her mountains, reclaim'd her as their own !

Nothing she heard around her, (though shouts rang
    forth again,)
Gone were the green Swiss valleys, the pasture, and the
    plain ;
Before her eyes one vision, and in her heart one cry,
That said, " Go forth, save Bregenz, and then, if need
    be, die ! "

With trembling haste and breathless, with noiseless
    step she sped ;
Horses and weary cattle were standing in the shed ;
She loosed the strong white charger,[1] that fed from
    out her hand,
She mounted and she turn'd his head toward her native
    land.

Out — out into the darkness — faster, and still more
    fast ;
The smooth grass flies behind her, the chestnut wood is
    pass'd ;
She looks up ; clouds are heavy :   Why is her steed so
    slow ? —
Scarcely the wind beside them can pass them as they
    go.

[1] **Charger**: a war-horse or one suitable for use in battle.

" Faster ! " she cries, " O, faster ! "   Eleven the church-
    bells chime :
" O God," she cries, " help Bregenz, and bring me there
    in time ! "
But louder than bells' ringing, or lowing of the kine,
Grows nearer in the midnight the rushing of the
    Rhine.

Shall not the roaring waters their headlong gallop
    check ?
The steed draws back in terror, she leans above his
    neck
To watch the flowing darkness, the bank is high and
    steep ;
One pause, — he staggers forward, and plunges in the
    deep.

She strives to pierce the blackness, and looser throws
    the rein ;
Her steed must breast the waters that dash above his
    mane ;
How gallantly, how nobly, he struggles through the
    foam,
And see, in the far distance shine out the lights of
    home !

Up the steep bank he bears her, and now they rush
    again
Towards the heights of Bregenz, that tower above the
    plain.

They reach the gate [1] of Bregenz just as the midnight
    rings,
And out come serf [2] and soldier to meet the news she
    brings.

Bregenz is saved! Ere daylight her battlements are
    mann'd ;
Defiance greets the army that marches on the land:
And, if to deeds heroic should endless fame be paid,
Bregenz does well to honor the noble Tyrol maid.

Three hundred years are vanish'd, and yet upon the
    hill
An old stone gateway rises, to do her honor still.
And there, when Bregenz women sit spinning in the
    shade,
They see in quaint old carving the charger and the maid.

And when, to guard old Bregenz, by gateway, street,
    and tower,
The warder paces all night long, and calls each passing
    hour:
"Nine," "ten," "eleven," he cries aloud, and then (O
    crown of fame !)
When midnight pauses in the skies he calls the maiden's
    name.

ADELAIDE A. PROCTER.

---

[1] **Gate**: Bregenz was formerly a walled town.

[2] **Serf**: a feudal dependent but one degree above a slave; a laborer
bound to the soil and unable to leave it without his lord's consent.

MARCO BOZZARIS.[1]

AT midnight, in his guarded tent,
  The Turk was dreaming of the hour
When Greece, her knee in suppliance bent,
  Should tremble at his power;
In dreams, through camp and court he bore
The trophies of a conqueror;
  In dreams, his song of triumph heard;
Then wore his monarch's signet-ring;[2]
Then press'd that monarch's throne — a king:
As wild his thoughts, and gay of wing,
  As Eden's garden bird.

At midnight, in the forest shades,
  Bozzaris ranged his Suliote[3] band,
True as the steel of their tried blades,
  Heroes in heart and hand.

---

[1] **Bozzaris** (Boz-zar'is): a Greek patriot who took a leading part in the war of independence begun in 1821, by which Greece threw off the yoke of the Turkish power. In 1823 Bozzaris attacked a Turkish force much larger than his own. The battle was begun in the night and was a complete surprise to the Turks. Bozzaris was mortally wounded, but the Greeks won a great and decisive victory. Six years later, the Turks, who had held Greece in subjection for nearly four centuries, were obliged to make peace.

[2] **Signet-ring**: a ring containing a signet or private seal, especially the seal used by a monarch in stamping documents.

[3] **Su'liote**: a name derived from the Suli Mountains and river in Northwestern Greece [the ancient Epirus]; Bozzaris was himself a Suliote.

There [1] had the Persian's thousands stood,
There had the glad earth drunk their blood,
  On old Platæa's [2] day;
And now there breathed that haunted air;
The sons of sires who conquer'd there,
With arm to strike, and soul to dare,
  As quick, as far, as they.

An hour pass'd on: the Turk awoke:
  That bright dream was his last.
He woke to hear his sentries shriek,
"To arms! they come! the Greek! the Greek!"
He woke, to die 'midst flame and smoke,
And shout, and groan, and sabre-stroke,
  And death-shots falling thick and fast
As lightnings from the mountain cloud,
And heard, with voice as trumpet loud,
  Bozzaris cheer his band:
"Strike! — till the last arm'd foe expires;
Strike! — for your altars and your fires;
Strike! — for the green graves of your sires;
  God, and your native land!"

They fought like brave men, long and well;
  They piled that ground with Moslem [3] slain;

---

[1] Bozzaris attacked the Turks in their camp not far from Missolonghi, near the entrance of the Gulf of Corinth. The scene of the battle can only be said to be near that of Platæa in the sense that both were on the shore of the gulf.

[2] Platæa (Pla-tē'a): in 479 B.C. the Greeks defeated an invading army of Persians at Platæa, a town northwest of Athens, and a short distance from the head of the Gulf of Corinth.

[3] Moslem: Mohammedans or Turks.

They conquer'd ; — but Bozzaris **fell,**
　Bleeding at every vein.
His few surviving comrades saw
His **smile** when rang their loud hurrah,
　And the red field was **won ;**
Then **saw** in death his eyelids close,
Calmly as to a night's repose, —
　Like flowers at set of sun.

Come to the bridal chamber, Death,
　Come to the mother's, when she feels,
For the first time, her first-born's breath ;
　Come, when the blessèd [1] seals [2]
That **close the** pestilence are **broke,**
And crowded cities **wail** its stroke :
Come **in** consumption's ghastly form,
The earthquake shock, the ocean storm ;
Come **when the** heart beats high and **warm**
　With banquet song **and** dance and wine ;
And thou art terrible : — the tear,
The groan, the knell, the pall, the **bier,**
And **all we** know, or dream, **or fear,**
　Of agony, are thine.

But to the hero, when his sword
　Has won the battle for the **free,**
Thy voice sounds like a prophet's word,
And **in** its hollow tones are heard
　The **thanks of** millions yet to be.

---

[1] **Blessèd** : pronounced here in two syllables, *bles'sed.*

[2] **Seals:** apparently an allusion to the opening of the seals in Rev. **vi.,** **or** to the pouring out of the vials of wrath, chapter **xvi.**

Come when his task of fame is wrought ;
Come, with **her** laurel-leaf,[1] blood-bought ;
   Come in her crowning hour, — and then
Thy sunken eye's unearthly light
To him is welcome as the sight
   Of sky and stars to prison'd men ;
Thy grasp is welcome as the hand
Of brother **in a** foreign land ;
Thy summons welcome as the cry
That told the Indian isles [2] were nigh
   To the world-seeking Genoese,[3]
When the land-wind, from woods of palm,
And orange groves, and fields of balm,[4]
   Blew o'er the Haytien seas.[5]

Bozzaris ! with the storied brave
   Greece nurtured in her glory's time,
Rest thee : there is no prouder grave,
   Even in her own proud clime.
She wore no funeral weeds [6] **for** thee,
   Nor **bade the** dark hearse wave its plume,
Like **torn** branch from death's leafless tree,
In sorrow's pomp and pageantry,
   The heartless luxury of the tomb ;
But she remembers thee as one
   Long loved, and **for a** season **gone;**

---

[1] **Laurel-leaf**: an allusion to the laurel crowns given by the Greeks to those who were **victors** in the ancient games.

[2] **Indian isles**: the West Indies.

[3] **Genoese: Columbus**; he however was not seeking a New World, but a new **way to the Old World, of** India, or Asia.

[4] **Balm**: here, any fragrant plants.

[5] **Haytien seas**: the seas about the island of Hayti.

[6] **Weeds**: mourning.

For thee her poet's lyre [1] is wreathed,
Her marble wrought, her music breathed;
For thee she rings the birthday bells;
Of thee her babes' first lisping tells;
For thine her evening prayer is said,
At palace couch and cottage bed:
Her soldier, closing with the foe,
Gives for thy sake a deadlier blow;
His plighted maiden, when she fears
For him, the joy of her young years,
Thinks of thy fate, and checks her tears;
    And she, the mother of thy boys,
Though in her eye and faded cheek
Is read the grief she will not speak,
    The memory of her buried joys, —
And even she who gave thee birth
Will, by their pilgrim-circled hearth,[2]
    Talk of thy doom without a sigh;
For thou art Freedom's now, and Fame's,
One of the few, th' immortal names
    That were not born to die.

FITZ-GREENE HALLECK.

[1] Lyre: a kind of harp.
[2] Pilgrim-circled hearth: the hearth of the widow of Bozzaris, round which travellers from foreign lands gathered to hear his story and that of Greek Independence.

THE NATION'S DEAD.

FOUR hundred thousand men,
   The **brave, the** good, the true,
In tangled wood, in mountain glen,
On battle plain, in prison pen,
   Lie dead for me and you.
Four hundred thousand of the brave
Have made our ransomed soil their grave,
      For me and you,
   Good friend, for me and you.

In many a fevered swamp,
   By many a black bayou,[1]
In many a cold and frozen camp,
The weary sentinel ceased his tramp,
   And died for me and you.
From western plain **to** ocean tide
Are stretched the **graves of those who died**
      For me and you,
   Good friend, for me and you.

On **many a bloody plain**
   Their **ready swords they** drew,
And poured their life-blood like the rain,
A home, a heritage, to gain,
      To gain for me and you.

---

[1] **Bayou** (bī-oo'): the narrow outlet of a lake or a channel of water or
creek in the valley of **the** lower Mississippi.

Our brothers mustered by our side,
They marched, and fought, and bravely died
    For me and you,
  Good friend, for me and you.

Up many a fortress wall
  They charged, those boys in blue ;
'Mid surging smoke and volleyed ball,
The bravest were the first to fall,
  To fall for me and you.
Those noble men, the nation's pride,
Four hundred thousand men, have died
    For me and you,
  Good friend, for me and you.

In treason's prison-hold
  Their martyr spirits grew
To stature like the saints of old,
While, amid agonies untold,
  They starved for me and you.
The good, the patient, and the tried,
Four hundred thousand men, have died
    For me and you,
  Good friend, for me and you.

A debt we ne'er can pay
  To them is justly due ;
And to the nation's latest day
Our children's children still shall say,
  " They died for me and you."
Four hundred thousand of the brave
Made this, our ransomed soil, their grave,
    For me and you,
  Good friend, for me and you.

ANONYMOUS.

SONG OF THE CORNISH MEN.[1]

A GOOD sword and a trusty hand !
  A merry heart and true !
King James's [2] men shall understand
  What Cornish lads can do.

And have they fixed the where and when ?
  And shall Trelawny die ?
Here's twenty thousand Cornish men
  Will know the reason why !

Outspake their captain, brave and bold,
  A merry wight [3] was he :
" If London Tower were Michael's hold,[4]
  We'll set Trelawny free !

[1] In 1688, King James II. of England ordered the clergy throughout the realm to read a royal proclamation which suspended all penal laws against Protestant Dissenters and Roman Catholics. The Archbishop of Canterbury and six bishops of the English Church, believing that the king's real object was to favor the Catholic party, petitioned His Majesty to be excused from reading the proclamation. He refused to consider their petition ; and as the proclamation was read by only a very few of the clergy, he sent the bishops prisoners to the Tower of London.

One of them was Trelawny, a native of Cornwall. The rough Cornish miners demanded his release, and from one end of Cornwall to the other people were heard singing this song.

The pressure brought to bear on the king and his servile bench of judges was so great that on their trial the bishops were all acquitted. Soon after, James fled the country, and William and Mary came to the throne.

[2] King James : James II.   [3] Wight : person.

[4] Michael's hold : St. Michael's castle and stronghold on the coast of Cornwall.

" We'll cross the **Tamar** [1] land to land,
   The Severn [1] is no stay —
With one and all, and hand-in-hand,
   And who shall bid us nay ?

" **And** when we come to **London wall,**—
   A pleasant sight to view, —
Come forth ! come forth, ye cowards **all,**
   To better men than you !

" **Trelawny he's in keep** and **hold,**[2]
   Trelawny he may die ;
But here's twenty **thousand** Cornish **bold**
   Will know the reason why ! "

ROBERT STEPHEN HAWKER.

[1] **Tamar** and **Severn** : rivers of the south of England. The Severn, however, would not be crossed by the Cornish men on their march to **London** ; perhaps the Avon is meant.

[2] **Keep and hold** : dungeon and fortress or stronghold.

THE RELIEF OF LUCKNOW.[1]

Oh, that last day in Lucknow fort!
 We knew that it was the last;
That the enemy's mines [2] crept surely in,
 And the end was coming fast.

To yield to that foe meant worse than death;
 And the men and we all worked on;
It was one day more of smoke and roar,
 And then it would all be done.

There was one of us, a corporal's wife,
 A fair, young, gentle thing,
Wasted with fever in the siege,
 And her mind was wandering.

---

[1] **The Relief of Lucknow**: In 1857 a fearful and wide-spread mutiny broke out among the native troops of India against their English rulers.

On the 1st of July a large number of English including about 130 women and children were besieged in the fort of Lucknow, a town of Northern India, on a tributary of the Ganges.

The garrison was too small to properly defend the place; food began to grow scarce, and fever, small-pox, and cholera carried off many.

For nearly three months the besieged waited for succor. At length, on Sept. 25, General Havelock came to their rescue, though the final relief of the place did not occur until Sir Colin Campbell rescued the garrison nearly a month later.

[2] **Mines**: excavations made by the enemy for the purpose of blowing up the fort.

She lay on the ground, in her Scottish plaid,
   And I took her head on my knee;
" When my father comes hame frae the pleugh,"[1] she
    said,
   " Oh! then please wauken[2] me."

She slept like a child on her father's floor,
   In the flecking[3] of wood-bine shade,
When the house-dog sprawls by the open door,
   And the mother's wheel[4] is stayed.[5]

It was smoke and roar and powder-stench,
   And hopeless waiting for death;
And the soldier's wife, like a full-tired child,
   Seemed scarce to draw her breath.

I sank to sleep; and I had my dream
   Of an English village-lane,
And wall and garden; but one wild scream
   Brought me back to the roar again.

There Jessie Brown stood listening
   Till a sudden gladness broke
All over her face; and she caught my hand
   And drew me near and spoke:

" The Hielanders![6] Oh! dinna ye hear
   The slogan[7] far awa?
The McGregor's?[8] Oh! I ken[9] it weel;[10]
   It's the grandest o' them a'!

---

[1] **Pleugh**: plough.   [2] **Wauken**: waken.
[3] **Flecking**: here, dappling or variegating with light and shade.
[4] **Wheel**: spinning-wheel.   [5] **Stayed**: stopped.
[6] **Hielanders**: Highlanders.   [7] **Slogan**: the war-cry.
[8] **McGregor's**: the Highland clan of that name.
[9] **Ken**: know.   [10] **Weel**: well.

" God bless thae [1] bonny [2] Hielanders !
  We're saved ! we're saved ! " she cried;
And fell on her knees ; and thanks to God
  Flowed forth like a full flood-tide.

Along the battery line her cry
  Had fallen among the men,
And they started back ; — they were there to die ;
  But was life so near them, then ?

They listened for life ; the rattling fire
  Far off, and the far-off roar,
Were all ; and the colonel shook his head,
  And they turned to their guns once more.

Then Jessie said, " That slogan's done ;
  But can ye hear them noo,[3]
" *The Campbells are comin'* " ? [4] It's no a dream ;
  Our succors [5] hae broken through."

We heard the roar and the rattle afar,
  But the pipes [6] we could not hear ;
So the men plied their work of hopeless war,
  And knew that the end was near.

It was not long ere it made its way,
  A thrilling, ceaseless sound :
It was no noise from the strife afar,
  Or the sappers [7] under ground.

---

[1] **Thae** : those.   [2] **Bonny** : handsome, good.   [3] **Noo** : now.
[4] "**The Campbells are comin'** " : a famous Scotch tune.
[5] **Succors** : rescuers.   [6] **Pipes** : bag-pipes.
[7] **Sappers** : the enemy's soldiers engaged in making the mines to blow
up the fort.

It *was* the pipers of the Highlanders !
　And now they played " *Auld Lang Syne.*"
It came to our men like the voice of God,
　And they shouted along the line.

And they wept, and shook one another's hands,
　And the women sobbed in a crowd ;
And every one knelt down where he stood,
　And we all thanked God aloud.

That happy day, when we welcomed them,
　Our men put Jessie first ;
And the general gave her his hand, and cheers
　Like a storm from the soldiers burst.

And the pipers' ribbons and tartan [1] streamed,
　Marching round and round our line ;
And our joyful cheers were broken with tears,
　As the pipes played " *Auld Lang Syne.*"

ROBERT TRAIL SPENCE LOWELL.

[1] **Tartan** : the Scotch plaid.

CASABIANCA.[1]

THE boy **stood** on the burning deck
   Whence all but him had fled ;
The flame that lit the battle's wreck
   Shone round him o'er the dead.

Yet beautiful and bright he stood,
   As born to rule the storm ;
A **creature of heroic** blood,
   A proud, though childlike form.

The flames rolled on — he would not go
   Without his father's **word** ;

---

[1] **Casabianca** (Ka-sa-be-an´ka) : There are several versions of the story of Casabianca, no one of **which can be** said to be capable of historical **proof,** yet all probably have some common foundation in fact.

The usual account represents him as a lad of ten, the son of Admiral Brueys, commander of the French man-of-war *L'Orient.*

At the battle of **the** Nile between Nelson and Napoleon in 1798, Admiral Brueys was mortally wounded, and left to die on the deck of his ship.

Shortly after nightfall the vessel was discovered **to be** in flames, and a number of English sailors went at Nelson's orders to rescue the officers **and** crew.

All left the doomed ship but Casabianca. He refused, **saying** that his **father,** who was now dead, had told him not to leave his post, and that he **would not disobey him.**

There was no time for delay ; the boat put off, and in a few minutes later **the French** frigate blew up. Whether Casabianca lost his life in the explosion or whether, as some suppose, **he** leaped overboard just before it occurred **in the** attempt to swim ashore with his father's corpse, is unknown ; but in either case the brave boy **perished.**

That father, faint in death below,
  His voice no longer heard.

He called aloud — " Say, father, say,
  If yet my task is done ? "
He knew not that the chieftain lay
  Unconscious of his son.

" Speak, father ! " once again he cried,
  " If I may yet be gone ! "
And but the booming shots [1] replied,
  And fast the flames rolled on.

Upon his brow he felt their breath,
  And in his waving hair,
And looked from that lone post of death
  In still, yet brave despair.

And shouted but once more aloud,
  " My father ! must I stay ? "
While o'er him fast, through sail and shroud,[2]
  The wreathing fires made way.

They wrapt the ship in splendor wild,
  They caught the flag on high,
And streamed above the gallant child,
  Like banners in the sky.

There came a burst of thunder sound [3] —
  The boy — oh ! where was he ? .

[1] Booming shots : the heat of the flames discharged the loaded cannon of *L'Orient.*

[2] Shroud : a large rope supporting a mast.

[3] Thunder sound : the explosion of the magazine.

Ask of the winds that far around
  With fragments strewed the sea! —

With mast, and helm, and pennon[1] fair
  That well had borne their part —
But the noblest thing that perished there
  Was that young, faithful heart!

FELICIA DOROTHEA HEMANS.

[1] **Pennon** : a long, pointed flag, or streamer.

THE BLUE AND THE GRAY.[1]

By the flow of the inland river,
  Whence the fleets of iron have fled,
Where the blades of the grave-grass quiver,
  Asleep are the ranks of the dead :
      Under the sod and the dew,
        Waiting the judgment-day ;
      Under the one, the Blue,
        Under the other, the Gray.

These in the robings of glory,
  Those in the gloom of defeat,
All with the battle-blood gory,
  In the dusk of eternity meet :
      Under the sod and the dew,
        Waiting the judgment-day ;
      Under the laurel, the Blue,
        Under the willow, the Gray.

From the silence of sorrowful hours
  The desolate mourners go,
Lovingly laden with flowers
  Alike for the friend and the foe :

---

[1] A poem suggested, it is said, by the fact that when on Decoration Day the women of Columbus, Ga., placed flowers on the graves of those who fell in the war, they remembered the Union soldiers as well as the Confederates.

Under the sod and the dew,
  Waiting the judgment-day;
Under the roses, the Blue,
  Under the lilies, the Gray.

So with an equal splendor
  The morning sun-rays fall,
With a touch impartially tender,
  On the blossoms blooming for all:
      Under the sod and the dew,
        Waiting the judgment-day;
      Broidered with gold, the Blue,
        Mellowed with gold, the Gray.

So, when the summer calleth,
  On forest and field of grain,
With an equal murmur falleth
  The cooling drip of the rain:
      Under the sod and the dew,
        Waiting the judgment-day;
      Wet with the rain, the Blue,
      Wet with the rain, the Gray.

Sadly, but not with upbraiding,
  The generous deed was done,
In the storm of the years that are fading,
  No braver battle was won:
      Under the sod and the dew,
        Waiting the judgment-day;
      Under the blossoms, the Blue,
        Under the garlands, the Gray.

No more shall the war-cry sever,
  Or the winding rivers be red;
They banish our anger forever
  When they laurel the graves of our dead!
    Under the sod and the dew,
      Waiting the judgment-day;
    Love and tears for the Blue,
      Tears and love for the Gray.

                  FRANCIS MILES FINCH.

CHEVY-CHASE.[1]

GOD prosper long our noble king,
  Our lives and safeties all;
A woful hunting once there did
  In Chevy-Chase befall.

To drive the deer with hound and horn
  Earl Percy[2] took his way;
The child may rue that is unborn
  The hunting of that day.

The stout earl of Northumberland
  A vow to God did make,
His pleasure in the Scottish woods
  Three summer days to take —

[1] Chev'y-Chase: that is, the hunt among the Chev'i-ot Hills which separate England from Scotland. This ballad contains an account not only of Chevy-Chase, but also of the Battle of Otterburn; in fact it is this latter battle, fought between the English and the Scotch in 1388 at Otterburn, in the border county of Northumberland, England, which gives the poem its real significance.

The Scots gained a decisive victory. Burton, in his history of Scotland, says that the fight "marks the fading from the defenders of Scotland of the dread of immediate absolute conquest by England."

[2] Earl Percy: Henry Percy, Earl of Northumberland. His son Henry — Shakespeare's "Hotspur," see "Henry IV.," Part 1st — killed the Scotch Earl of Douglas in the battle of Otterburn; though in the ballad Douglas is represented as meeting his death from the arrow of an English archer.

The chiefest **harts**[1] in Chevy-Chase
    To kill and bear away.
These tidings **to Earl** Douglas came,
    In Scotland where he lay;

Who sent Earl Percy present word
    He would prevent his sport.
The English earl, not fearing that,
    Did to the woods resort,

With fifteen hundred bowmen bold,
    All **chosen men** of might,
Who knew full well **in time of need**
    To aim their shafts **aright.**

The gallant greyhounds swiftly **ran**
    To chase the fallow[2] deer;
On Monday they began **to hunt**
    When **daylight** did appear;

And long before high noon they had
    A hundred fat bucks slain;
Then having dined, the drovers[3] went
    To rouse the deer again.

The bowmen mustered **on the hills,**
    Well able to endure;
And all their rear, with special care,
    That day was **guarded sure.**

The hounds ran swiftly through the woods,
    The nimble **deer to** take,

---

[1] **Harts**: bucks.   [2] **Fallow**: pale red or pale yellow.
[3] **Drovers**: those whose duty it was to rouse or beat up the game for the archers.

That with **their** cries the hills and dales
   An echo shrill did make.

Lord Percy to the quarry[1] went,
   To **view** the slaughtered deer;
Quoth he, "Earl Douglas promised
   This day to meet me here;

"But if I thought he would not come,
   No longer would I stay;"
With that a brave **young gentleman**
   Thus to the earl did say:

"**Lo, yonder** doth Earl Douglas come,
   His men in armor bright;
Full twenty hundred Scottish spears
   All marching in our sight;

"All men of pleasant Teviotdale,
   Fast by[2] the river Tweed;[3]"
"Then cease your sports," Earl Percy said,
   "And take your bows with speed;

"**And now** with me, my countrymen,
   Your courage forth advance;
For never was there champion yet,
   In Scotland or in France,

"That **ever** did on horseback come,
   But if my hap[4] it were,

---

[1] **Quarry**: a heap of dead game.   [2] **Fast by**: near by.
[3] **Tweed**: the Tweed forms part of the boundary between England and Scotland. It empties into the North Sea, or German Ocean.
[4] **Hap**: chance, luck.

I durst encounter man for man,
  With him to break a spear." [1]

Earl Douglas on his milk-white steed,
  Most like a baron bold,
Rode foremost of his company,
  Whose armor shone like gold.

"Show me," said he, "whose men you be,
  That hunt so boldly here,
That, without my consent, do chase
  And kill my fallow-deer."

The first man that did answer make,
  Was noble Percy he —
Who said, "We list not to declare,
  Nor show whose men we be:

"Yet will we spend our dearest blood
  Thy chiefest harts to slay."
Then Douglas swore a solemn oath,
  And thus in rage did say:

"Ere thus I will out-braved be,
  One of us two shall die;
I know thee well, an earl thou art —
  Lord Percy, so am I.

"But trust me, Percy, pity it were,
  And great offence, to kill
Any of these our guiltless men,
  For they have done no ill.

[1] **Break a spear**: to fight with spears on horseback.

" Let you and me the battle try,
    And set our men aside."
" Accursed be he," Earl Percy said,
    " By whom this is denied."

Then stepped a gallant squire [1] forth,
    Witherington was his name,
Who said, " I would not have it told
    To Henry, our king,[2] for shame,

" That e'er [3] my captain fought on foot,
    And I stood looking on.
You two be earls," said Witherington,
    " And I a squire alone ;

" I'll do the best that do I may,
    While I have power to stand ;
While I have power to wield my sword,
    I'll fight with heart and hand."

Our English archers bent their bows —
    Their hearts were good and true ;
At the first flight of arrows sent,
    Full fourscore Scots they slew.

Yet stays Earl Douglas on the bent,[4]
    As chieftain stout and good ;
As valiant captain, all unmoved,
    The shock he firmly stood.

[1] **Squire:** the attendant of a knight.
[2] **Henry, our king** : Richard II. was king of England in 1388 when the
battle of Otterburn was fought. The ballad mixes up a traditional chase
of the reign of Henry VI. with the battle.   [3] **E'er** : ever.
[4] **Bent** : here, ground ; from " bent," a kind of grass ; hence a moor covered with bent.

His host he parted had in three,
　As leader ware[1] and tried;[2]
And soon his spearmen on their foes
　Bore down on every side.

Throughout the English archery
　They dealt full many a wound;
But still our valiant Englishmen
　All firmly kept their ground.

And throwing straight their bows away,
　They grasped their swords so bright;
And now sharp blows, a heavy shower,
　On shields and helmets light.

They closed full fast on every side —
　No slackness there was found;
And many a gallant gentleman
　Lay gasping on the ground.

In truth, it was a grief to see
　How each one chose his spear,
And how the blood out of their breasts ·
　Did gush like water clear.

At last these two stout earls did meet;
　Like captains of great might,
Like lions wode,[3] they laid on lode,[4]
　And made a cruel fight.

They fought until they both did sweat,
　With swords of tempered steel,

---

[1] **Ware**: wary, cautious.
[2] **Tried**: experienced.
[3] **Wode**. mad, furious.
[4] **Lode**: blows.

Until the blood, like drops of rain,
   They trickling down did feel.

" Yield thee, Lord Percy," Douglas said;
   " In faith I will thee bring
Where thou shalt high advanced be
   By James,[1] our Scottish king.

" Thy ransom I will freely give,
   And this report of thee,
Thou art the most courageous knight
   That ever I did see."

" No, Douglas," saith Earl Percy then,
   " Thy proffer I do scorn;
I will not yield to any Scot
   That ever yet was born."

With that there came an arrow keen
   Out of an English bow,
Which struck Earl Douglas to the heart,
   A deep and deadly blow;

Who never spake more words than these:
   " Fight on, my merry men all;
For why, my life is at an end;
   Lord Percy sees my fall."

Then leaving life, Earl Percy took
   The dead man by the hand;
And said, " Earl Douglas, for thy life
   Would I had lost my land.

---

[1] James: the first Scottish king of that name was crowned in 1405.
Robert II. ruled Scotland in 1388, when the battle was fought.

"In truth, my very heart doth **bleed**
  With sorrow **for thy** sake;
For sure a more redoubted [1] knight
  Mischance did never take."

A knight amongst the Scots there was
  Who saw Earl Douglas die,
Who straight in wrath did vow revenge
  Upon the Earl Percy.

Sir Hugh Mountgomery was he called,
  Who, **with a** spear full bright,
Well mounted **on a** gallant steed,
  Ran fiercely through the fight;

And past the English archers all,
  Without a dread or **fear;**
And through Earl **Percy's** body then
  He thrust his hateful spear;

With such vehement **force and might**
  He did his body gore,
The staff ran through **the other side**
  A large cloth-yard [2] and more.

So thus **did** both these nobles die,
  Whose courage none could stain.
An English archer then perceived
  The noble **earl** was slain.

He had **a bow** bent in **his hand,**
  Made of a trusty tree;

[1] **Redoubted** : valiant.
[2] **Cloth-yard** : that is, the length of a yard-stick **used in measuring cloth.**

An arrow of a cloth-yard long
　　To the hard head [1] haled [2] he.

Against Sir Hugh Mountgomery
　　So right the shaft he set,
The gray goose wing [3] that was thereon
　　In his heart's blood was wet.

This fight did last from break of day
　　Till setting of the sun:
For when they rung the evening-bell,
　　The battle scarce was done.

With stout Earl Percy there were slain
　　Sir John of Egerton,
Sir Robert Ratcliff, and Sir John,
　　Sir James, that bold baron.

And with Sir George and stout Sir James,
　　Both knights of good account,
Good Sir Ralph Raby there was slain,
　　Whose prowess did surmount.

For Witherington my heart is wo
　　That ever he slain should be,
For when his legs were hewn in two,
　　He knelt and fought on his knee.

And with Earl Douglas there was slain
　　Sir Hugh Mountgomery,
Sir Charles Murray, that from the field
　　One foot would never flee.

[1] **Hard head**: the steel point of the arrow.　　[2] **Haled**: drew.
[3] **Gray goose wing**: the feathers fastened to an arrow, near the notched end, to guide its flight.

Sir Charles Murray of Ratcliff, too —
  His sister's son was he;
Sir David Lamb, so well esteemed,
  But saved he could not be.

And the Lord Maxwell in like case
  Did with Earl Douglas die:
Of twenty hundred Scottish spears,
  Scarce fifty-five did fly.

Of fifteen hundred Englishmen,
  Went home but fifty-three;
The rest in Chevy-Chase were slain,
  Under the greenwood tree.

Next day did many widows come,
  Their husbands to bewail;
They washed their wounds in brinish tears,
  But all would not prevail.

Their bodies, bathed in purple blood,
  They bore with them away;
They kissed them dead a thousand times,
  Ere they were clad in clay.[1]

The news was brought to Edinburgh,
  Where Scotland's king did reign,
That brave Earl Douglas suddenly
  Was with an arrow slain:

" Oh heavy news," King James did say;
  " Scotland can witness be
I have not any captain more
  Of such account as he."

[1] Clad in clay: buried.

Like tidings to King Henry came
  Within as short a space,
That Percy of Northumberland
  Was slain in Chevy-Chase:

"Now God be with him," said our king,
  "Since 'twill no better be;
I trust I have within my realm
  Five hundred as good as he:

"Yet shall not Scots or Scotland say
  But I will vengeance take:
I'll be revenged on them all,
  For brave Earl Percy's sake."

This vow full well the king performed
  After at Humbledown; [1]
In one day fifty knights were slain,
  With lords of high renown;

And of the best, of small account,
  Did many hundreds die:
Thus endeth the hunting of Chevy-Chase,
  Made by the Earl Percy.

God save the king, and bless this land,
  With plenty, joy, and peace;
And grant, henceforth, that foul debate [2]
  'Twixt noblemen may cease!

                                    ANONYMOUS.

[1] **Humbledown**: Humbleton, Northumberland, England. Here the English gained a great victory over the Scotch in 1402.
[2] **Debate**. contest.

THE BALLAD OF AGINCOURT.[1]

FAIR stood the wind for France,
When we our sails advance,
Nor now to prove our chance
    Longer will tarry;
But putting to the main,[2]
At Kaux,[3] the mouth of Seine,
With all his martial train,
    Landed King Harry.

And taking many a fort,
Furnished in warlike sort,
Marched towards Agincourt
    In happy hour —

[1] Agincourt (Ah-zhan-koor') : to divert the attention of his people from dangerous political questions at home, and also to gratify hopes of conquest, Henry V. of England began a war with France in 1415. The battle of Agincourt was fought that year. It gets its name from the little village of Agincourt, in the Department of Calais, about forty miles southwest of that port.

The French greatly outnumbered Henry's forces; but the English had the good fortune to be able to use their bowmen to the best possible advantage, as a hard rain had fallen the night before, and the heavily armed French troops could with difficulty get over the muddy ploughed land.

The English king gained a great victory, and went back to London in triumph. Later he renewed the war, and obtained the hand of the French princess Katherine in marriage, and the promise of the crown of France on the death of Charles VI., her father, who was then insane, and in feeble health.

[2] To the main: to sea.

[3] Kaux (Kō).

Skirmishing day by day
With those that stopped his way,
Where the French gen'ral lay
    With all his power,

Which in his height of pride,
King Henry to deride,
His ransom [1] to provide
    To the king sending;
Which he neglects the while,
As from a nation vile,
Yet, with an angry smile,
    Their fall portending.

And turning to his men,
Quoth our brave Henry then:
Though they to one be ten,
    Be not amazed;
Yet have we well begun —
Battles so bravely won
Have ever to the sun
    By fame been raised.

And for myself, quoth he,
This my full rest shall be;
England ne'er mourn for me,
    Nor more esteem me.
Victor I will remain,
Or on this earth lie slain;
Never shall she sustain
    Loss to redeem me.

[1] **Ransom**: it was the custom then for the victors to extort heavy ransoms from all prisoners of rank taken in war. The French king demands Henry's ransom in advance of the battle by way of deriding his power.

Poitiers and Cressy [1] tell,
When most their pride did swell,
Under our swords they fell;
    No less our skill is
Than when our grandsire [2] great,
Claiming the regal seat,
By many a warlike feat
    Lopped the French lilies.[3]

The Duke of York so dread
The eager vaward [4] led;
With **the main** [5] **Henry** sped,
    Amongst **his** henchmen.[6]
Excester [7] had **the** rear —
A braver man not there:
O Lord! how **hot** they were
    On the **false** Frenchmen!

They now **to** fight are gone;
Armor on armor shone;
Drum now to drum did **groan** —
    To hear was wonder;

---

[1] **Poitiers and Cressy**: two famous battles fought by **the English** in France in 1356 **and** 1346, in both of which the English **gained decisive** victories. The French pronunciation of Poitiers is nearly Pwi'-te-â'.

[2] **Grandsire**: Edward III. of England, who gained the victory of Cressy. He claimed the throne of France.

[3] **Lilies**: the lilies or fleur-de-lis **on the arms** of France.

[4] **Vaward**: vanward, front.

[5] **Main**: main body of troops. According to some early accounts Henry had only six or seven thousand soldiers to fifty thousand of the enemy.

[6] **Henchmen**: followers.

[7] **Excester** (Exe Cester or Exe Chester; meaning the fortified place on the river Exe, in Devonshire, in the southwest of England, the modern Exeter): Sir Thomas Beaufort, Duke of Exeter, one of Henry's chief men.

That with the cries they make
The very earth did shake;
Trumpet to trumpet spake,
    Thunder to thunder.

Well it thine age became,
O noble Erpingham ![1]
.Which did the signal aim
    To **our** hid forces;
When, **from** a meadow by,
Like a storm suddenly,
The English archery
    Struck the French horses,

With Spanish yew [2] so strong,
Arrows a cloth-yard long,
That like to serpents stung,
    Piercing the weather; [3]
None from his fellow **starts,**
But playing manly parts,
And like true English hearts,
    Stuck close together.

When down their bows they threw,
And forth their bilbows [4] drew,
And on the French they **flew,**
    Not one was tardy:

[1] **Erpingham**: Sir Thomas Erpingham was the marshal of the army.
He tossed up his baton, shouting, "Now strike!" and the battle began.

[2] **Yew**: the best bows were made of yew-tree wood.

[3] **Weather**: the withers or shoulders of a horse.

[4] **Bilbow**. a kind of sword, so called, it is said, because the best of these
weapons were made in Bilboa, Spain.

Arms were from shoulders sent ;
Scalps to the teeth were rent ;
Down the French peasants went ;
    Our men were hardy.[1]

This while our noble king,
His broadsword brandishing,
Down the French host did ding,[2]
    As to o'erwhelm it ;
And many a deep wound lent,
His arms with blood besprent,[3]
And many a cruel dent
    Bruised his helmet.

Glo'ster,[4] that duke so good,
Next of the royal blood,
For famous England stood,
    With his brave brother —
Clarence,[5] in steel so bright,
Though but a maiden knight,[6]
Yet in that furious fight
    Scarce such another.

Warwick [7] in blood did wade ;
Oxford [8] the foe invade,
And cruel slaughter made,
    Still as they ran up.

---

[1] **Hardy** : brave, daring.
[2] **Ding** : strike.   **Besprent** : bespattered.
[4] **Glo'ster** : the Duke of Gloucester ; a younger brother of King Henry.
[5] **Clarence** : the Duke of Clarence ; King Henry's eldest brother.
[6] **Maiden knight** : one who had not had experience in battle.
[7] **Warwick** (pronounced War'ick) : the Earl of Warwick.
[8] **Oxford** : the Earl of Oxford.

Suffolk [1] his axe [2] did ply ;
Beaumont [3] and Willoughby [4]
Bare [5] them right doughtily,[6]
    Ferrers [7] and Fanhope.[7]

Upon Saint Crispin's [8] day
Fought was this noble fray,
Which fame did not delay
    To England to carry;
Oh, when shall Englishmen
With such acts fill a pen,[9]
Or England breed again
    Such a King Harry?

MICHAEL DRAYTON.

[1] **Suffolk**: the **Duke** of Suffolk.

[2] **Axe**: battle-axe.

[3] **Beaumont**: Baron Beaumont.

[4] **Willoughby**: Lord Willoughby, a distinguished military commander.

[5] **Bare them**: bore themselves, conducted themselves.

[6] **Doughtily**: valiantly.

[7] **Ferrers** ; **Fanhope**: neither of these **names** can be found in Tyler's Memoirs of Henry V.

[8] **Saint Crispin's day**: October 25. See Shakspeare's "Henry V.," Act IV. Scene 3.

[9] **Fill a pen**: fill the pages of history; employ the historian's pen.

THE BONNETS OF BONNIE DUNDEE.[1]

———✦———

To the Lords of Convention[2] 'twas Claverhouse who
    spoke,
" Ere the king's crown[3] shall fall, there are crowns[4] to
    be broke ;
So let each cavalier who loves honor and me
Come follow the bonnets of bonnie Dundee ! "[5]

Come fill up my cup, come fill up my can ;
Come saddle your horses, and call up your men ;
Come open the Westport[6] and let us gang[7] free,
And it's room for the bonnets[8] of bonnie Dundee !

[1] **Bonnie Dundee**: John Graham of Claverhouse — hence **generally called**
Claverhouse — was created **Viscount of Dundee in 1688 by** James II. In
the previous reign Claverhouse had persecuted the Covenanters of Scotland
with remorseless vigor (see note 1, p. 82).

After the revolution in England, when William of Orange (William III.)
had landed, and the cowardly James II. had fled from London, Claverhouse
entered Edinburgh with a body of troops. His intention was to raise a
force in Scotland, drive out William, and reinstate James; finding, however,
that the feeling in Edinburgh was strongly against him, he suddenly left
that city. He was killed in the battle of Killiecrankie (1689), fighting in
behalf of the lost cause of the unworthy King James. Claverhouse was **a**
man of wonderful dash and courage, but one who in the name of loyalty
perpetrated such horrible cruelties that he fully earned the name the country
people gave him of " Bloody Claver'se."

[2] **Lords of Convention** : the Scottish Parliament assembled in Edinburgh
March, 1689. They later declared that James II. had forfeited the crown,
and finally declared William (William III.) and Mary king and queen.

[3] **King's crown** : the crown of James II.   [4] **Crowns** : heads.

[5] **Dundee** : Claverhouse, Viscount of Dundee.

[6] **Westport:** the western gate of the city of Edinburgh; it was then a
walled town.   [7] **Gang**: go.   [8] **Bonnets** : Scotch caps.

Dundee he is mounted, he rides up the **street**,
The bells are rung backward,[1] the drums they are **beat**;
But the provost, douce[2] man, **said**, "Just e'en[3] let
    him be,
The gude toun[4] is **well** quit[5] **of** that deil[6] of Dundee!"

As he rode doun[7] the sanctified bends[8] of the Bow,[9]
Ilk carline[10] **was** flyting[11] and shaking **her pow**;[12]
But the young plants of grace[13] **they** looked cowthie[14]
    and slee,[15]
Thinking, Luck to thy bonnet, thou bonnie Dundee!

With sour-featured whigs[16] the Grass-Market[17] was
    thranged,[18]
As if half the west had set tryst[19] to be hanged;
There was spite in each look, there was fear in each ee,[20]
As they watched for the bonnets of bonnie Dundee.

---

[1] **Rung backward**: to give the alarm.
[2] **Douce**: sedate, grave.   [3] **E'en**: even.   [4] **Gude toun**: good town.
[5] **Quit**: rid.   [6] **Deil**: devil.   [7] **Doun**: down.
[8] **Sanctified bends**: because in a hall in Bow street the Scottish Church formerly held its annual assembly.
[9] **Bow**: or the West Bow; the name of a street in Edinburgh. It got its name from a bend in the city wall.   [10] **Ilk carline**: every old woman.
[11] **Flyting**: scolding, brawling.   [12] **Pow**: head.
[13] **Young plants of grace**: the Scottish maidens.
[14] **Cowthie**: kindly, lovingly.   [15] **Slee**: sly.
[16] **Whigs**: those who favored William III. Scott was a strong tory, or conservative, and **hence** the expression "sour-featured" applied to the whigs, though, as many if not most of them were Covenanters and very austere, they may have justified the use of the phrase by their looks.
[17] **Grass-Market**: a famous square in Edinburgh where executions formerly took place.   [18] **Thranged**: thronged.
[19] **Half the west had set tryst**: the covenanting whigs were especially strong in certain parts of the West. "To set tryst" is to make an appointment.   [20] **Ee**: eye.

These cowls[1] of Kilmarnock[2] had spits[3] and had
    spears,
And lang-hafted[4] gullies[5] to kill cavaliers;
But they shrunk to close-heads,[6] and the causeway[7] was
    free
At the toss of the bonnet of bonnie Dundee.

He spurred to the foot of the proud castle rock,[8]
And with the gay Gordon[9] he gallantly spoke:
" Let Mons Meg[10] and her marrows[11] speak twa[12] words
    or three,
For the love of the bonnet of bonnie Dundee."

The Gordon demands of him which way he goes.
" Where'er shall direct me the shade[13] of Montrose![14]
Your grace[15] in short space shall hear tidings of me,
Or that low lies the bonnet of bonnie Dundee.

---

[1] **Cowls:** literally, hoods worn by monks; here, however, the word is used
to ridicule the Protestant Covenanters, or Puritan monks, as Scott would
call them.

[2] **Kilmarnock**: the chief town of Ayre, in the west of Scotland, where
the "sour-faced whigs" were numerous.

[3] **Spits**: long sharp-pointed bars of iron on which it was formerly the
custom to roast meat.

[4] **Lang-hafted**: long-handled.   [5] **Gullies**: large-knives.

[6] **Close-heads:** close together.   [7] **Causeway**: the street.

[8] **Castle rock:** a high, precipitous rock on which stands the castle of
Edinburgh.

[9] **Gordon: the Duke of** Gordon, who held the castle for King James, and
was therefore friendly to Claverhouse.

[10] **Mons Meg**: an immense cannon within the walls of the castle.

[11] **Marrows**: companions; the other cannon of the castle.

[12] **Twa**: two.   [13] **Shade**: ghost or spirit.

[14] **Montrose**: see note 1, p. 87.

[15] **Grace**: a title given to a duke.

"There are hills beyond Pentland[1] and lands beyond
    Forth;[2]
If there's lords in the lowlands,[3] there's chiefs[4] in the
    north;
There are wild Duniewassals[5] three thousand times three
Will cry 'Hoigh!' for the bonnet of bonnie Dundee.

"There's brass on the target[6] of barkened[7] bull-hide,
There's steel in the scabbard that dangles beside;
The brass shall be burnished, the steel shall flash free,
At a toss of the bonnet of bonnie Dundee.

"Away to the hills, to the caves, to the rocks,
Ere I own an usurper I'll couch[8] with the fox:
And tremble, false whigs, in the midst of your glee,
You have not seen the last of my bonnet and me."

He waved his proud hand, and the trumpets were blown,
The kettle-drums clashed, and the horsemen rode on,
Till on Ravelston's cliffs[9] and on Clermiston's lea[10]
Died away the wild war-notes of bonnie Dundee.

    Come fill up my cup, come fill up my can,
    Come saddle the horses, and call up the men;
    Come open your doors and let me gae free,
    For it's up with the bonnets of bonnie Dundee.

                    SIR WALTER SCOTT.

  [1] **Pentland**: the Pentland Hills on the south of Edinburgh County.
  [2] **Forth**: an arm of the sea, the Firth of Forth. Claverhouse means that Edinburgh does not represent all Scotland, and that he will seek aid elsewhere — especially in the Highlands.
   [3] **Lowlands**: the lords in the Lowlands were favorable to William III.
   [4] **Chiefs**: Highland chiefs who were friendly to King James.
   [5] **Duniewassals**: Highland chiefs or noblemen and their principal followers. [6] **Target**: a shield. [7] **Barkened**: hardened. [8] **Couch**: hide.
   [9] **Ravelston's cliffs** and **Clermiston's lea**: places in the vicinity of Edinburgh.   [10] **Lea**: a meadow.

THE DESTRUCTION OF SENNACHERIB.[1]

———•◦•———

THE Assyrian came down like the wolf on the fold,[2]
And his cohorts[3] were gleaming in purple and gold;
And the sheen[4] of their spears was like stars on the sea,
When the blue wave rolls nightly on deep Galilee.

Like the leaves of the forest when summer is green,
That host with their banners at sunset were seen;
Like the leaves of the forest when autumn hath flown,
That host on the morrow lay withered and strown.

For the angel of death spread his wings on the blast,
And breathed in the face of the foe as he passed;
And the eyes of the sleepers waxed deadly and chill,
And their hearts but once heaved, and for ever grew
     still!

And there lay the steed with his nostril all wide,
But through it there rolled not the breath of his pride;
And the foam of his gasping lay white on the turf,
And cold as the spray of the rock-beating surf.

---

[1] Sennacherib (Sen-nak'er-ib), king of Assyria, marched on Libnah and
Lachish, two frontier towns of Egypt, about 699 B.C., to punish them for
the aid they had given or promised to Hezekiah, king of Judah, who had
revolted against the authority of the Assyrian monarch. For what befell
Sennacherib and his host, see 2 Kings xix.

[2] Fold : a pen or enclosure for sheep, and hence the sheep thus enclosed.

[3] Cohorts : a body of troops.

[4] Sheen : brightness, splendor.

And there lay the rider distorted and pale,
With the dew on his brow and the rust on his mail;
And the tents were all silent, the banners alone,
The lances unlifted, the trumpet unblown.

And the widows of Ashur[1] are loud in their wail;
And the idols are broke in the temple of Baal;[2]
And the might of the Gentile,[3] unsmote by the sword,
Hath melted like snow in the glance of the Lord!

LORD BYRON.

[1] **Ashur: or** Asshur; the same as Assyria.
[2] **Baal** (Ba'al) : a heathen god, represented by the sun or some heavenly body, worshipped by the Assyrians.
[3] **Gentile** : the heathen; those who did not worship the God of the Jews.

INCIDENT OF THE FRENCH CAMP.[1]

You know we French stormed Ratisbon : [2]
  A mile or so away,
On a little mound, Napoleon
  Stood on our storming-day ;
With neck out-thrust, you fancy how,
  Legs wide, arms locked behind,
As if to balance the prone [3] brow,
  Oppressive with its mind.

Just as perhaps he mused, " My plans
  That soar, to earth may fall,
Let once my army-leader Lannes [4]
  Waver at yonder wall," —
Out 'twixt the battery-smokes there flew
  A rider, bound on bound
Full-galloping ; nor bridle drew
  Until he reached the mound.

[1] In 1809 Napoleon began a victorious campaign against Austria. On his march against Vienna, the Austrian capital, he stormed and carried the walled city of Rat'isbon, in Bavaria, on the Danube. A soldier (here represented as a boy) received his death-wound in planting the French flag within the walls of the captured town. Though dying, he gallops out to the emperor — a mile or two away — to announce the victory.

[2] Ratisbon: a city of Bavaria, on the Danube, on the route to Vienna. The place is walled, and a breach had to be battered by cannon in order to take the town. [3] Prone: bent forward ; but here, apparently, prominent.

[4] Lannes (Lan) : Marshal Lannes, one of Napoleon's generals. He led the attack at Ratisbon.

Then off there flung in smiling joy,
  And held himself erect
By just his horse's mane, a boy:
  You hardly could suspect —
(So tight he kept his lips compressed,
  Scarce any blood came through)
You looked twice ere you saw his breast
  Was all but shot in two.

"Well," cried he, "Emperor, by God's grace
  We've got you Ratisbon!
The marshal's in the market-place,
  And you'll be there anon [1]
To see your flag-bird [2] flap his vans [3]
  Where I, to heart's desire,
Perched him!" The chief's eye flashed; his plans
  Soared up again like fire.

The chief's eye flashed; but presently
  Softened itself, as sheathes
A film the mother eagle's eye
  When her bruised eaglet breathes;
"You're wounded!" "Nay," his soldier's pride
  Touched to the quick, he said:
"I'm killed, sire!" And, his chief beside,
  Smiling, the boy fell dead. [4]

ROBERT BROWNING.

[1] **Anon**: presently.
[2] **Flag-bird**: the eagle on the French flag. [3] **Vans**: wings.
[4] **Fell dead**: a similar incident occurred at the Battle of Gettysburg, 1863.
An officer of the Sixth Wisconsin approached Lieutenant-Colonel
Dawes, the commander of the regiment, after the sharp fight in the rail-
road cut. The colonel supposed, from the firm and erect attitude of the
man, that he came to report for orders of some kind; but the compressed
lips told a different story. With a great effort the officer said, ' *Tell them
at home I died like a man and a soldier.*' He threw open his coat, displayed a ghastly wound, and dropped dead at the colonel's feet. — *Chancellorsville and Gettysburg, by Major-General Doubleday.*

YE MARINERS OF ENGLAND.

Ye mariners of England,
  That guard our native seas,
Whose flag has braved, a thousand years,
  The battle and the breeze,
Your glorious standard launch again,
  To match another foe !
And sweep through the deep
  While the stormy winds do blow —
While the battle rages loud and long,
  And the stormy winds do blow.

The spirits of your fathers
  Shall start from every wave !
For the deck it was their field of fame,
  And ocean was their grave.
Where Blake [1] and mighty Nelson [2] fell
  Your manly hearts shall glow,
As ye sweep through the deep

---

[1] **Blake**: a distinguished English **admiral** (1599–1657). "**He is con**-sidered as the founder of the naval supremacy of England." His **great** battles were with the Dutch and the Spanish.

[2] **Nelson**: Southey **calls** Lord Nelson **(1758–1805)** "**the** greatest naval hero of our own and of all former times." He won the battle of the Nile over Napoleon, battle of the **Baltic**, and **the great and** decisive battle of Trafalgar, which destroyed Napoleon's **combined French and** Spanish fleets and made "England mistress **of the seas.**" **In this last** engagement (1805) Nelson was mortally wounded.

While the stormy winds do blow —
While the battle rages loud and long,
   And the stormy winds do blow.

Britannia [1] needs no bulwarks,
   No towers along the steep;
Her march is o'er the mountain-wave,
   Her home is on the deep.
With thunders from her native oak [2]
   She quells the floods below,
As they roar on the shore
   When the stormy winds do blow —
When the battle rages loud and long,
   And the stormy winds do blow.

The meteor [3] flag of England
   Shall yet terrific burn,
Till danger's troubled night depart,
   And the star of peace return.
Then, then, ye ocean-warriors!
   Our song and feast shall flow
To the fame of your name,
   When the storm has ceased to blow —
When the fiery fight is heard no more,
   And the storm has ceased to blow.

                              THOMAS CAMPBELL.

[1] **Britannia**: the Roman or Latin name of Britain.
[2] **Oak**: formerly all men-of-war were built of oak.
[3] **Meteor**: so called from its bright, fiery red. Milton uses the same expression, "The imperial ensign . . . shone like a meteor."

BATTLE OF THE BALTIC.[1]

Of Nelson[2] and the north
  Sing the glorious day's renown,
When to battle fierce came forth
  All the might of Denmark's crown,
And her **arms** along **the** deep proudly shone;
  By **each** gun the lighted brand
  In a bold, determined hand,
  And the prince of **all** the land
Led them on.

Like leviathans[3] afloat
  Lay their bulwarks on the brine;
While the sign **of** battle flew
  On the lofty British **line** —
It was ten of April morn by the chime.
  As they drifted on their path
  There **was** silence deep as death;
  And the boldest held his **breath**
For a time.

[1] **Battle of the Baltic**: during the wars with Napoleon, England claimed the right to search all neutral vessels, the object being to prevent **trade** with **France**.

In 1800 **Russia,** Denmark, and Sweden entered into a treaty or coalition known as the "**Second** Armed Neutrality" to resist England's claim.

In 1801 the "Battle of the Baltic" was fought, in which Nelson bombarded Copenhagen, destroyed a great part of the Danish fleet, and gained such a victory that, with the death of the Czar, which shortly after followed, the coalition was broken up.

[2] **Nelson**: see note 2, p. 179.   [3] **Leviathans**: sea-monsters.

But the might of England flushed
  To anticipate the scene ;
And her van the fleeter rushed
  O'er the deadly space between.
" Hearts of oak ! " our captain cried ; when each gun
  From its adamantine [1] lips
  Spread a death-shade round the ships,
  Like the hurricane eclipse
Of the sun.

Again ! again ! again !
  And the havoc did not slack,
Till a feeble cheer the Dane
  To our cheering sent us back ;
Their shots along the deep slowly boom —
  Then ceased — and all is wail,
  As they strike the shattered sail,
  Or in conflagration pale,
Light the gloom.

Out spoke the victor then,
  As he hailed them o'er the wave :
" Ye are brothers ! ye are men !
  And we conquer but to save ;
So peace instead of death let us bring ;
  But yield, proud foe, thy fleet,
  With the crews, at England's feet,
  And make submission meet
To our king."

Then Denmark blessed our chief,
  That he gave her wounds repose ;

[1] **Adamantine** : which cannot be broken.

And the sounds of joy and grief
  From her people wildly rose,
As death withdrew his shades from the day.
  While the sun looked smiling bright
  O'er a wide and woeful sight,
  Where the fires of funeral light
Died away.

Now joy, old England, raise!
  For the tidings of thy might,
By the festal cities' blaze,
  Whilst the wine-cup shines in light;
And yet, amidst that joy and uproar,
  Let us think of them that sleep
  Full many a fathom deep,
  By thy wild and stormy steep,
Elsinore![1]

Brave hearts! to Britain's pride
  Once so faithful and so true,
On the deck of fame that died,
  With the gallant, good Riou[2] —
Soft sigh the winds of heaven o'er their grave!
  While the billow mournful rolls,
  And the mermaid's song condoles,
  Singing glory to the souls
Of the brave!

THOMAS CAMPBELL.

[1] Elsinore: a town of Denmark, north of, Copenhagen, on the sound where the battle was fought.

[2] Riou (RĪ-oo): Captain Riou of the English forces. He was killed in the battle.

GEORGE NIDIVER.

MEN have done brave deeds,
    And bards [1] have sung them well ;
I of good George Nidiver
    Now the tale will tell.

In Californian mountains
    A hunter bold was he ;
Keen his eye and sure his aim
    As any you should see.

A little Indian boy
    Followed him everywhere,
Eager to share the hunter's joy,
    The hunter's meal to share.

And when the bird or deer
    Fell by the hunter's skill,
The boy was always near
    To help with right good-will.

One day as through the cleft
    Between two mountains steep,
Shut in both right and left,
    Their questing [2] way they keep,

[1] **Bards** : poets.
[2] **Questing** : here, roving or searching for game.

They see **two** grizzly bears,
  With **hunger** fierce and fell,
Rush at them unawares
  Right down the narrow dell.[1]

The boy turned round with screams,
  And ran with terror wild;
One of the pair of savage beasts
  Pursued the shrieking child.

The hunter raised his gun,
  He knew *one* charge **was all,**
And through the boy's pursuing foe
  He sent his only ball.

The **other on** George **Nidiver**
  Came on with dreadful pace;
The hunter stood unarmed,
  And met him face to face.

I say *unarmed* **he stood;**
  Against those frightful paws,
The rifle-butt, or club of wood,
  Could stand no more than **straws.**

George Nidiver stood still,
  And looked **him** in the face;
The wild beast stopped amazed,
  Then came with slackening **pace.**

Still firm **the hunter stood,**
  Although his **heart** beat **high;**
Again the creature stopped,
  And gazed with wondering eye.

---

[1] **Dell** : a narrow valley, a ravine.

The hunter met his gaze,
  Nor yet an inch gave way;
The bear turned slowly round,
  And slowly moved away.

What thoughts were in his mind
  It would be hard to spell;[1]
What thoughts were in George Nidiver
  I rather guess than tell.

But sure that rifle's **aim,**
  Swift choice of generous part,
Showed in its passing gleam
  The depths of a brave heart.

ANONYMOUS.

[1] **Spell**: tell.

SHAN VAN VOCHT.[1]

THE sainted isle of old,
  Says the Shan Van Vocht,
The parent and the mould
Of the beautiful and bold,
Has her sainted heart waxed cold?
  Says the Shan Van Vocht.

Oh ! **the** French are on the say,[2]
  Says the Shan Van Vocht ;
The French are on the say,
  Says the Shan Van Vocht.
Oh ! the French are in the bay ; [3]

---

[1] **Shan Van Vocht**: an Irish phrase meaning the Poor Old Woman ; here personifying Ireland. The song was written just before the Irish **rebellion** of 1798.

Before the union of Ireland with Great Britain in 1800 that country **was** governed, or rather misgoverned, by a national parliament largely under the control of the English and of those whom the English had bought **up.**

From this parliament all Irish Catholics were rigidly excluded, and this contributed in no small degree to intensify the hatred not only **of England,** but of the Orangemen, or Irish Protestants, and allies of England **in the** North.

At the time the song was written, **the United Irishmen — a** strong **body** of Catholics pledged to reform — were expecting the French to land a **force** on the shores of Bantry Bay and aid them in a desperate attempt to secure liberty for their country. The attempt ended in disastrous failure, but the " Shan Van Vocht " hopes yet, through the influence of Mr. Gladstone and his party, to obtain the rights which have been so long and so unjustly withheld from her.   [2] **Say**: sea.

[3] **Bay**: Bantry Bay, on the south of Ireland, county of Cork.

They'll be here without delay,
And the Orange [1] will decay,
   Says the Shan Van Vocht.
     Oh! the French are in the bay,
     They'll be here by break of day,
     And the Orange will decay,
      Says the Shan Van Vocht.

And where will they have their camp?
   Says the Shan Van Vocht;
Where will they have their camp?
   Says the Shan Van Vocht.
On the Currach of Kildare; [2]
The boys they will be there
With their pikes [3] in good repair,
   Says the Shan Van Vocht.
     To the Currach of Kildare
     The boys they will repair,
     And Lord Edward [4] will be there,
      Says the Shan Van Vocht.

Then what will the yeomen do?
   Says the Shan Van Vocht;
What will the yeomen do?
   Says the Shan Van Vocht.
What should the yeomen do,

---

[1] **The Orange**: the Orange organization in the North.

[2] **Currach of Kildare**: the plain of Kildare in the county of that name, west of Dublin. It was a noted place for military gatherings.

[3] **Pikes**: spear-like weapons.

[4] **Lord Edward**: Lord Edward Fitzgerald, a younger son of the Duke of Leinster, and a leader in the cause of Catholic emancipation. He was arrested for plotting the insurrection of 1798 and died in prison.

But throw off the red and blue,[1]
And swear that they'll be true
To the Shan Van Vocht?
What should the yeomen do,
But throw off the red and blue,
And swear that they'll be true
To the Shan Van Vocht?

And what color will they wear?
Says the Shan Van Vocht;
What color will they wear?
Says the Shan Van Vocht.
What color *should* be seen,
Where our fathers' homes have been,
But our own immortal green?[2]
•   Says the Shan Van Vocht.
What color should be seen,
Where our fathers' homes have been,
But our own immortal green?
Says the Shan Van Vocht.

[1] **The red and blue**: the English colors.
[2] **Green**: the Irish national color — the shamrock, or clover.
The favorite Irish song, "The wearin' o' the Green," well expresses the Irishman's intense love of that color.

> "Then take the shamrock from your hat
> And fling it on the sod,
> And never fear, 'twill take root there
> Tho' under foot 'tis trod.
> When law can stop the blades of grass
> From growing as they grow,
> And when the leaves in summer time
> Their color cease to show,
> Oh! then I'll change the favor *
> That I wear in my cawbeen; †
> But till that time, please God, I'll stick
> To wearin' o' the green."

* **Favor**: here a token or badge of loyalty to one's native land.
† **Cawbeen**: hat.

And will Ireland then be free ?
 Says the Shan Van Vocht;
Will Ireland then be free ?
 Says the Shan Van Vocht.
Yes! Ireland *shall* be free,
From the centre to the sea ;
Then hurrah for liberty !
 Says the Shan Van Vocht.

  Yes! Ireland shall be free,
  ***From** the centre to the **sea** ;*
  Then hurrah for liberty!
  ***Says** the Shan Van Vocht.*

ANONYMOUS.

HOW THEY BROUGHT THE GOOD NEWS FROM GHENT TO AIX.[1]

I sprang to the stirrup, and Joris and he:
I galloped, Dirck galloped, we galloped all three;
" Good speed!" cried the watch as the gate-bolts un-
    drew,
" Speed!" echoed the wall to us galloping through,
Behind shut the postern,[2] the lights sank to rest,
And into the midnight we galloped abreast.

Not a word to each other; we kept the great pace —
Neck by neck, stride by stride, never changing our
    place;
I turned in my saddle and made its girths tight,
Then shortened each stirrup and set the pique[3] right,
Rebuckled the check-strap, chained slacker the bit,
Nor galloped less steadily Roland a whit.

'Twas a moonset at starting; but while we drew near
Lokeren, the cocks crew and twilight dawned clear;

---

[1] This is said to be a purely imaginary poem. Aix (Āks), a town of
Rhenish Prussia, is in peril, but may be saved if certain " good news " can
be carried to it without delay. Three horsemen start on a gallop from
Ghent (Ḡhent, G hard), in Belgium, over a hundred miles away, to announce the glad tidings.

One rider of the three succeeds in reaching the city.

[2] Postern: a small gate.

[3] Pique (peek): the point or pommel of the saddle.

At Boom a great yellow **star came out** to see;
At **Düffeld** 'twas morning as plain as could **be**;
And from **Mecheln** church-steeple we heard **the** half
        chime —
So Joris broke silence with **" Yet** there is time ! "

At Aerschot up leaped **of a sudden** the sun,
And against him **the** cattle **stood black every** one,
To **stare** through **the** mist at us galloping past;
And I saw **my** stout galloper Roland at last,
With resolute shoulders, each butting away
The haze, **as some** bluff river headland its spray;

And his low head and crest, just one sharp ear bent back
For my **voice,** and the other pricked out on his track;
And one eye's black intelligence, — **ever that** glance
O'er its white edge at me, **his** own master, askance;
And the thick heavy spume-flakes,[1] which aye and anon
His **fierce** lips shook upward in galloping **on**.

By **Hasselt** Dirck groaned; and cried Joris, "Stay spur !
Your Roos galloped bravely, the fault's not in her;
We'll remember at Aix " — for one heard the quick
        wheeze
Of her chest, saw the stretched neck, **and** staggering
        knees,
And sunk tail, **and** horrible heave of the flank,
As down on her haunches she shuddered and sank.

So **we were** left galloping, Joris and I,
Past **Looz and** past Tongres, no cloud in the sky;

_____
[1] **Spume-flakes** : foam-flakes.

The broad sun above laughed a pitiless laugh ;
'Neath our feet broke the brittle, bright stubble like
    chaff ;
Till over by Dalhem a dome-spire sprang white,
And "Gallop," gasped Joris, "for Aix is in sight!"

"How they'll greet us!"—and all in a moment his roan
Rolled neck and croup [1] over, lay dead as a stone ;
And there was my Roland to bear the whole weight
Of the news which alone could save Aix from her fate,
With his nostrils like pits full of blood to the brim,
And with circles of red for his eye-sockets' rim.

Then I cast loose my buff-coat,[2] each holster [3] let fall,
Shook off both my jack-boots [4] let go belt and all,
Stood up in the stirrup, leaned, patted his ear,
Called my Roland his pet-name, my horse without
    peer —
Clapped my hands, laughed and sung, any noise, bad or
    good,
Till at length into Aix Roland galloped and stood.

And all I remember is friends flocking round,
As I sate with his head 'twixt my knees on the ground ;
And no voice but was praising this Roland of mine,
As I poured down his throat our last measure of wine,
Which (the burgesses [5] voted by common consent)
Was no more than his due who brought good news from
    Ghent.

ROBERT BROWNING.

[1] **Croup**: rump.   [2] **Buff-coat**: a leather coat.
[3] **Holster**: a leather case for holding a horse-pistol.
[4] **Jack-boots**: large, heavy boots coming up above the knee.
[5] **Burgesses**: the citizens, those who had a right to vote.

BATTLE-HYMN OF THE REPUBLIC.

MINE eyes have seen the glory of the coming of the
    Lord ;
He is trampling out the vintage where the grapes of
    wrath are stored,
He hath loosed the fateful lightning of his terrible swift
    sword ;
    His truth is marching on.

I have seen him in the watch-fires of a hundred circling
    camps ;
They have builded him an altar in the evening dews and
    damps,
I have read his righteous sentence by the dim and flaring
    lamps ;
    His day is marching on.

I have read a fiery gospel writ in burnished rows of steel :
" As ye deal with my contemners, so with you my grace
    shall deal :
Let the hero born of woman crush the serpent with his
    heel,
    Since God is marching on."

He has sounded forth the trumpet that shall never call
    retreat ;

He is sifting out the hearts of men before his judgment-
　　seat:
Oh, be swift, my soul, to answer him, — be jubilant, my
　　feet!
　　Our God is marching on.

In the beauty of the lilies Christ was born across the sea,
With a glory in his bosom that transfigures you and me:
As he died to make men holy, let us die to make men
　　free,
　　While God is marching on.

Julia Ward Howe.

THE LANDING OF THE PILGRIM FATHERS
IN NEW ENGLAND.[1]

"Look now abroad — another race has filled
   Those populous borders — wide the wood recedes,
And towns shoot up, and fertile realms are tilled;
   The land is full of harvests and green meads."

BRYANT.

THE breaking waves dashed high
   On a stern and rock-bound coast,
And the woods against a stormy sky
   Their giant branches tossed;

And the heavy night hung dark,
   The hills and waters o'er,
When a band of exiles moored their bark
   On the wild New England shore.

Not as the conqueror comes,
   They, the true-hearted, came;
Not with the roll of the stirring drums,
   And the trumpet that sings of fame;

Not as the flying come,
   In silence and in fear;
They shook the depths of the desert gloom
   With their hymns of lofty cheer.

Amidst the storm they sang,
   And the stars heard, and the sea;

[1] December 21, 1620, is the traditional date of the landing.

And the sounding aisles of the dim woods rang
  To the anthem of the free.

The ocean eagle soared
  From his nest by the white wave's foam ;
And the rocking pines of the forest roared —
  This was their welcome home.

There were men with hoary hair
  Amidst that pilgrim band :
Why had they come to wither there,
  Away from their childhood's land?

There was woman's fearless eye,
  Lit by her deep love's truth ;
There was manhood's brow, serenely high,
  And the fiery heart of youth.

What sought they thus afar ?
  Bright jewels of the mine ?
The wealth of seas, the spoils of war ?
  They sought a faith's pure shrine !

Ay, call it holy ground,
  The soil where first they trod ;
They have left unstained what there they found —
  Freedom to worship God.

FELICIA HEMANS.

MONTEREY.[1]

We were not many, we who stood
　　Before the iron sleet that day ;
Yet many a gallant spirit would
Give half his years if but he could
　　Have been with us at Monterey.

Now here, now there, the shot it hailed
　　In deadly drifts of fiery spray,
Yet not a single soldier quailed
When wounded comrades round them wailed
　　Their dying shout at Monterey.

And on, still on our column kept
　　Through walls of flame its withering way ;
Where fell the dead, the living stept,
Still charging on the guns which swept
　　The slippery streets of Monterey.

The foe himself recoiled aghast,
　　When, striking where he strongest lay,
We swooped his flanking batteries past,
And braving full their murderous blast,
　　Stormed home the towers of Monterey.

[1] During the Mexican War, in 1846, General Taylor with less than six
thousand men took the strongly fortified city of Monterey by storm. The
city was defended by a garrison numbering nearly two to one of the attack-
ing force, but it fell before the impetuous assault of the Americans.

Our banners on those turrets wave,
  And there our evening bugles play ;
Where orange-boughs above their grave,
Keep green the memory of the brave
  Who fought and fell at Monterey.

We are not many, we who pressed
  Beside the brave who fell that day ;
But who of us has not confessed
He'd rather share their warrior rest
  Than not have been at Monterey?

CHARLES FENNO HOFFMAN.

OUR STATE.

THE south-land boasts its teeming cane,
The prairied west its heavy grain,
And sunset's radiant gates unfold
On rising marts and sands of gold.

Rough, bleak, and hard, our little State
Is scant of soil, of limits strait ;
Her yellow sands are sands alone,
Her only mines are ice and stone !

From autumn frost to April rain,
Too long her winter woods complain ;
From budding flower to falling leaf,
Her summer time is all too brief.

Yet, on her rocks, and on her sands,
And wintry hills, the school-house stands ;
And what her rugged soil denies
The harvest of the mind supplies.

The riches of the commonwealth
Are free, strong minds, and hearts of health ;
And more to her than gold or grain
The cunning hand and cultured brain.

For well she keeps her ancient stock,
The stubborn strength of Pilgrim Rock ;
And still maintains, with milder laws,
And clearer light, the good old cause !

Nor heeds the sceptic's puny hands,
While near her school the church-spire stands ;
Nor fears the blinded bigot's rule,
While near her church-spire stands the school.

JOHN GREENLEAF WHITTIER.

CARMEN BELLICOSUM.[1]

In their ragged regimentals
Stood the old Continentals,[2]
   Yielding not,
When the grenadiers [3] were lunging,[4]
And like hail fell the plunging
   Cannon-shot ;
   When the files
   Of the isles,
From the smoky night encampment, bore the banner of
   the rampant [5]
   Unicorn,[6]
And grummer, grummer, grummer, rolled the roll of
   the drummer,
   Through **the morn** !

Then **with** eyes to the front all,
And with guns horizontal,
   Stood our sires ;
And the balls whistled **deadly,**
And in streams **flashing redly**

[1] **Carmen Bellicosum** : a war-song (of the **Revolution**).
[2] **Continentals**: the American forces.
[3] **Grenadiers**: English soldiers.
[4] **Lunging** : thrusting with their swords.
[5] **Rampant**: standing in a fighting attitude.
[6] **Unicorn**: the Unicorn on the British coat-of-arms.

Blazed the fires;
As the roar
On the shore,
Swept the strong battle-breakers o'er the green-sodded
acres
Of the plain;
And louder, louder, louder, cracked the black gun-
powder,
Cracking amain!

Now like smiths at their forges
Worked the red St. George's
Cannoniers;[1]
And the " villanous saltpetre "
Rung a fierce, discordant metre
Round their ears;
As the swift
Storm-drift,
With hot sweeping anger, came the horse-guards'[2] clangor
On our flanks.
Then higher, higher, higher, burned the old-fashioned
fire
Through the ranks!

Then the old-fashioned colonel
Galloped through the white infernal
Powder-cloud;
And his broad sword was swinging,
And his brazen throat was ringing

---

[1] St. George's cannoniers the British artillery-men.
[2] Horse-guards: the British cavalry.

Trumpet loud.
Then the blue
Bullets flew,
And the trooper-jackets redden at the touch of the
  leaden
      Rifle-breath;
And rounder, rounder, rounder, roared the iron six-
  pounder,
      Hurling death!

GUY HUMPHREY McMASTER

ROLL-CALL.

"Corporal Green!" the Orderly [1] cried.
    "Here!" was the answer, loud and clear,
    From the lips of the soldier who stood near;
And "Here!" was the word the next replied.

"Cyrus Drew!" — then silence fell —
    This time no answer followed the call;
    Only his rear man had seen him fall,
Killed or wounded, he could not tell.

There they stood in the falling light,
    These men of battle, with grave, dark looks,
    As plain to be read as open books,
While slowly gathered the shades of night.

The fern on the hillsides was splashed with blood,
    And down in the corn, where the poppies grew,
    Were redder stains than the poppies knew;
And crimson-dyed was the river's flood.

For the foe had crossed from the other side
    That day, in the face of a murderous fire
    That swept them down in its terrible ire,
And their life-blood went to color the tide.

---

[1] **Orderly**: a non-commissioned officer who attends a superior officer to bear his orders or do other service.

" Herbert Kline ! "   At the call there came
  Two stalwart soldiers into the line,
  Bearing between them this Herbert Kline,
Wounded and bleeding, to answer his name.

" Ezra Kerr ! " — and a voice answered " Here ! "
  " Hiram Kerr ! " — but no man replied.
  They were brothers, these two ; the sad wind sighed,
And a shudder crept through the cornfield near.

" Ephraim Deane ! " — then a soldier spoke :
  " Deane carried our regiment's colors," he said ;
  " Where our ensign was shot I left him dead,
Just after the enemy wavered and broke.

" Close to the roadside his body lies ;
  I paused a moment and gave him drink ;
  He murmured his mother's name, I think,
And death came with it, and closed his eyes."

'Twas a victory, yes, but it cost us dear —
  For that company's roll, when called at night,
  Of a hundred men who went into the fight,
Numbered but twenty that answered " Here ! "

NATHANIEL GRAHAM SHEPHERD

THE BATTLE-FIELD.

ONCE this soft turf, this rivulet's sands,
   Were trampled by a hurrying crowd,
And fiery hearts and armed hands
   Encountered in the battle-cloud.

Ah! never shall the land forget
   How gushed the life-blood of her brave —
Gushed, warm with hope and courage yet,
   Upon the soil they sought to save.

Now all is calm, and fresh, and still:
   Alone the chirp of flitting bird,
And talk of children on the hill,
   And bell of wandering kine are heard.

No solemn host goes trailing by
   The black-mouthed gun and staggering wain [1];
Men start not at the battle-cry —
   Oh, be it never heard again!

Soon rested those who fought; but thou
   Who minglest in the harder strife
For truths which men receive not now,
   Thy warfare only ends with life.

[1] **Wain**: a heavy wagon.

A friendless warfare ! lingering **long**
   Through weary day and weary year ;
A wild and many-weaponed throng
   Hang on thy front, and flank, and rear.

Yet nerve thy spirit to the proof,
   And blench not at **thy** chosen lot ;
The timid good may stand aloof,
   The sage may frown — yet faint thou not.

Nor heed the shaft too surely cast,
   The foul and hissing bolt of scorn ;
For with **thy** side shall dwell, at last,
   The victory **of** endurance born.

Truth, crushed **to** earth, shall **rise** again —
   The eternal years **of** God are **hers** ;
But Error, wounded, writhes in pain,
   And dies among his worshippers.

Yea, though thou **lie upon the dust,**
   When they who helped thee flee in fear,
Die full of hope and manly **trust,**
   Like those who fell in battle here !

Another hand thy sword shall wield,
   Another hand the standard wave,
Till from the trumpet's mouth is pealed
   The **blast of** triumph o'er thy grave.

WILLIAM CULLEN BRYANT.

BARBARA FRIETCHIE.[1]

Up from the meadows rich with corn,
Clear in the cool September morn,

The clustered spires of Frederick[2] stand
Green-walled by the hills of Maryland.

Round about them orchards sweep,
Apple and peach tree fruited deep,

Fair as a garden of the Lord
To the eyes of the famished rebel horde,

On that pleasant morn of the early fall
When Lee marched over the mountain wall, —

Over the mountains, winding down,
Horse and foot into Frederick town.

Forty flags with their silver stars,
Forty flags with their crimson bars,[3]

[1] During the Civil War, early in September, 1862, General Lee of the Confederate army crossed the Potomac, took possession of Frederick City, Md., and prepared to move on to Baltimore or Philadelphia. The battle of Antietam (Sept. 17) compelled him to retreat into Virginia.

[2] Frederick: the capital of Frederick County, Md.

[3] Bars: for the sake of the rhyme "bars" is here used for stripes. The "forty flags," according to the story, were National flags displayed in Frederick; the Confederates hauled them down.

Flapped in the morning wind; the sun
Of noon looked down, and saw not one.

Up rose old Barbara Frietchie [1] then,
Bowed with her fourscore years and ten;

Bravest of all in Frederick town,
She took up the flag the men hauled down;

In her attic-window the staff she set,
To show that one heart was loyal yet.

Up the street came the rebel tread,
"Stonewall" Jackson [2] riding ahead.

Under his slouched hat left and right
He glanced: the old flag met his sight.

"Halt!" — the dust-brown ranks stood fast;
"Fire!" — out blazed the rifle-blast.

It shivered the window, pane and sash;
It rent the banner with seam and gash.

[1] **Barbara Frietchie**: the story of Barbara Frietchie is accepted as true by Lossing in his "Pictorial History of the War" (II. 466), and he gives a sketch of her house; but neither Greeley, Draper, nor the Comte de Paris mentions the incident.

[2] **"Stonewall" Jackson**: Thomas J. Jackson, lieutenant-general in the Confederate army, was one of the bravest and most conscientious of the Southern men who came into prominence during the Civil War.

He received the name of "Stonewall" as a compliment to his courage at Bull Run, where during a furious charge of Union troops he stood "like a stone wall." His example inspired others on his side, and was one great cause of the South's winning the day.

"Stonewall" Jackson died in 1863, shortly after the battle of Chancellorsville; his English admirers, since the war, subscribed for a bronze statue of the general, which was erected in the city of Richmond, Va., Jackson's native State.

Quick, as it fell, from the broken staff
Dame Barbara snatched the silken scarf;

She leaned far out on the window-sill,
And shook it forth with a royal will.

"Shoot, if you must, this old gray head,
But spare your country's flag," she said.

A shade of sadness, a blush of shame,
Over the face of the leader came;

The nobler nature within him stirred
To life at that woman's deed and word:

"Who touches a hair of yon gray head
Dies like a dog! March on!" he said.

All day long through Frederick street
Sounded the tread of marching feet;

All day long that free flag tost
Over the heads of the rebel host.

Ever its torn folds rose and fell
On the loyal winds that loved it well;

And through the hill-gaps sunset light
Shone over it with a warm good-night.

Barbara Frietchie's work is o'er,
And the rebel rides on his raids no more.

Honor to her! and let a tear
Fall, for her sake, on "Stonewall's" bier.

Over Barbara Frietchie's grave,
Flag of freedom and union, wave!

Peace, and order, and beauty draw
Round thy symbol of light and law;

And ever the stars above look down
On thy stars below in Frederick town!

JOHN GREENLEAF WHITTIER

THE BURIAL OF SIR JOHN MOORE.[1]

1809.

Not a drum was heard, not a funeral note,
  As his corse to the rampart we hurried ;
Not a soldier discharged his farewell shot
  O'er the grave where our hero we buried.

We buried him darkly at dead of night,
  The sod with our bayonets turning ;
By the struggling moonbeam's misty light,
  And the lantern dimly burning.

No useless coffin enclosed his breast,
  Not in sheet nor in shroud we wound him ;
But he lay like a warrior taking his rest,
  With his martial cloak around him !

Few and short were the prayers we said,
  And we spoke not a word of sorrow ;
But we steadfastly gazed on the face that was dead,
  And we bitterly thought of the morrow.

We thought, as we hollowed his narrow bed,
  And smoothed down his lonely pillow,
That the foe and the stranger would tread o'er his head,
  And we far away on the billow !

---

[1] The burial of the English general, Sir John Moore, was an incident of
Wellington's campaign against Napoleon in Spain. Sir John was killed at
Corunna in 1809. He was buried on the ramparts of the city.

Lightly they'll talk of the spirit that's gone,
 And o'er his cold ashes upbraid him;
But little he'll reck if they let him sleep on,
 In the grave where a Briton has laid him.

But half of our heavy task was done,
 When the clock struck the hour for retiring;
And we heard the distant random gun
 That the foe was sullenly firing.

Slowly and sadly we laid him down,
 From the field of his fame fresh and gory;
We carved not a line, and we raised not a stone —
 But we left him alone in his glory!

CHARLES WOLFE.

THE CUMBERLAND.[1]

March 8, 1862.

At anchor in Hampton Roads we lay,
  On board of the Cumberland, sloop-of-war ;
And at times from the fortress across the bay
    The alarum of drums swept past,
    Or a bugle blast
  From the camp on the shore.

Then far away to the south uprose
  A little feather of snow-white smoke,
And we knew that the iron ship of our foes
    Was steadily steering its course
    To try the force
  Of our ribs of oak.

Down upon us heavily runs,
  Silent and sullen, the floating fort ;
Then comes a puff of smoke from her guns,
    And leaps the terrible death,
    With fiery breath,
  From each open port.

We are not idle, but send her straight
  Defiance back in a full broadside !

---

[1] The Cumberland : during the American Civil War, the *Merrimac*, an iron-clad Confederate gunboat, attacked and crushed in the side of the Union frigate *Cumberland* at Hampton Roads, Va.

The *Cumberland* speedily sunk, carrying down all the sick and wounded, or one hundred and twenty-one in all.

As hail rebounds from a roof of slate,
  Rebounds our heavier hail
  From each iron scale
Of the monster's hide.

"Strike your flag!" the Rebel cries,
  In his arrogant old plantation strain.
"Never!" our gallant Morris [1] replies;
  "It is better to sink than to yield!"
  And the whole air pealed
With the cheers of our men.

Then, like a kraken [2] huge and black,
  She crushed our ribs in her iron grasp!
Down went the Cumberland all a wreck,
  With a sudden shudder of death,
  And the cannon's breath
For her dying gasp.

Next morn, as the sun rose over the bay,
  Still floated our flag at the mainmast-head.
Lord, how beautiful was thy day!
  Every waft of the air
  Was a whisper of prayer,
Or a dirge for the dead.

Ho! brave hearts that went down in the seas!
  Ye are at peace in the troubled stream;
Ho! brave land! with hearts like these,
  Thy flag, that is rent in twain,
  Shall be one again,
And without a seam!

HENRY WADSWORTH LONGFELLOW.

[1] Lieutenant George Upham Morris, commander of the *Cumberland*.
[2] Kraken: a terrible sea-monster said to have been seen off the coast of Norway.

THE PRIVATE OF THE BUFFS.[1]

Last night, among his fellow-roughs,
  He jested, quaffed, and swore ;
A drunken private of the Buffs,[2]
  Who never looked before.
To-day, beneath the **foeman**'s frown,
  He stands in Elgin's place,[3]
Ambassador from Britain's crown,
  And type of all her race.

Poor, reckless, rude, low-born, untaught,
  Bewildered, and alone,
A heart with English instinct fraught
  He yet can call his own.
Aye, tear his body limb from limb,
  Bring cord, or axe, or flame ;
He only knows, that not through *him*
  Shall England come **to** shame.

[1] During the English war with China in 1858 a private of the Buffs **with** some Indian troops fell into the hands of the Chinese. They were **ordered** to salute the authorities in the Chinese fashion by prostrating **themselves** and touching the ground with the forehead. The Indians obeyed, **but the English soldier** swore that he would **not prostrate himself to any** Chinaman living. He was knocked on the head and his body cast out on a dung-hill.

[2] **Buffs** : a regiment from Kent, England, so called because the facings **of** their uniforms are of buff or light yellow color.

[3] **He stands** : like Lord Elgin (*g* hard) ; a representative of England's manliness and courage.

Far **Kentish** hop-fields round him seemed
　Like dreams to come and go;
Bright leagues of cherry-blossoms gleamed,
　One sheet of living **snow**;
The smoke above his father's door,
　In gray, soft eddyings **hung**:
Must he then watch **it** rise no more,
　Doomed by **himself** so young?

Yes, honor calls.!　With strength like steel
　He puts the vision by;
Let dusky Indians [1] whine and kneel;
　An English lad must die.
And thus, with eyes that would not shrink,
　With knee to man unbent,
Unfaltering on its dreadful brink,
　To his red grave he went.

Vain, mightiest fleets, of iron framed;
　Vain, those all-shattering guns;
Unless proud England keep, untamed,
　The strong heart of her sons.
So let **his** name through Europe ring —
　A man of mean estate,
Who died, as firm as Sparta's king,[2]
　Because his soul was great.

Sir Francis Hastings Doyle.

[1] **Indians**: native troops from India employed by the English in this war with China.

[2] Leonidas, king of Sparta, who with three hundred men held the pass of Thermopylæ against a Persian army, until he and all his band were slain.

LOCHINVAR.

O, YOUNG Lochinvar [1] is come out of the west,
Through all the wide Border [2] his steed was the best;
And save his good broadsword, he weapon had none,
He rode all unarmed, and he rode all alone.
So faithful in **love**, and so dauntless in **war**,
There never was knight like **the young Lochinvar**.

He **staid not for** brake, [3] and he stopped not for stone,
He swam the Eske [4] river where ford there was none;
But ere he alighted at Netherby [5] gate,
The bride had consented, the gallant **came late**:
For a laggard in love, and a dastard in war,
Was to wed the fair Ellen of young Lochinvar.

So boldly he entered the Netherby Hall,
Among bridesmen and kinsmen, and brothers, and all:
Then spake the bride's father, his hand on his sword,
(For the poor craven bridegroom **said** never a word,)
"O come ye in peace here, or come ye in war,
Or to dance at our bridal, young Lord Lochinvar?"

---

[1] **Lochinvar** (Lok-in-var').
[2] **Border**: that part of Scotland which **borders on** England.
[3] **Brake**: here, ground overgrown with brakes and bushes.
[4] **Eske** (or Esk): a river on the border, emptying into Solway Firth.
[5] **Netherby**: Netherby Castle, Cumberland, England. It is on the eastern bank of the **Eske**.

"I long wooed your daughter, my suit you denied;
Love swells like the Solway, but ebbs like its tide —
And now am I come, with this lost love of mine,
To lead but one measure,[1] drink one cup of wine.
There are maidens in Scotland more lovely by far,
That would gladly be bride to the young Lochinvar."

The bride kissed the goblet : the knight took it up,
He quaffed off the wine, and he threw down the cup.
She looked down to blush, and she looked up to sigh,
With a smile on her lips and a tear in her eye.
He took her soft hand, ere her mother could bar, —
"Now tread we a measure !" said young Lochinvar.

So stately his form, and so lovely her face,
That never a hall such a galliard[2] did grace ;
While her mother did fret, and her father did fume,
And the bridegroom stood dangling his bonnet and
          plume ;
And the bride-maidens whispered, "'Twere better by
          far,
To have matched our fair cousin with young Lochinvar."

One touch to her hand, and one word in her ear,
When they reached the hall-door, and the charger stood
          near ;
So light to the croupe the fair lady he swung,
So light to the saddle before her he sprung.
"She is won ! we are gone over bank, bush and scaur ;[3]
They'll have fleet steeds that follow," quoth young
          Lochinvar.

---

[1] Measure : a dance.
[2] Galliard : a gay, lively dance.
[3] Scaur : a steep, precipitous place.

There was mounting 'mong Graemes of the Netherby
  clan ;

Forsters, Fenwicks, and Musgraves, they rode and they
  ran :

There was racing and chasing on Cannobie Lee,[1]

But the lost bride of Netherby ne'er did they see.

So daring in love, and so dauntless in war,

Have ye e'er heard of gallant like young Lochinvar ?

Sir Walter Scott.

[1] **Cannobie** (or **Cannonby**) **Lee**: the Cannobie meadows in the vicinity
of Netherby Castle.

"'STONEWALL' JACKSON'S WAY."[1]

———•◦•———

COME, stack arms, men! Pile on the rails,[2]
  Stir up the camp-fire bright;
No matter if the canteen fails,
  We'll make a roaring night.
Here Shenandoah[3] brawls along,
There burly Blue Ridge echoes strong,
To swell the brigade's rousing song
  Of "'Stonewall' Jackson's way."

We see him now — the old slouched hat
  Cocked o'er his eye askew,
The shrewd, dry smile, the speech so pat,
  So calm, so blunt, so true.
The "Blue-Light Elder"[4] knows 'em well;

[1] "Stonewall" Jackson: see note 2, p. 210.

[2] Rails: fence rails; this must be regarded as "poetic license," since "Stonewall" Jackson gave his men strict orders not to take the fence rails for fuel — occasionally, however, on bitter cold or very wet nights these orders would be secretly violated.

[3] Shenandoah: Jackson always spoke of the Shenandoah Valley with particular affection, — his home at Lexington, Va., was in it, — and he used to say that if the South lost, "The Valley," Virginia, would be lost.

[4] "Blue-Light Elder": Jackson was a rigid Presbyterian, and a man of exemplary piety. The name "Blue-Light Elder" was playfully given to him by his former pupils at the Lexington Military Academy; it meant no disrespect, — it could not, — for Jackson was one who, by his sincerity and force of character, compelled all to respect him whether they agreed with him or not.

Says he, "That's Banks [1] — he's fond of shell,[2]
Lord save his soul! We'll give him " — well,
That's "'Stonewall' Jackson's way."

Silence! ground arms! kneel all! caps off!
"Old Blue-Light's" going to pray.
Strangle the fool that dares to scoff!
Attention! it's his way.
Appealing from his native sod,
In forma pauperis [3] to God —
"Lay bare thine arm, stretch forth thy rod!
Amen!" That's "'Stonewall's' way."

He's in the saddle now, — Fall in!
Steady! the whole brigade!
Hill's [4] at the ford, cut off — we'll win
His way out, ball and blade! [5]
What matter if our shoes are worn?
What matter if our feet are torn?
"Quick-step! [6] we're with him before dawn!"
That's "'Stonewall' Jackson's way."

The sun's bright lances rout the mists
Of morning, and, by George!
Here's Longstreet [7] struggling in the lists,[8]

[1] **Banks:** General Banks of the Union army, who undertook to drive
Jackson out of "The Valley."   [2] **Shell:** a contraction of bombshell.

[3] **In forma pauperis**: literally, as a pauper; as one who sorely needs
God's help.   [4] **Hill:** General Hill of the Confederate army.

[5] **Ball and blade**: by bullet and sword.

[6] **Quick-step**: nothing could equal the rapidity of Jackson's movements;
he always seemed to be on the "double-quick," and his brigade of infantry
got the name of Jackson's *foot-cavalry*.

[7] **Longstreet**: General Longstreet of the Confederate army.

[8] **Lists**: literally an enclosure where a tournament or battle between
knights was fought.

Hemmed in an ugly gorge.
Pope [1] and his Yankees, whipped before, —
" Bay'nets and grape ! " [2] hear " Stonewall " roar ;
" Charge, Stuart ! [3]   Pay off Ashby's [4] score ! "
In " ' Stonewall ' Jackson's way."

Ah ! maiden, wait and watch and yearn
   For news of " Stonewall's " band !
Ah ! widow, read with eyes that burn
   That ring [5] upon thy hand.
Ah ! wife, sew on, pray on, hope on !
Thy life shall not be all forlorn ;
The foe had better ne'er been born
   That gets in " ' Stonewall's ' way."

J. W. PALMER.

(Written, it is said, within hearing of the battle of
Antietam, Sept. 17th, 1862.)

[1] **Pope** : General Pope of the Union army.
[2] **Grape** : grapeshot.
[3] **Stuart** : General Stuart of the Confederate cavalry.
[4] **Ashby** : a cavalry general in Jackson's army.
[5] Ring : wedding ring.

THE OLD SERGEANT.[1]

THE carrier [1] cannot sing to-night the ballads
  With which he used to go
Rhyming the grand round of the Happy New Years
  That are now beneath the snow;

For the same awful and portentous shadow
  That overcast the earth,
And smote the land last year with desolation,
  Still darkens every hearth.

And the carrier hears Beethoven's [2] mighty Deadmarch
  Come up from every mart,
And he hears and feels it breathing in his bosom,
  And beating in his heart.

And to-day, like a scarred and weather-beaten veteran,
  Again he comes along,
To tell the story of the Old Year's struggles,
  In another New Year's song.

And the song is his, but not so with the story;
  For the story, you must know,

---

[1] The carrier of the *Louisville* (Kentucky) *Journal.* This poem was distributed by the *Journal* to its patrons on New Year's Day, 1863.

[2] **Beethoven** (Bay'to-ven): a celebrated German musical composer.

Was told in prose to Assistant-Surgeon Austin,
  By a soldier of Shiloh,[1] —

By Robert Burton, who was brought up on the Adams,
  With his death-wound in his side,
And who told the story to the Assistant-Surgeon
  On the same night that he died.

But the singer feels it will better suit the ballad,
  If all should deem it right,
To sing the story as if what it speaks of
  Had happened but last night.

"Come a little nearer, doctor, — thank you, — let me
    take the cup;
Draw your chair up, — draw it closer, — just another
    little sup!
May be you may think I'm better; but I'm pretty well
    used up, —
Doctor, you've done all you could do, but I'm just
    a-going up!

"Feel my pulse, sir, if you want to, but it ain't much
    use to try — "
"Never say that," said the surgeon, as he smothered
    down a sigh;
"It will never do, old comrade, for a soldier to say die!"
"What you *say* will make no difference, doctor, when
    you come to die.

[1] **Shiloh**: this was the first really great battle of the Civil War. It was
fought at Shiloh Church (or Pittsburgh Landing), Tenn., April 6, 7, 1862,
between General Grant and General Johnston. Johnston was killed, and
the Confederate force driven from the field.

" Doctor, what has been the matter ? "   " You were
 very faint, they say ;
You must try to get some sleep now."   " Doctor, have
 I been away ? "
" Not that anybody knows of ! "   " Doctor, — doctor,
 please to say !
There is something I must tell you, and you won't have
 long to stay !

" I have got my marching orders, and I'm ready now to
 go ;
Doctor, did you say I fainted ? — but it couldn't ha'
 been so, —
For as sure as I'm a sergeant and was wounded at
 Shiloh,
I've this very night been back there, on the old field of
 Shiloh !

" This is all that I remember ! The last time the lighter
 came,
And the lights had all been lowered, and the noises
 much the same,
He had not been gone five minutes before something
 called my name :
ORDERLY SERGEANT — ROBERT BURTON ! just that way
 it called my name.

" And I wondered who could call me so distinctly and
 so slow,
Knew it couldn't be the lighter, — he could not have
 spoken so, —

And I tried to answer, 'Here, sir!' but I couldn't make
    it go!
For I couldn't move a muscle, and I couldn't make
    it go!

— "Then I thought: 'It's all a nightmare, all a hum-
    bug and a bore;
Just another foolish *grapevine*,[1] — and it won't come
    any more;'
But it came, sir, notwithstanding, just the same way as
    before:
ORDERLY SERGEANT — ROBERT BURTON! even plainer
    than before.

"That is all that I remember, till a sudden burst of
    light,
And I stood beside the river,[2] where we stood that Sun-
    day night,
Waiting to be ferried over to the dark bluffs opposite,
When the river was perdition and all hell was opposite!

" And the same old palpitation came again in all its
    power,
And I heard a bugle sounding, as from some celestial
    tower;
And the same mysterious voice said: 'IT IS THE
    ELEVENTH HOUR!
ORDERLY SERGEANT — ROBERT BURTON, — IT IS THE
    ELEVENTH HOUR!'

" Doctor Austin! what *day* is this?"   "It is Wednesday
    night, you know."

---

[1] Army slang for false news.
[2] The Tennessee River, where the battle was fought.

" Yes, — to-morrow will be New Year's, and a right good
      time below !
What *time* is **it,** Doctor Austin?" "**Nearly** twelve."
      " Then don't you **go** !
Can it **be that** all this happened — **all** this — not an hour
      ago ?

" There was where the gunboats opened on the **dark**
      rebellious host ;
And where Webster semicircled his last guns upon the
      coast ;
There were still **the two log-houses,** just the same, or
      else their **ghost, —**
And the same **old** transport [1] came and took me over, —
      or its ghost !

" And the old field lay before me all deserted far **and**
      wide ;
There was where they fell on Prentiss, — **there McCler-**
      nand met the tide ;
There was where stern Sherman rallied, and where
      Hurlbut's heroes died, —
Lower down **where** Wallace charged them, and kept
      charging **till** he died.

" There was where Lew **Wallace** [2] showed them **he was**
      of the canny [3] kin,
There was **where** old Nelson thundered, and where
      Rousseau waded in ;

---

[1] **Transport** : the transport boat.
[2] **Lew Wallace** : General Lewis Wallace of the Union army ; he distinguished himself at the battle of **Shiloh.** The other names are those **of**
Union commanders in the battle.   [3] **Canny** : knowing, shrewd.

There McCook sent 'em to breakfast, and we all began
    to win, —
There was where the grapeshot took me, just as we
    began to win.

"Now a shroud of snow and silence over everything
    was spread;
And but for this old blue mantle and the old hat on
    my head,
I should not have even doubted, to this moment, I was
    dead, —
For my footsteps were as silent as the snow upon the
    dead!

"Death and silence! death and silence! all around me
    as I sped!
And behold a mighty tower, as if builded to the dead,
To the heaven of the heavens lifted up its mighty head,
Till the stars and stripes of heaven all seemed waving
    from its head!

"Round and mighty-based it towered, up into the in-
    finite, —
And I knew no mortal mason could have built a shaft
    so bright;
For it shone like solid sunshine; and a winding stair of
    light
Wound around it and around it, till it wound clear out
    of sight!

"And behold, as I approached it, with a rapt[1] and
    dazzled stare, —

---

[1] Rapt: raptured.

Thinking that I saw old comrades just ascending the
    great stair, —
Suddenly the solemn challenge broke of — 'Halt, and
    who goes there?'
'I'm a friend,' I said, 'if you are.' 'Then advance, sir,
    to the stair!'

"I advanced! — That sentry, doctor, was Elijah Bal-
    lantyne! —
First of all to fall on Monday, after we had formed the
    line! —
'Welcome, my old sergeant, welcome! Welcome by
    that countersign!'
And he pointed to the scar there, under this old cloak
    of mine!

"As he grasped my hand, I shuddered, thinking only
    of the grave;
But he smiled and pointed upward with a bright and
    bloodless glaive; [1]
'That's the way, sir, to headquarters.' 'What head-
    quarters?' 'Of the brave.'
'But the great tower?' 'That,' he answered, 'is the
    way, sir, of the brave!'

"Then a sudden shame came o'er me at his uniform of
    light, —
At my own so old and tattered, and at his so new and
    bright.
'Ah!' said he, 'you have forgotten the new uniform
    to-night, —

[1] **Glaive**: sword.

Hurry back, for you must be here at just twelve o'clock
     to-night!'

"And the **next** thing I remember, you were sitting
     there, and I—
Doctor,—did **you** hear a footstep?   Hark!—God bless
     you **all**!   Good-by!
Doctor, please to give my musket and my knapsack,
     when I **die**,
To my son—my son that's coming,—he won't **get** here
     till I **die**!

"Tell him his old father blessed him as he never did
     before,—
And to carry that old musket"—Hark! a knock is at
     the door—
"Till the Union"—See! it opens!—"Father! Father!
     speak **once** more!"—
"**Bless you**!" gasped the old gray sergeant, and he lay
     and said **no more**.

FORCEYTHE WILLSON.

BARCLAY OF URY.[1]

Up the streets of Aberdeen,
By the kirk [2] and college-green,
    Rode the Laird [3] of Ury;
Close behind him, close beside,
Foul of mouth and evil-eyed,
    Pressed the mob in fury.

Flouted him the drunken churl,[4]
Jeered at him the serving-girl,
    Prompt to please her master;
And the begging carlin,[5] late
Fed and clothed at Ury's gate,
    Cursed him as he passed her.

Yet with calm and stately mien,
Up the streets of Aberdeen

---

[1] **Barclay of Ury**: David Barclay, proprietor of Ury, an estate near Aberdeen, Scotland, was one of the early Friends, or Quakers. He served under the famous Swedish general, Gustavus Adolphus, when that commander was mortally wounded in the terrible battle of Lützen, Germany, in the Thirty Years' War.

Barclay with thirty other Quakers was cast into prison in Aberdeen in 1676, on account of his religious faith, but was shortly after released. His son, Robert, a man of commanding talents and great moral courage, — qualities which he inherited from his father, — was the author of a defence of the religion held and taught by the Friends, which is considered the ablest work of the kind yet produced.

[2] **Kirk**: church.

[3] **Laird**: a landed proprietor, squire.

[4] **Churl**: a low fellow.

[5] **Carlin**: old woman.

Came he slowly riding;
And, to all he saw and heard,
Answering not with bitter word,
   Turning not for chiding.

Came a troop with broadswords swinging,
Bits and bridles sharply ringing,
   Loose and free and froward;[1]
Quoth the foremost, "Ride him down!
Push him! prick him![2] through the town
   Drive the Quaker coward!"

But from out the thickening crowd
Cried a sudden voice and loud:
   "Barclay! Ho! a Barclay!"
And the old man at his side
Saw a comrade, battle-tried,
   Scarred and sunburned darkly, —

Who with ready weapon bare,
Fronting to the troopers there,
   Cried aloud: "God save us!
Call ye coward him who stood
Ankle deep in Lützen's[3] blood,
   With the brave Gustavus?"

"Nay, I do not need thy sword,
Comrade mine," said Ury's lord;
   "Put it up, I pray thee;

---

[1] **Froward**: ungovernable, perverse.
[2] **Prick him**: prick him with your swords.
[3] **Lutzen** and **Gustavus**: see note 1, p. 233.

Passive to his holy will,
Trust I in my Master still,
  Even though he slay me.

" Pledges of thy love and faith,
Proved on many a field of death,
  Not by me are needed."
Marvelled much that henchman [1] bold
That his laird, so stout [2] of old,
  Now so meekly pleaded.

" Woe's the day ! " he sadly said,
With a slowly shaking head,
  And a look of pity ;
" Ury's honest lord reviled,   .
Mock of knave and sport of child,
  In his own good city !

" Speak the word, and, master mine,
As we charged on Tilly's [3] line,
  And his Walloon [4] lancers,
Smiting through their midst we'll teach
Civil look and decent speech
  To these boyish prancers ! "

" Marvel not, mine ancient friend,
Like beginning, like the end : "
  Quoth the Laird of Ury,
" Is the sinful servant more

---

[1] Henchman : servant or follower.   [2] Stout : brave.
[3] Tilly : Gustavus Adolphus defeated Marshal Tilly at Leipsic, 1631.
[4] Walloon : an inhabitant of Southern Belgium.

Than his gracious Lord who bore
　　Bonds and stripes in Jewry?[1]

"Give me joy that in His name
I can bear, with patient frame,
　　All these vain ones offer;
While for them He suffereth long,
Shall I answer wrong with wrong,
　　Scoffing with the scoffer?

"Happier I, with loss of all,
Hunted, outlawed, held in thrall,[2]
　　With few friends to greet me,
Than when reeve[3] and squire were seen,
Riding out from Aberdeen,
　　With bared heads to meet me.

"When each goodwife, o'er and o'er,
Blessed me as I passed her door;
　　And the snooded[4] daughter,
Through her casement glancing down,
Smiled on him who bore renown
　　From red fields of slaughter.

"Hard to feel the stranger's scoff,
Hard the old friend's falling off,
　　Hard to learn forgiving;
But the Lord his own rewards,
And his love with theirs accords,
　　Warm and fresh and living.

---

[1] Jewry: Judea.　　[2] Thrall: captivity.　　[3] Reeve: sheriff.
[4] Snooded: having the hair bound with a fillet or ribbon.

"Through this dark and **stormy night**
Faith beholds a feeble **light**
   Up the blackness **streaking;**
Knowing God's own **time is best,**
In a patient hope **I rest**
   For the full day-breaking!"
       *   *   *   *   *

             JOHN GREENLEAF WHITTIER.

THE LORD OF BUTRAGO.[1]

1385.

" YOUR horse is faint, my **King** — my lord! your gallant
    horse is sick —
His limbs **are torn**, his breast is gored, on his eye the
    film **is** thick;
Mount, mount on mine, oh, mount apace,[2] **I** pray thee,
    mount and fly!
Or in mine arms I'll **lift your** Grace — these trampling
    hoofs are nigh!

"**My King** — my King! you're wounded sore — the
    blood runs from your **feet**;
But only lay a hand before, **and** I'll **lift you to** your
    seat:
Mount, Juan,[3] for **they gather fast**! — I hear their com-
    ing cry;
Mount, mount, and ride for jeopardy[4] — I'll save you
    though I die!

"Stand, noble **steed**! this hour of **need** — be **gentle** as
    a lamb:

---

[1] The incident which is related in the following ballad is supposed to have occurred on the famous field of Aljubarrota, where King Juan the First, of Castile, was defeated by the Portuguese. The King, who was at the time in a feeble state of health, exposed himself very much during the action; and being wounded, had great difficulty in making his escape.

[2] **Apace**: quickly.

[3] **Juan**: Spanish pronunciation, Hoo-an' or **Wan**.

[4] For **jeopardy**: on account of the peril.

I'll kiss the foam from off thy mouth, thy master dear
    I am.
Mount, Juan, mount: whate'er betide, away the bridle
    fling,
And plunge the rowels in his side. My horse shall
    save my king!

"Nay, never speak; my sires, Lord King, received their
    land from yours,
And joyfully their blood shall spring, so be it thine
    secures;
If I should fly, and thou, my King, be found among the
    dead,
How could I stand 'mong gentlemen, such scorn on my
    gray head?

"Castile's proud dames shall never point the finger of
    disdain,
And say there's ONE that ran away when our good
    lords were slain!
I leave Diego[1] in your care — you'll fill his father's
    place:
Strike, strike the spur, and never spare — God's bless-
    ing on your Grace!"

So spake the brave Montañez, Butrago's lord was he,
And turned him to the coming host in steadfastness and
    glee.
He flung himself among them, as they came down the
    hill;
He died, God wot![2] but not before his sword had drunk
    its fill.

J. G. LOCKHART.
Translated from the Spanish.

---

[1] **Diego**: Spanish pronunciation, De-ā'go.   [2] **Wot**: knows.

THE CAVALIER'S ESCAPE.[1]

TRAMPLE! trample! went the roan,
    Trap! trap! went the gray;
But pad! *pad!* PAD! like a thing that was mad,
    My chestnut broke away.
It was just five miles from Salisbury[2] town,
    And but one hour to day.

Thud! THUD! came on the heavy roan,
    Rap! RAP! the mettled gray;
But my chestnut mare was of blood so rare,
    That she showed them all the way.
Spur on! spur on! — I doffed my hat,
    And wished them all good-day.

They splashed through miry rut and pool, —
    Splintered through fence and rail;
But chestnut Kate switched over the gate, —
    I saw them droop and tail.
To Salisbury town — but a mile of down,[3]
    Once over this brook and rail.

[1] An incident of the Civil War in England between Charles I. and Parliament. The cavaliers were on the royalist side. Here one of their number escapes, thanks to his good horse, from a band of "Roundheads" of the Parliamentary party.

[2] **Salisbury**: a noted cathedral town of Southern England.

[3] **Down**: see note 11, p. 55.

Trap! trap! I heard their echoing hoofs
  Past the walls of mossy stone;
The roan flew on at a staggering pace,
  But blood is better than bone.
I patted old Kate, and gave her the spur,
  For I knew it was all my own.

But trample! trample! came their steeds,
  And I saw their wolf's eyes burn;
I felt like a royal hart at bay,
  And made me ready to turn.
I looked where highest grew the May,[1]
  And deepest arched the fern.

I flew at the first knave's sallow throat;
  One blow, and he was down.
The second rogue fired twice, and missed;
  I sliced the villain's crown, —
Clove through the rest, and flogged brave Kate,
  Fast, fast to Salisbury town!

Pad! pad! they came on the level sward,
  Thud! thud! upon the sand, —
With a gleam of swords and a burning match,[2]
  And a shaking of flag and hand;
But one long bound, and I passed the gate,
  Safe from the canting[3] band.

WALTER THORNBURY.

[1] **May**: the hawthorn.

[2] **Match**: a slow-match kept burning to discharge the guns then in use, neither flint nor percussion locks having been invented.

[3] **Canting**: hypocritical; a term of reproach given to the Puritan or "Roundhead" party.

SONG OF MARION'S MEN.

1780–1781.

OUR band is few, but true and tried,
  Our leader frank and bold;
The British soldier trembles
  When Marion's [1] name is told.
Our fortress is the good greenwood,
  Our tent the cypress-tree;
We know the forest round us,
  As seamen know the sea;
We know its walks of thorny vines,
  Its glades [2] of reedy grass,
Its safe and silent islands
  Within the dark morass.

Woe to the English soldiery
  That little dread us near!
On them shall light at midnight
  A strange and sudden fear;
When, waking to their tents on fire,
  They grasp their arms in vain,

---

[1] **Marion : General** Francis Marion, a hero of the American Revolution. He was born in South Carolina and was of Huguenot descent. When the British besieged Charleston, Marion raised a force of twenty followers, and kept up a three years' warfare which rendered great service to the cause of liberty. His epitaph states with entire truth, that "He lived without fear, and died without reproach."

[2] **Glades** : here, a contraction of everglades; a low, marshy tract of country interspersed with land covered with high grass.

And they who stand to face us
  Are beat to earth again;
And they who fly in terror deem
  A mighty host behind,
And hear the tramp of thousands
  Upon the hollow wind.

Then sweet the hour that brings release
  From danger and from toil;
We talk the battle over,
  And share the battle's spoil.
The woodland rings with laugh and shout,
  As if a hunt were up,
And woodland flowers are gathered
  To crown the soldier's cup.
With merry songs we mock the wind
  That in the pine-top grieves,
And slumber long and sweetly
  On beds of oaken leaves.

Well knows the fair and friendly moon
  The band that Marion leads —
The glitter of their rifles,
  The scampering of their steeds.
'Tis life to guide the fiery barb [1]
  Across the moonlight plain;
'Tis life to feel the night-wind
  That lifts his tossing mane.
A moment in the British camp —
  A moment — and away,
Back to the pathless forest,
  Before the peep of day.

[1] Barb: a horse remarkable for speed and spirit.

Grave men there are by broad Santee,[1]
　Grave men with hoary hairs;
Their hearts are all with Marion,
　For Marion are their prayers.
And lovely ladies greet our band,
　With kindest welcoming,
With smiles like those of summer,
　And tears like those of spring.
For them we wear these trusty arms,
　And lay them down no more
Till we have driven the Briton,
　Forever, from our shore.

WILLIAM CULLEN BRYANT.

[1] **Santee**: the Santee River.

ABRAHAM LINCOLN.

OH, slow to smite and swift to spare,
    Gentle and merciful and just!
Who, in the fear of God, didst bear
    The sword of power — a nation's trust.

In sorrow by thy bier we stand,
    Amid the awe that hushes all,
And speak the anguish of a land
    That shook with horror at thy fall.

Thy task is done — the bond are free;
    We bear thee to an honored grave,
Whose noblest monument shall be
    The broken fetters of the slave.

Pure was thy life; its bloody close
    Hath placed thee with the sons of light,
Among the noble host of those
    Who perished in the cause of right.

WILLIAM CULLEN BRYANT.

HOW HE SAVED ST. MICHAEL'S.

It was long ago it happen'd, ere ever the signal gun
That blazed above Fort Sumter had waken'd **the** North
    as one ; [1]
Long ere the wonderous pillar of battle-cloud **and fire**
Had mark'd where the unchain'd millions march'd on to
    their **heart's** desire.

On the **roofs** and the glittering turrets, that night, as
    the sun went down,
The mellow glow of the twilight shone like a jewell'd
    crown ;
And, bathed in the living **glory, as** the people lifted
    their eyes,
They saw the pride of the city, the spire of St. Michael's,[2]
rise.

High over the lesser steeples, tipp'd with a golden ball,
That hung like a radiant planet caught in its earthward
    fall, —
First glimpse of home to **the** sailor who made the harbor-
    round,
And last **slow-fading vision dear to** the outward bound.

[1] Before the Civil War, which began in 1861 with the attack of the South on Fort Sumter, in Charleston harbor, the fort being then garrisoned by United States troops.
[2] St. Michael's: this church is considered the finest in Charleston; it has a spire of remarkable beauty.

The gently gathering shadows **shut** out the waning
    light;
The children pray'd at their bedsides, as you will pray
    to-night;
The noise of buyer and seller from the busy **mart was**
    gone;
And in dreams of a peaceful morrow the city slumber'd
    on.

But another **light than sunrise aroused** the sleeping
    street;
For a cry was **heard** at **midnight, and the rush of tram-**
    pling feet;
Men stared in each other's faces through mingled fire
    and smoke,
While the **frantic** bells went clashing, **clamorous stroke**
    on stroke.

By the glare **of** her blazing roof-tree [1] the **houseless**
    mother fled,
With the babe she press'd to her bosom shrieking in
    nameless dread,
While the fire-king's **wild** battalions scaled wall and
    capstone high,
And planted their flaring banners against an inky sky.

From the death that raged behind them, **and** the crash
    of **ruin loud,**
To the great **square of** the city was **driven the** surging
    crowd;

---

[1] **Roof-tree**: the beam in the angle of a roof; hence the roof itself.

Where yet, firm in all the tumult, unscathed by the
    fiery flood,
With its heavenward-pointing finger the Church of St.
    Michael stood.

But e'en as they gazed upon it there rose a sudden
    wail, —
A cry of horror, blended with the roaring of the gale,
On whose scorching wings up-driven, a single flaming
    brand
Aloft on the towering steeple clung like a bloody hand.

"Will it fade?" The whisper trembled from a thou-
    sand whitening lips;
Far out on the lurid harbor they watched it from the
    ships, —
A baleful[1] gleam that brighter and ever brighter shone,
Like a flickering, trembling will-o'-wisp[2] to a steady
    beacon grown.

"Uncounted gold shall be given to the man whose
    brave right hand,
For the love of the perill'd city, plucks down yon burn-
    ing brand!"
So cried the mayor of Charleston, that all the people
    heard;
But they look'd each one at his fellow; and no man
    spoke a word.

---

[1] **Baleful**: fraught with evil; threatening
[2] **Will-o'-wisp**: a flickering, moving light seen at times in marshy places and church-yards. It is supposed to be the result of animal and vegetable decomposition.

Who is it leans from the belfry, with face upturn'd **to**
    the sky,
Clings to a column, and measures **the dizzy** spire with
    his **eye**?
Will **he dare it,** the hero undaunted, that terrible, sick-
    ening height?
Or will the hot blood of his courage **freeze** in his veins
    at the sight?

But see! he has stepp'd **on the** railing; he **climbs with**
    his feet and his hands;
And firm on **a** narrow projection, with the belfry be-
    neath him, he stands;
Now once, and once only, **they cheer** him, — a single
    tempestuous breath, —
And there falls on the multitude gazing a **hush** like **the**
    stillness of death.

Slow, steadily mounting, unheeding aught save the goal
    of the fire,
Still higher and higher, **an atom, he** moves on the face
    of the **spire.**
He stops! Will he fall? **Lo!** for answer, a gleam like
    a meteor's track,
And, hurl'd on the stones **of** the pavement, the **red**
    brand lies shatter'd and black.

Once more the shouts **of the people have** rent the quiv-
    ering air:
At the church-door mayor **and council wait** with their
    feet on the stair;

And the eager throng **behind them** press for a touch of
    his hand, —
The **unknown hero,** whose daring **could compass a** deed
    so grand.

But **why does a** sudden tremor **seize** on them while they
    gaze?
And **what meaneth that** stifled **murmur of** wonder and
    amaze?
He stood in the gate **of the temple** he **had** perill'd his
    life to save; .
And the **face** of **the hero** undaunted was the **sable** face
    of a slave.

With folded arms he was speaking, in tones that were
    clear, **not loud,**
And his eyes, ablaze in their **sockets, burnt** into the
    eyes of the crowd:
"**You** may keep **your gold; I scorn it!** — but answer
    me, ye who can,
If the deed I have **done** before you be not **the deed of**
    a *man?*"

He stepp'd but a short space backward; and from all
    the women and men
There were **only** sobs for answer; **and the mayor** call'd
    for **a pen,**
And the great **seal** of the **city, that he** might read who
    ran:
And the slave who saved St. Michael's **went out** from
    its **door, a** *man.*

ANONYMOUS.

CURFEW MUST NOT RING TO-NIGHT.

ENGLAND'S sun was slowly setting o'er the hills so far
    away,
Filling all the land with beauty at the close of one sad
    day;
And the last rays kiss'd the forehead of a man and
    maiden fair,
He with step so slow and weaken'd, she with sunny,
    floating hair;
He with sad bow'd head, and thoughtful, she with lips
    so cold and white,
Struggling to keep back the murmur, " Curfew[1] must
    not ring to-night."

" Sexton," — Bessie's white lips falter'd, pointing to the
    prison old,
With its walls so dark and gloomy, walls so dark and
    damp and cold, —
" I've a lover in that prison, doom'd this very night to
    die
At the ringing of the Curfew, and no earthly help is
    nigh.

---

[1] **Curfew** (French *couvre-feu*, cover-fire): **a** bell formerly rung in England in the evening as a signal to the inhabitants to rake the ashes over
their fires and retire to rest. The curfew is still rung in some parts of
England, but no longer for its original purpose.

Cromwell[1] will not come till sunset"; and her face
grew strangely white,
As she spoke in **husky** whispers, " Curfew must not ring
to-night."

" Bessie," calmly spoke the sexton, — every word pierced
her young heart
Like a thousand gleaming arrows, like a deadly poison'd
dart, —
" Long, long years I've rung the Curfew from that gloomy
shadow'd tower ;
Every evening, just at sunset, it has told the twilight
hour;
I have **done** my duty ever, tried to do it just and right ;
Now I'm old, I **will** not miss **it**; girl, the Curfew rings
to-night ! "

Wild her eyes and pale **her** features, stern and white
her thoughtful brow,
And within her heart's deep **centre** Bessie made a solemn
vow :
She had **listen'd** while the judges read, without a tear
or sigh,
" At the ringing of the Curfew Basil Underwood *must
die.*"
And her breath came fast **and faster,** and her eyes grew
large and bright, —
One low **murmur, scarcely** spoken, " Curfew *must not*
ring **to-night !** "

---

[1] **Cromwell**: Oliver Cromwell, " Protector," a ruler of England 1654 to
1658. He was one of the great leaders in the English Civil War.

She with light **step bounded** forward, sprang within the
    old church-door,
Left the old man coming slowly, paths he'd trod so oft
    before;
Not one moment paused the maiden, but, with cheek
    and brow aglow,
Stagger'd up the gloomy tower, where the bell swung
    to and fro:
Then she climb'd the slippery ladder, dark, without **one**
    ray of light,
Upward still, her pale **lips. saying,** "Curfew *must not*
    ring to-night."

She has reach'd the topmost ladder, o'er her hangs the
    great **dark** bell,
And the **awful** gloom beneath her, like **the** pathway
    down to Hell;
See, the ponderous tongue is swinging, **'tis the** hour of
    Curfew now;
And the sight has chilled her bosom, stopp'd her breath
    and paled her brow.
Shall she **let** it ring?   No, never! her eyes flash with
    sudden **light,**
As she springs and grasps it **firmly,** " Curfew *shall not*
    ring to-night!"

Out she **swung,** far out; **the** city seem'd a **tiny speck**
    below;
There 'twixt **heaven** and **earth** suspended, **as** the bell
    swung to and fro;
And the half-deaf **sexton** ringing, **(years** he had **not**
    heard the bell,)

And he thought the twilight Curfew rang young Basil's
  funeral knell:
Still the maiden clinging firmly, cheek and brow so pale
  and white,
Still'd her frighten'd heart's wild beating, " *Curfew shall
  not ring to-night.*"

It was o'er; the bell ceased swaying, and the maiden
  stepp'd once more
Firmly on the damp old ladder, where **for** hundred
  years before
Human foot had not been planted; and what she this
  night had done
Should be told **in** long years after: **as** the rays of setting sun
Lit the sky **with mellow** beauty, agèd [1] sires, with heads
  of white,
Tell their children why the Curfew **did not** ring that
  one sad night.

O'er the distant hills came Cromwell; Bessie **saw** him,
  and her brow,
Lately white with sickening terror, glows with sudden
  beauty **now**:
At his feet she told her story, show'd her hands all
  bruised and torn;
And her **sweet** young face **so** haggard, with **a** look so
  sad **and worn,**
Touch'd his **heart** with sudden pity, lit his eyes with
  misty light:
" **Go, your** lover lives!" **cried** Cromwell; "Curfew shall
  not ring to-night."

[1] **Aged**: to be pronounced in two syllables, — *a'ged*.

Wide they flung the massive portals, led the prisoner
    forth to die,
All his bright young life before him.   'Neath the dark-
    ening English sky,
Bessie came with flying footsteps, eyes aglow with love-
    light sweet;
Kneeling on the turf beside him, laid his pardon at his
    feet.
In his brave, strong arms he clasp'd her, kiss'd the face
    upturn'd and white,
Whisper'd, " Darling, you have saved me ; Curfew must
    not ring to-night."

. ROSE A. HARTWICK THORPE.

THE LOSS OF THE BIRKENHEAD.[1]

SUPPOSED TO BE NARRATED BY A SOLDIER WHO SURVIVED.

RIGHT on our flank the crimson sun went down,
 The deep sea rolled around in dark repose,
When, like the wild shriek from some captured town,
  A cry of women rose.

The stout ship Birkenhead lay hard and fast,
 Caught, without hope, upon a hidden rock;
Her timbers thrilled as nerves, when through them passed
  The spirit of that shock.

And ever like base cowards, who leave their ranks
 In danger's hour, before the rush of steel,
Drifted away, disorderly, the planks
  From underneath her keel.

Confusion spread, for, though the coast seemed near,
 Sharks hovered thick along that white sea-brink.
The boats could hold? — not all ; and it was clear
  She was about to sink.

---

[1] **The Birkenhead**: an English war-steamer was wrecked on a reef on the African coast in 1852. She had on board, her crew, one hundred and thirty-two in number, and about five hundred other persons consisting of soldiers with their wives and children. The women and children were sent off in the boats. The men remained on board to face almost certain death. Many of them were young soldiers who had been but a short time in the service, but they were as patient and resolute as veterans. All of these brave men were swept into the sea by the waves, and nearly all were lost. They died that others might live.

"Out with those boats, and let us haste away,"
  Cried one, "ere yet yon sea the bark devours."
The man thus clamoring was, I scarce need say,
    No officer of ours.

We knew our duty better than to care
  For such loose babblers, and made no reply,
Till our good colonel gave the word, and there
    Formed us in line to die.

There rose no murmur from the ranks, no thought,
  By shameful strength, unhonored life to seek;
Our post to quit we were not trained, nor taught
    To trample down the weak.

So we made women with their children go,
  The oars ply back again, and yet again;
Whilst, inch by inch, the drowning ship sank low,
    Still under steadfast men.

What follows, why recall? The brave who died,
  Died without flinching in the bloody surf;
They sleep as well, beneath that purple tide,
    As others, under turf; —

They sleep as well, and, roused from their wild grave,
  Wearing their wounds like stars, shall rise again,
Joint-heirs with Christ, because they bled to save
    His weak ones, not in vain.

If that day's work no clasp[1] or medal mark,
  If each proud heart no cross of bronze[2] may press,

[1] **Clasp**: here, a decoration of honor.
[2] **Cross of bronze**: a cross given by Queen Victoria to men who have distinguished themselves by brave deeds in battle or otherwise.

Nor cannon thunder loud from Tower and Park,[1]
  This feel we, none the less:

That those whom God's high grace there saved from ill —
  Those also, left His martyrs in the bay —
Though not by siege, though not in battle, still
  Full well had earned their pay.

Sir Francis Hastings Doyle.

[1] Tower and Park: the Tower of London and Hyde Park, London, where salutes are fired in honor of great victories.

THE SONG OF THE CAMP.[1]

———•◦•———

" GIVE us a song!" the soldiers cried,
   The outer trenches guarding,
When the heated guns of the camps allied
   Grew weary of bombarding.

The dark Redan,[2] in silent scoff,
   Lay, grim and threatening, under;
And the tawny mound of the Malakoff [3]
   No longer belched its thunder.

There was a pause.   A guardsman said:
   " We storm the forts to-morrow;
Sing while we may, another day
   Will bring enough of sorrow."

They lay along the battery's side,
   Below the smoking cannon, —
Brave hearts, from Severn and from Clyde,[4]
   And from the banks of Shannon.[5]

They sang of love, and not of fame;
   Forgot was Britain's glory;

[1] Song of the Camp: an incident of the English and French siege of the Russian stronghold of Sebastopol in the Crimean War, 1855.
   [2] Redan: a Russian fort.   [4] Severn and Clyde: rivers of Britain.
   [3] Malakoff: a Russian fort.   [5] Shannon: a river of Ireland.

Each heart recalled a different name,
   But all sang *Annie Laurie*.[1]

Voice after voice caught up the song,
   Until its tender passion
Rose like an anthem, rich and strong,
   Their battle-eve confession.

Dear girl, her name he dared not speak,
   But, as the song grew louder,
Something upon the soldier's cheek
   Washed off the stains of powder.

Beyond the darkening ocean burned
   The bloody sunset's embers,
While the Crimean valleys learned
   How English love remembers.

And once again a fire of hell
   Rained on the Russian quarters,
With scream of shot, and burst of shell,
   And bellowing of the mortars!

[1] **Annie Laurie:** a famous Scotch song, beginning:—

> "Maxwelton banks are bonnie,
>   Where early fa's the dew;
>   Where me and Annie Laurie
>   Made up the promise true;
>
> Made up the promise true,
>   And never forget will I;
>   And for bonnie Annie Laurie
>   I'll lay me down and die."
>
>   See J. T. FIELDS, *British Poetry*.

And Irish Nora's eyes are dim
  For a singer, dumb and gory;
And English Mary mourns for him
  Who sang of *Annie Laurie.*

Sleep, soldiers! still in honored rest
  Your truth and valor wearing;
The bravest are the tenderest, —
  The loving are the daring.

BAYARD TAYLOR

THE "REVENGE." [1]

A Ballad of the Fleet.

August, 1591.

At Flores in the Azores, Sir Richard Grenville lay,
And a pinnace,[2] like a fluttered bird, came **flying** from
    far away :
"Spanish ships-of-war at sea! we have sighted fifty-
    three!"
Then sware **Lord** Thomas Howard: "'Fore [3] God I am
    no coward ;
But I cannot meet them here, for **my ships** are out of
    gear,
And the half **my men are sick.** I must fly but follow
    quick.
We are six ships of the line ; [4] can **we fight with** fifty-
    three?"

[1] **During the** war between Queen Elizabeth of England and Philip II. of Spain, Sir **Richard** Grenville, commander of the *Revenge*, was overtaken at the Azores (1591) by fifty-three Spanish men-of-war, several of them of immense size and carrying a great number of heavy guns. The *Revenge* was a small vessel, and one of a fleet of six. Five of the English ships fled from so unequal and hopeless a fight; but Grenville refused to accompany them. He with his crew fought the Spaniards all alone all the afternoon and following night. Finally the little *Revenge* could hold out no longer, and the enemy took the ship. Sir Richard, **who** was mortally wounded, was **carried on board of one of the Spanish ships.** His last words were, "Here **die I, Richard Grenville, with a joyful and** quiet mind; for I have ended my **life as a** good soldier ought to do, **who** has fought for his country and his queen, for his honor and religion."

[2] **Pinnace:** a small sailing-vessel.   [3] **'Fore:** before.

[4] **Ships of the line** men-of-war large enough to take their place in line of battle.

Then spake Sir Richard Grenville : " I know you are
     no coward ;
You fly them for a moment to fight with them again.
But I've ninety men and more that are lying sick ashore.
I should count myself the coward if I left them, my
     Lord Howard,
To these Inquisition [1] dogs and the devildoms [2] of
     Spain."

So Lord Howard passed away with five ships of war
     that day,
Till he melted like a cloud in the silent summer heaven;
But Sir Richard bore in hand all his sick men from the
     land
Very carefully and slow,
Men of Bideford in Devon,[3]
And we laid them on the ballast down below ;
For we brought them all aboard,
And they blest him in their pain, that they were not
     left to Spain,
To the thumbscrew [4] and the stake, for the glory of the
     Lord.

He had only a hundred seamen to work the ship and
     to fight,

---

[1] **Inquisition**: a Roman Catholic tribunal for inquiring into and punish-
ing heresy. It was established in 1233. It was most active in Spain, where
multitudes of Mohammedans and Jews secretly practised their religion. It
never obtained a real foothold in Germany, and never in England, though
both countries were formerly zealous upholders of the Catholic faith. The
Inquisition practically ceased to exist, even in Spain, many years ago.

[2] **Devildoms**: here, cruelties.

[3] **Devon**: Devonshire, England.

[4] **Thumbscrew**: an instrument of torture for crushing the thumbs.

And he sailed away from Flores till the Spaniard came
  in sight,
With his huge sea-castles [1] heaving upon the weather-
  bow.[2]
" Shall we fight or shall we fly ?
Good Sir Richard, tell us now,
For to fight is but to die !
There'll be little of us left by the time this sun be set."
And Sir Richard said again : " We be all good English-
  men.
Let us bang these dogs of Seville, the children of the
  devil,
For I never turned my back upon don [3] or devil yet."

Sir Richard spoke and he laughed, and we roared a
  hurrah, and so
The little *Revenge* ran on sheer into the heart of the
  foe,
With her hundred fighters on deck, and her ninety sick
  below ;
For half of their fleet to the right and half to the left
  were seen,
And the little *Revenge* ran on through the long sea-
  lane between.

Thousands of their soldiers looked down from their
  decks and laughed,
Thousands of their seamen made mock at the mad little
  craft

---

[1] **Sea-castles** : the Spanish vessels were built very high at the bow and
stern, so that they loomed up like castles.

[2] **Weather-bow: the** side of a ship's bow against which the wind strikes.

[3] **Don** : a Spanish title like our Mr., but here equivalent to Spaniard.

Running on and on, till delayed
By their mountain-like *San Philip* that, of fifteen hun-
    dred tons,
And up-shadowing high **above** us with her yawning
    tiers of guns,
Took **the breath** from our sails, and we stayed.

And while now the great *San Philip* hung above us
    like a cloud,
Whence the thunderbolt will fall
Long and loud,
Four galleons [1] **drew** away
From the Spanish fleet that day,
And two upon the larboard [2] **and two** upon the star-
    board [3] **lay,**
And the battle-thunder [4] broke from them all.

But anon the great *San Philip,* she bethought herself
    and went,
Having that within **her womb that had left her** ill-
    content;
And the rest they came aboard us, and they fought us
    hand to hand,
For a dozen times they **came with** their pikes and **mus-**
    queteers,[5]
And a **dozen** times **we shook 'em off** as a **dog** that
    shakes his ears,
When he leaps from the water to the land.

[1] **Galleons** : large vessels.
[2] **Larboard** : the left side of a ship.
[3] **Starboard** : the right side **of** a ship.
[4] **Battle-thunder** : discharge of the **guns** ; broadsides.
[5] **Musqueteers** : men armed **with muskets.**

And the sun went down, and the stars came out far
  over the summer sea,
But never a moment ceased the fight of the one and
  the fifty-three.
Ship after ship, the whole night long, their high-built
  galleons came,
Ship after ship, the whole night long, with her battle-
  thunder and flame ;
Ship after ship, the whole night long, drew back with
  her dead and her shame.
For some were sunk and many were shattered, and so
  could fight us no more —
God of battles, was ever a battle like this in the world
  before ?

For he [1] said " Fight on ! fight on ! "
Though his vessel was all but a wreck ;
And it chanced that, when half of the summer night
  was gone,
With a grisly [2] wound to be drest, he had left the deck,
But a bullet struck him that was dressing it suddenly
  dead,
And himself, he was wounded again in the side and the
  head.
And he said " Fight on ! fight on ! "

And the night went down, and the sun smiled out far
  over the summer sea,
And the Spanish fleet with broken sides lay round us
  all in a ring ;

---

[1] He: Sir Richard.   [2] Grisly: terrible.

But they dared not touch us again, for they **feared** that
   we still could sting,
So they watched what the end would **be.**
And we had not fought them **in vain,**
But in perilous plight were we,
Seeing forty of **our** poor hundred were slain,
And half of the rest of us maimed for life
In the crash of the cannonades and the desperate strife ;
And the sick men down in the hold were most of them
   stark and cold,
And the pikes were all broken or bent, and the powder
   was all of it spent ;
And the masts **and** the rigging were lying over the
   side ;
But Sir Richard cried in his English pride,
" **We have** fought such a fight, for a day and a night,
As may never be fought again !
We have won great glory, my **men !**
And a day less or more
At sea or ashore,
We **die** — does it matter when ?
Sink me the ship, Master Gunner — sink her, split her
   in twain !
Fall into the hands of God, **not into** the hands of
   Spain ! "

And **the gunner said " Ay,** ay," but the seamen **made**
   reply :
" **We** have children, **we have wives,**
And the Lord hath spared **our** lives.
We will make the Spaniard promise, if we yield, to let
   us go ;

We shall live to fight again and to strike another blow."
And the lion [1] there lay dying, and they yielded to the
　　foe.

And the stately Spanish men to their flagship [2] bore
　　him then,
Where they laid him by the mast, old Sir Richard
　　caught at last,
And they praised him to his face with their courtly
　　foreign grace;
But he rose upon their decks, and he cried:
"I have fought for Queen [3] and Faith like a valiant
　　man and true;
I have only done **my** duty as a man is bound to do:
With a joyful spirit I, Sir Richard Grenville, die!"
And he fell upon their decks, and he died.

And they stared at the **dead** that **had been** so valiant
　　and true,
And had holden the power **and** glory of Spain so cheap
That he dared her with **one** little ship and his English
　　few;
Was he devil or man? He was devil for aught they
　　knew,
But they sank his body with honor down into the deep,
And they manned the *Revenge* **with a** swarthier, alien [4]
　　crew,
And away **she** sailed with her loss and longed for her
　　own;

1 **The lion**: Sir Richard.
2 **Flagship**: the ship of the commander of the Spanish fleet.
3 **Queen**: Queen Elizabeth.
4 **Alien**: foreign; **a crew of Spaniards.**

When a wind from the lands they had ruined awoke
    from sleep,
And the water began to heave and the weather to moan,
And or ever that evening ended, a great gale blew,
And a wave like the wave that is raised by an earth-
    quake grew,
Till it smote on their hulls and their sails and their
    masts and their flags,
And the whole sea plunged and fell on the shot-shat-
    tered navy of Spain,
And the little *Revenge* herself went down by the island
    crags,
To be lost evermore in the main.[1]

ALFRED TENNYSON.

[1] **Main** : the open or high sea.

THE EVE OF WATERLOO.[1]

THERE was a sound of revelry by night,
  And Belgium's capital had gathered then
Her beauty and her chivalry, and bright
  The lamps shone o'er fair women and brave men.
A thousand hearts beat happily; and when
  Music arose with its voluptuous swell,
Soft eyes looked love to eyes which spake again,
  And all went merry as a marriage bell;
  But hush! hark! a deep sound strikes like a rising
    knell!

Did ye not hear it?—No; 'twas but the wind,
  Or the car[2] rattling o'er the stony street;

---

[1] The battle of Waterloo was fought on Sunday, June 18, 1815, at Water-loo, near Brussels.

The opposing forces were those of Napoleon on the one side, and the allied English and Prussian armies under Wellington and Blucher (Bloo'ker) on the other.

The battle resulted in a decisive victory for the allies, and the final downfall of Napoleon, who was not long after banished to St. Helena, where he died.

Three nights before the battle the Duchess of Richmond gave a ball in Brussels at which the Duke of Wellington is said to have been present.

Wellington received news of the advance of the French on that evening, June 15, but the information was kept secret in order not to alarm the people of Brussels. In the course of the evening, the Duke sent many of his officers from the ball-room to their posts, and he eventually followed them to prepare for the great battle.

[2] Car: here, poetically used of any vehicle.

On with the dance! let joy be unconfined;
  No sleep till morn, when youth and pleasure meet
To chase the glowing hours with flying feet.
But hark!—that heavy sound breaks in once more,
  As if the clouds its echo would repeat;
And nearer, clearer, deadlier than before;
Arm! arm! it is—it is—the cannon's opening roar!

Within a windowed niche of that high hall [1]
  Sate Brunswick's fated chieftain; [2] he did hear
That sound the first amidst the festival,
  And caught its tone with death's prophetic ear;
  And when they smiled because he deemed it near,
His heart more truly knew that peal too well
  Which stretched his father on a bloody bier,
And roused the vengeance blood alone could quell;
He rushed into the field, and, foremost fighting, fell.

Ah! then and there was hurrying to and fro,
  And gathering tears, and tremblings of distress,
And cheeks all pale, which, but an hour ago,
  Blushed at the praise of their own loveliness.
  And there were sudden partings, such as press
The life from out young hearts, and choking sighs
  Which ne'er might be repeated; who would guess
If ever more should meet those mutual eyes,
Since upon night so sweet such awful morn could rise!

---

[1] **The hall**: the hall where the ball was given is no longer standing. It was near the centre of the modern city of Brussels.

[2] **Brunswick's fated chieftain**: Frederick William, the German Duke of Brunswick; he fought with the allies, and was killed in the battle of Quatre Bras, June 16, two days before the great and final battle of Waterloo.

And there was mounting in hot haste; the steed,
  The mustering squadron, and the clattering car,
Went pouring forward with impetuous speed,
  And swiftly forming in the ranks of war;
  And the deep thunder, peal on peal afar;
And near, the beat of the alarming drum
  Roused up the soldier ere the morning star;
While thronged the citizens with terror dumb,
Or whispering, with white lips — " The foe! they come!
    they come!"

Lord Byron (from Childe Harold).

HOHENLINDEN.[1]

On Linden [2] when the sun was low,
All bloodless lay the untrodden snow,
And dark as winter was the flow
Of Iser,[3] rolling rapidly.

But Linden saw another sight
When the drum beat, at dead of night,
Commanding fires of death to light
The darkness of her scenery.

By torch and trumpet fast arrayed
Each horseman drew his battle blade,
And furious every charger neighed,
To join the dreadful revelry.

Then shook the hills with thunder riven,
Then rushed the steed to battle driven,
And louder than the bolts of heaven
Far flashed the red artillery.

[1] Hohenlinden: this is a little village of Upper Bavaria situated in a pine forest on the river Iser, about twenty miles from Munich. Here in December, 1800, the combined French and Bavarian forces under General Moreau, representing Napoleon, gained a decisive victory over the Austrians. The battle was fought in the forest, in the midst of a snowstorm so blinding that it is said that the armies could only see each other by the flash of their guns.

The Austrian ruler was obliged to accept such terms of peace as Napoleon saw fit to offer, as the only means of saving his capital of Vienna.

.[2] Linden: a contraction of Hohenlinden.   [3] Iser (Ee'zer).

And redder yet those fires shall glow
On Linden's hills of blood-stained snow,
And darker yet shall be the flow
Of Iser, rolling rapidly.

'Tis morn, but scarce yon lurid[1] sun
Can pierce the war-clouds, rolling dun,
Where furious Frank[2] and fiery Hun[3]
Shout in their sulphurous canopy.

The combat deepens.   On, ye brave,
Who rush to glory, or the grave!
Wave, Munich,[4] all thy banners wave!
And charge with all thy chivalry!

Ah! few shall part where many meet!
The snow shall be their winding-sheet,
And every turf beneath their feet
Shall be a soldier's sepulchre.

THOMAS CAMPBELL.

[1] **Lurid**: pale yellow, dismal.
[2] **Frank**: here, a name given to the French.
[3] **Hun**: here, applied to the Austrians.
[4] **Munich** (Mu'nik): the capital of Bavaria.

THE HAPPY WARRIOR.

WHO is the happy warrior? who is he
Whom every man in arms should wish to be?

*   *   *   *   *   *

— 'Tis he whose law is reason; who depends
Upon that law as on the best of friends;

*   *   *   *   *   *

— Who, if he rise to station of command,
Rises by open means; and there will stand
On honorable terms, or else retire,
And in himself possess his own desire;
Who comprehends his trust, and to the same
Keeps faithful with a singleness of aim;
And therefore does not stoop, nor lie in wait
For wealth, or honors, or for worldly state:
Whom they must follow; on whose head must fall,
Like showers of manna, if they come at all.

*   *   *   *   *   *

Who if he be called upon to face
Some awful moment to which Heaven has joined
Great issues, good or bad for human kind,
Is happy as a lover; and attired
With sudden brightness like a man inspired;
And through the heat of conflict, keeps the law
In calmness made, and sees what he foresaw;

Or if an unexpected call succeed,
Come when it will, is equal to the need:

   *   *   *   *   *   *

Who, whether praise of him must walk the earth
Forever, and to noble deeds give birth,
Or he must go to dust without his fame,
And leave a dead, unprofitable name, —
Finds comfort in himself and in his cause;
And while the mortal mist is gathering, draws
His breath in confidence of Heaven's applause:
This is the happy warrior: this is he
Whom every man in arms should wish to be.

                       WILLIAM WORDSWORTH.

ABRAHAM LINCOLN.

You lay a wreath on murdered Lincoln's bier!
You who with mocking pencil wont to trace,
Broad for the self-complacent British sneer,
His **length of shambling limb, his furrowed face,**

His gaunt, gnarled hands, his unkempt, bristling hair,
His garb uncouth, his bearing ill at ease,
His lack of all we prize as debonair,[1]
Of power or will to shine, of art to **please**!

You, whose smart pen backed up **the** pencil's **laugh,**
Judging each step, as though the way were plain ;
Reckless, so it could point its paragraph
Of chief's perplexity, or people's pain!

Beside **this** corpse, that bears **for** winding-sheet
The stars and stripes he lived to rear anew,
Between the mourners at **his** head **and** feet,
Say, scurrile jester, is there room for *you?*

Yes, **he had lived to shame me from my sneer** —
To blame my pencil and confute my pen —
To make me own this hind, of princes peer,
This rail-splitter a true-born king of men.

---

[1] **Debonair: courteous, elegant.**

My shallow judgment I had learnt to rue,
Noting how to occasion's height he rose;
How his quaint wit made home-truth seem more true;
How, iron-like, his temper grew by blows;

How humble, yet how hopeful he could be;
How in good fortune and in ill the same;
Nor bitter in success, nor boastful he,
Thirsty for gold, nor feverish for fame.

He went about his work — such work as few
Ever had laid on head, and heart, and hand —
As one who knows where there's a task to do,
Man's honest will must Heaven's good grace command;

Who trusts the strength will with the burden grow,
That God makes instruments to work his will,
If but that will we can arrive to know,
Nor tamper with the weights of good and ill.

So he went forth to battle, on the side
That he felt clear was Liberty's and Right's,
As in his pleasant boyhood he had plied
His warfare with rude nature's thwarting mights; —

The uncleared forest, the unbroken soil,
The iron bark that turns the lumberer's axe,
The rapid, that o'erbears the boatman's toil,
The prairie, hiding the mazed wanderer's tracks,

The ambushed Indian, and the prowling bear —
Such were the needs that helped his youth to train :
Rough culture — but such trees large fruit may bear,
If but their stocks be of **right girth** and grain.

So he grew up, a destined work to do,
And lived to do it : four long-suffering years'
Ill-fate, ill-feeling, ill-report, lived through,
And then he heard the hisses change to cheers,

The taunts to tribute, the abuse to praise,
And took both **with** the same unwavering mood ;
Till, **as** he came **on** light, **from** darkling days,
And seemed to touch **the goal** from where he **stood,**

A felon hand, between the goal and **him,**
Reached from behind his back, a trigger **prest** —
And those perplexed and patient eyes were dim,
Those gaunt, long-laboring limbs were laid **to rest !**

The words of mercy were upon **his lips,**
Forgiveness in his heart and on his pen,
When this vile murderer brought swift eclipse
To thoughts of peace on earth, **good-will to** men.

The old world **and the new,** from sea to sea,
Utter one voice **of** sympathy **and shame !**
Sore heart, so stopped when **it** at last beat high ;
Sad life, cut short just as its triumph came.

A deed accurst! Strokes have been struck before
By the assassin's hand, whereof **men doubt**
If more of horror or disgrace **they** bore;
But thy foul crime, like Cain's, stands darkly out.

Vile hand, that brandest murder on a strife,
Whate'er its grounds, stoutly and nobly striven;
And with the martyr's crown crownest a **life**
With much to praise, little to be forgiven!

Tom **Taylor,** in *London Punch.*

COMMEMORATION ODE.[1]

READ AT HARVARD UNIVERSITY, JULY 21, 1865.

MANY loved Truth, and lavished life's best oil
  Amid the dust of books to find her,
Content at last, for guerdon[2] of their toil,
  With the cast mantle she hath left behind her.
    Many in sad faith sought for her,
    Many with crossed hands sighed for her;
    But these, our brothers,[3] fought for her,
    At life's dear peril wrought for her,
    So loved her that they died for her,
    Tasting the raptured fleetness
    Of her divine completeness:
      Their higher instinct knew
Those love her best who to themselves are true,
And what they dare to dream of dare to do;
    They followed her and found her
    What all may hope to find,
Not in the ashes of the burnt-out mind,
But beautiful, with danger's sweetness round her;
    Where faith made whole with deed
    Breathes its awakening breath
    Into the lifeless creed,

[1] Extracts from the Ode.
[2] Guerdon: reward, recompense.
[3] Our brothers: the students and graduates of Harvard University who died in the Civil War.

They saw her plumed and mailed,[1]
With sweet, stern face unveiled,
And all-repaying eyes, look proud on them in death.

Life may be given in many ways,
     And loyalty to Truth be sealed
As bravely in the closet as the field,
          So generous is fate;
          But then to stand beside her
          When craven churls deride her,
To front a lie in arms and not to yield, —
          This shows, methinks, God's plan
          And measure of a stalwart man,
          Limbed like the old heroic breeds,
          Who stand self-poised on manhood's solid earth,
          Not forced to frame excuses for his birth,
Fed from within with all the strength he needs.

          Such was he, our Martyr-chief,[2]
          Whom late the Nation he had led,
          With ashes on her head
Wept with the passion of an angry grief:

          Nature, they say, doth dote,
          And cannot make a man
          Save on some worn-out plan,
          Repeating us by rote:
For him her Old-World moulds aside she threw,
And, choosing sweet clay from the heart
          Of the unexhausted West,

---

[1] **Mailed**: clad in armor.   [2] **Our Martyr-chief**: Abraham Lincoln.

With stuff untainted shaped a hero new,
Wise, steadfast in the strength of God, and true.

Our children shall behold his fame,
The kindly-earnest, brave, foreseeing man,
Sagacious, patient, dreading praise, not blame,
New birth of our new soil, the first American.

We sit here in the Promised Land
That flows with Freedom's honey and milk;
But 'twas *they* won it, sword in hand,
Making the nettle danger soft for us as silk.
We welcome back our bravest and our best; —
Ah, me! not all! some come not with the rest,
Who went forth brave and bright as any here!
I strive to mix some gladness with my strain,
But the sad strings complain,
And will not please the ear;
I sweep them for a pæan,[1] but they wane
Again and yet again
Into a dirge, and die away in pain.
In these brave ranks I only see the gaps,
Thinking of dear ones whom the dumb turf wraps,
Dark to the triumphs which they died to gain:
Fitlier may others greet the living,
For me the past is unforgiving;
I with uncovered head
Salute the sacred dead,
Who went and who returned not. — Say not so!

---

[1] Pæan : a song of triumph.

'Tis not the grapes of Canaan that repay,[1]
But the high faith that failed not by the way;
Virtue treads paths that end not in the grave;
No ban [2] of endless night exiles the brave;
  And to the saner mind
We rather seem the dead that stayed behind.
Blow, trumpets, all your exultations blow!
For never shall their aureoled [3] presence lack :
I see them muster in a gleaming row,
With ever-youthful brows that nobler show;
We find in our dull road their shining track;
  In every nobler mood
We feel the orient [4] of their spirit glow,
Part of our life's unalterable good,
Of all our saintlier aspiration;
  They come transfigured back,
Secure from change in their high-hearted ways,
Beautiful evermore, and with the rays
Of morn on their white Shields of Expectation!

Bow down, dear land, for thou hast found release!
 Thy God, in these distempered days,
 Hath taught thee the sure wisdom of His ways,
And through thine enemies hath wrought thy peace!
  Bow down in prayer and praise!
O Beautiful! my Country! ours once more!
Smoothing thy gold of war-dishevelled hair
O'er such sweet brows as never other wore,

---

[1] Grapes of Canaan: see Numbers xiii. 17-30.
[2] Ban curse.
[3] Au'reoled: surrounded by a halo of holy light.
[4] Orient: the dawning or perfect light.

And letting thy set **lips,**
    Freed from wrath's pale **eclipse,**
The rosy edges of their smile lay bare,
What words divine of lover or of poet
Could tell our love and make thee know it,
Among **the** Nations bright beyond compare?
    What were our lives without thee?
    What **all** our lives to save thee?
    We reck [1] not what we gave thee,
    We will **not dare to** doubt thee,
But ask whatever else, and we will dare!

JAMES RUSSELL LOWELL

[1] **Reck**: care.

SONG OF THE SWORD.[1]

THOU sword at my left side,
What means thy flash of pride?
Thou smilest so on me,
I take delight in thee.
    Hurrah!

" I grace a warrior's side,
And hence my flash of pride;
What rapture thus to be
The guardian of the free!"
    Hurrah!

Good sword, yes, I *am* free,
And fondly I love thee,
As wert thou, at my side,
My sweet affianced bride.
    Hurrah!

" And I to thee, by Heaven,
My light steel life have given;
O were the knot but tied!
When wilt thou fetch thy bride?"
    Hurrah!

[1] Charles Theodore **Körner** (Kur'ner), a young German poet and soldier, was killed in 1813, while fighting for his country against the forces of Napoleon. He was but twenty-two when he died. He wrote this song a few hours before his death, and had just finished reading it to a companion when the signal was given for battle. His comrades buried him at the foot of an old oak on the battle-field, and cut his name deep in the bark of the tree. This poem is, however, his best monument.

The clanging trumps betray
The blushing bridal day;
When cannons, far and wide,
Shall roar, I'll fetch my bride.
          Hurrah!

" O blessed, blessed meeting!
My heart is wildly beating;
Come, bridegroom, come for **me**;
My garland waiteth thee."
          Hurrah!

Why in thy sheath doth clash,
As wouldst thou brightly flash
In battle, wild and proud?
Why clashest thou so **loud**?
          Hurrah!

" Yes, in my sheath I clash;
I long to gleam and flash
In battle, wild and proud.
'Tis why I clash so loud."
          Hurrah!

Stay in thy narrow cell;
What **wilt** thou here?   O tell!
In thy small chamber bide,
Soon will I fetch my bride.
          Hurrah!

" O do not long delay!
To Love's fair fields away,
Where blood-red roses blow,
And death blooms round us so!"
          Hurrah!

Then quit thy sheath that I
On thee may feast mine eye.
Come forth, my sword, and view
The Father's mansion blue!
        Hurrah!

" O lovely blue expanse!
Where golden sunbeams dance,
How in the nuptial reel
Will gleam the bridal steel!"
        Hurrah!

Up, warriors! awake,
Ye German brave!   O take,
Should not your hearts be warm,
Your bride into your arm.
        Hurrah!

At first she did but cast
A stolen glance; at last
Hath truly God allied
The right hand to the bride.
        Hurrah!

Then press with fervent zeal
The bridal lips of steel
To thine; and woe betide
Him who deserts his bride!
        Hurrah!

Now let her sing and clash,
That glowing sparks may flash!
Morn wakes in nuptial pride —
Hurrah, thou Iron Bride!
        Hurrah!   From the German of KÖRNER.

SHERIDAN'S RIDE.[1]

OCTOBER 19, 1864.

Up from the South at break of day,
Bringing to Winchester fresh dismay,
The affrighted air with a shudder bore,
Like a herald in haste, to the chieftain's door,
The terrible grumble, and rumble, and roar,
Telling the battle was on once more,
And Sheridan twenty miles away.

And wider still those billows of war
Thundered along the horizon's bar;
And louder yet into Winchester rolled
The roar of that red sea uncontrolled,
Making the blood of the listener cold,
As he thought of the stake in that fiery fray,
And Sheridan twenty miles away.

But there is a road from Winchester town,
A good broad highway leading down;

[1] During the Civil War, in September, 1864, General Sheridan of the Union army defeated General Early with his Confederate troops, and sent him "whirling up the Shenandoah Valley." Some weeks afterward, Early surprised Sheridan's men at Cedar Creek, about twenty miles from Winchester. Sheridan was absent, and Early drove the Union forces before him. Sheridan heard the noise of the cannon at Winchester, and riding rapidly reached the field a little before noon. As he rode up he shouted, "Face the other way, boys; we're going back!" The "boys" did go back, and attacked the Confederates with such vigor that they speedily cleared the valley of them. In return for this victory, President Lincoln made Sheridan a major-general.

And there, through the flush of the morning light,
A steed as black as the steeds of night
Was seen to pass, as with eagle flight,
As if he knew the terrible need ;
He stretched away with his utmost speed ;
Hills rose and fell ; but his heart was gay,
With Sheridan fifteen miles away.

Still sprung from those swift hoofs, thundering South,
The dust, like smoke from the cannon's mouth ;
Or a trail of a comet, sweeping faster and faster,
Foreboding to traitors the doom of disaster.
The heart of the steed and the heart of the master
Were beating like prisoners assaulting their walls,
Impatient to be where the battle-field calls ;
Every nerve of the charger was strained to full play,
With Sheridan only ten miles away.

Under his spurning feet the road
Like an arrowy Alpine river flowed,
And the landscape sped away behind
Like an ocean flying before the wind ;
And the steed, like a bark fed with furnace ire,
Swept on with his wild eye full of fire.
But lo ! he is nearing his heart's desire ;
He is snuffing the smoke of the roaring fray,
With Sheridan only five miles away.

The first that the General saw were the groups
Of stragglers, and then the retreating troops.
What was done ? what to do ? A glance told him both.
Then, striking his spurs, with a terrible oath,

He dashed down the line, mid a storm of huzzas,
And the wave of retreat checked its course there,
    because
The sight of the master compelled it to pause.
With foam and with dust the black charger was gray ;
By the flash of his eye, and the red nostril's play,
He seemed to the whole great army to say,
" I have brought you Sheridan all the way
From Winchester down to save the day ! "

Hurrah ! hurrah for Sheridan !
Hurrah ! hurrah for horse and man !
And when their statues are placed on high,
Under the dome of the Union sky,
The American soldier's Temple of Fame, —
There with the glorious General's name,
Be it said, in letters both bold and bright,
" Here is the steed that saved the day
By carrying Sheridan into the fight,
From Winchester, twenty miles away ! "

THOMAS BUCHANAN READ.

THE PLACE WHERE MAN SHOULD DIE.

How little recks [1] it where man lie,
  When once the moment's past
In which the dim and glazing eye
  Has looked on earth its last —
Whether beneath the sculptured urn
  The coffined form shall rest,
Or in its nakedness return
  Back to its mother's breast!

Death is a common friend or foe,
  As different men may hold,
And at his summons each must go,
  The timid and the bold;
But when the spirit free and warm,
  Deserts it as it must,
What matter where the lifeless form
  Dissolves again to dust?

The soldier falls 'mid corses piled
  Upon the battle-plain,
Where reinless war-steeds gallop wild
  Above the mangled slain;

[1] **Recks**: matters.

But though his corse be grim to see,
　　Hoof-trampled on the sod,
What recks it, when the spirit free
　　Has soared aloft to God?

　　*　　　　*　　　　*　　　　*

'Twere sweet, indeed, to close our eyes,
　　With those we cherish near,
And wafted upwards by their sighs,
　　Soar to some calmer sphere.
But whether on the scaffold high,
　　Or in the battle's van,
The fittest place where man can die
　　Is where he dies for man!

MICHAEL JOSEPH BARRY.

CONCORD FIGHT.[1]

By the rude bridge that arched the flood,
Their flag to April's breeze unfurled,
Here once the embattled farmers stood,
And fired the shot heard round the **world.**

The foe long since in silence slept;
Alike the conqueror silent sleeps;
And **Time** the ruined bridge has swept
Down the dark **stream which** seaward creeps.

On the green bank, by this soft stream,
We set to-day a votive **stone** ;[2]
That memory may **her dead** redeem,
When, like our sires, **our sons are gone.**

Spirit, that made those heroes dare
To die, and leave their children free,
Bid Time and Nature gently spare
The shaft we raise **to** them **and thee.**

R. W. EMERSON.

[1] The battle of Concord, Mass., April 19, 1775, was the opening battle
of the Revolution. "There," as Emerson says, "the Americans first shed
British blood." This hymn was sung at the completion of the battle monument erected April 19, 1836, on the bank of Concord River.

[2] **Votive stone** : a stone or monument raised in grateful commemoration
of some event.

PAUL REVERE'S RIDE.

LISTEN, my children, and you shall hear
Of the midnight ride of Paul Revere,[1]
On the eighteenth of April, in **Seventy-Five**:
Hardly a man is now alive
Who remembers **that** famous day and **year.**

He said to **his friend,** — "If the British march
By land or sea **from the town** to-night,

[1] **Paul Revere**: At the outbreak of the Revolution, large quantities of provisions and ammunition were stored at Concord, Mass., for the American provincial army. Concord is about eighteen miles from Boston. General Gage, who had the command of the British troops in Boston, determined to destroy the "**rebel stores**" at that town, and **sent a detachment** of eight hundred troops for this purpose, and also to arrest the "traitors," John Hancock and Samuel Adams, who were then at Lexington.

The British troops embarked secretly on the night of April 18, 1775, **and** crossing over from Boston to Cambridge, began their march to Concord by way of Lexington.

But the Boston patriots were on the alert, and as soon as it was known that **the** British had started, Paul Revere was sent to give the alarm. Mounting a swift horse at Charlestown, opposite Boston, he succeeded in reaching Lexington in time to warn Hancock and Adams of their danger, and then started for Concord, but was stopped by British troops at Lincoln, and brought back to Lexington. Dr. **Samuel Prescott of Concord** had been passing the evening at Lexington, and he carried the alarm to Concord.

The British succeeded in destroying a considerable part of **the supplies** at that place **and** then began the memorable march back to Boston.

They were hotly pursued by the enraged farmers, and their march soon became a retreat, and a running retreat at that. When they reached Lexington and stopped to **rest, it is said** that their tongues hung out of their mouths "like dogs after a chase." Had it not been for reinforcements, few of them would ever have reached Boston; as it was, their loss was very heavy.

Hang a lantern aloft in the belfry-arch
Of the North-Church [1] tower, as a signal-light, —
One if by land, and two if by sea ;
And I on the opposite shore [2] will be,
Ready to ride and spread the alarm
Through every Middlesex village and farm,
For the country-folk to be up and to arm."

Then he said good-night, and with muffled oar
Silently row'd to the Charlestown shore,
Just as the moon rose over the bay,
Where swinging wide at her moorings lay
The Somerset, British man-of-war:
A phantom ship, with each mast and spar
Across the moon, like a prison-bar,
And a huge, black hulk, that was magnified
By its own reflection in the tide.

Meanwhile his friend, through alley and street
Wanders and watches with eager ears,
Till in the silence around him he hears
The muster of men at the barrack-door,
The sound of arms, and the tramp of feet,
And the measured tread of the grenadiers
Marching down to their boats on the shore.

Then he climb'd to the tower of the church,
Up the wooden stairs, with stealthy tread,
To the belfry-chamber overhead,
And startled the pigeons from their perch

[1] The North Church: Christ Church, Salem Street, Boston. It still stands, and bids fair to do so for at least another century.
[2] Opposite shore: the Charlestown shore, opposite Boston.

On the sombre rafters, that round him made
Masses and moving shapes of shade;
Up the light ladder, slender and tall,
To the highest window in the wall,
Where he paused to listen and look down
A moment on the roofs of the quiet town,
And the moonlight flowing over all.

Beneath, in the church-yard, lay the dead
In their night-encampment on the hill,
Wrapp'd in silence so deep and still,
That he could hear, like a sentinel's tread,
The watchful night-wind as it went
Creeping along from tent to tent,
And seeming to whisper, "All is well!"
A moment only he feels the spell
Of the place and the hour, the secret dread
Of the lonely belfry and the dead;
For suddenly all his thoughts are bent
On a shadowy something far away,
Where the river widens to meet the bay, —
A line of black, that bends and floats
On the rising tide, like a bridge of boats.

Meanwhile, impatient to mount and ride,
Booted and spurr'd, with a heavy stride,
On the opposite shore walk'd Paul Revere.
Now he patted his horse's side,
Now gazed on the landscape far and near,
Then impetuous stamp'd the earth,
And turn'd and tighten'd his saddle-girth;
But mostly he watch'd with eager search
The belfry-tower of the old North Church,

As it rose above the graves on the hill,
Lonely, and spectral, and sombre, and still.

And, lo! as he looks, on the belfry's height,
A glimmer, and then a gleam of light!
He springs to the saddle, the bridle he turns,
But lingers and gazes, till full on his sight
A second lamp in the belfry burns!

A hurry of hoofs in a village street,
A shape in the moonlight, a bulk in the dark,
And beneath from the pebbles, in passing, a spark
Struck out by a steed that flies fearless and fleet:
That was all! And yet, through the gloom and the light,
The fate of a nation was riding that night;
And the spark struck out by that steed, in his flight,
Kindled the land into flame with its heat.

It was twelve by the village clock,
When he cross'd the bridge into Medford town,
He heard the crowing of the cock,
And the barking of the farmer's dog,
And felt the damp of the river-fog,
That rises when the sun goes down.

It was one by the village clock,
When he rode into Lexington.
He saw the gilded weathercock
Swim in the moonlight as he pass'd,
And the meeting-house windows, blank and bare,
Gaze at him with a spectral glare,
As if they already stood aghast
At the bloody work they would look upon.

It was two by the village clock,
When he came to the bridge in Concord town.[1]
He heard the bleating of the flock,
And the twitter of birds among the trees,
And felt the breath of the morning-breeze
Blowing over the meadows brown.
And one was safe and asleep in his bed
Who at the bridge would be first to fall,[2]
Who that day would be lying dead,
Pierced by a British musket-ball.

You know the rest. In the books you have read
How the British regulars fired and fled;
How the farmers gave them ball for ball,
From behind each fence and farmyard-wall,
Chasing the red-coats down the lane,
Then crossing the fields to emerge again
Under the trees at the turn of the road,
And only pausing to fire and load.

So through the night rode Paul Revere;
And so through the night went his cry of alarm
To every Middlesex village and farm,—
A cry of defiance, and not of fear,—
A voice in the darkness, a knock at the door,
And a word that shall echo for evermore!

---

[1] **Concord**: Revere himself did not succeed in reaching Concord; but the alarm was carried there by Dr. Samuel Prescott of Concord, who had spent the evening at Lexington.

[2] **First to fall**: Shattuck's History of Concord states that the first to fall were Captain Davis and Abner Hosmer of Acton. Three British soldiers were killed. The bodies of two of them were buried where they fell.

For, borne on the night-wind of the Past,
Through all our history, to the last,
In the hour of darkness, and peril, and need,
The people will waken and listen to hear
The hurrying hoof-beat of that steed,
And the midnight message of Paul Revere.

                                H. W. LONGFELLOW.

SAXON GRIT.

WORN with the battle, by **Stamford** town,[1]
Fighting the Norman, by Hastings Bay,
Harold, the Saxon's sun, **went** down
While the acorns were falling **one** autumn day.
Then the Norman **said,** "I am **lord of** the land:
By tenor of conquest **here** I sit;
I **will rule** you now with **the** iron hand";
But he had **not** thought of **the** Saxon grit.

    *   *   *   *   *

To the merry **green-wood** went bold Robin Hood,[2]
With his strong-hearted yeomanry ripe for the fray,
Driving the arrow into the marrow
Of all the proud Normans who came in **his way;**
Scorning the fetter, fearless and free,

[1] Early **in January, 1066, Edward the** Confessor, king **of England, died,**
and Harold, the last of the Saxon or English kings, came to the throne.

William, Duke of Normandy, a distant kinsman of Harold's, demanded
the crown, declaring that Harold had sworn to uphold his claim to it.

Harold refused to recognize William's claim, and the duke, raising a
large force, invaded England late in September, landing at Hastings on the
south coast.

Harold **was then in** the north, where he had gone to repel an invasion from **Norway.** He gained the battle **of** Stamford Bridge, in York-
shire, and then **hurried** south to meet William. In the terrible battle
of Hastings which ensued, the English army was utterly defeated and
Harold himself slain. William became king of England, and eventually
Norman wit and Saxon grit united to make the English race the foremost
people of the globe.

[2] **Robin Hood:** according to tradition he was an English outlaw, com-

Winning by valor, or foiling by wit,
Dear to our Saxon folk ever is he,
This merry old rogue with the Saxon grit.

And Ket,[1] the tanner, whipped out his knife,
And Wat,[1] the smith, his hammer brought down,
For ruth[2] of the maid he loved better than life,
And by breaking a head, made a hole in the Crown.
From the Saxon heart rose a mighty roar,
"Our life shall not be by the King's permit;
We will fight for the right, we want no more";
Then the Norman found out the Saxon grit.

For slow and sure as the oak had grown
From the acorns falling that autumn day,
So the Saxon manhood in thorpe[3] and town
To a nobler stature grew alway;
Winning by inches, holding by clinches,
Standing by law and the human right,
Many times failing, never once quailing,
So the new day came out of the night.

manding a band of outlaws in Sherwood Forest, in the twelfth century,
and warring against the rich and cruel Norman oppressors. He figures
conspicuously in Scott's "Ivanhoe," under the name of Locksley.

[1] **Ket** and **Wat**: they were both leaders of insurrections against tyranny.
Wat's rising took place in the reign of Richard II. (1381); and, though it
failed at the time, it eventually helped to bring about the emancipation of
the English laboring classes from a condition but little better than that of
slaves. Ket's insurrection occurred under Henry VIII., a century and
a half later. Just how Wat's rising can be said to have "made a hole in
the Crown" is not clear; possibly, because as the people gained power, the
Crown lost it. Richard was deposed and died in prison, but Wat's rebellion
seems to have had no direct connection with the king's fall.

[2] **Ruth**: pity.

[3] **Thorpe**: a Saxon name for a cluster of farm-houses; a hamlet.

*   *   *   *   *

Then rising afar in the western sea,
A new world stood in the morn of the day,
Ready to welcome the brave and free,
Who could wrench out the heart and march away
From the narrow, conservative, dear old land,
Where the poor are held by a cruel bit,
To ampler spaces for heart and hand —
For here was a chance for the Saxon grit.

Steadily steering, eagerly peering,
Trusting in God your fathers came,
Pilgrims and strangers, fronting all dangers,
Cool-headed Saxons with hearts aflame.
Bound by the letter,[1] but free from the fetter,
And hiding their freedom in Holy Writ,
They gave Deuteronomy [2] hints in economy,
And made a new Moses of Saxon grit.

They whittled and waded through forest and fen,
Fearless as ever of what might befall;
Pouring out life for the nurture of men;
In faith that by manhood the world wins all.
Inventing baked beans and no end of machines;
Great with the rifle, and great with the axe —
Sending their notions over the oceans,
To fill empty stomachs and straighten bent backs.

[1] The letter: the letter of the Scriptures.
[2] Deuteronomy: the Book of Deuteronomy is largely made up of rules
and regulations for the government of the Israelites on their way to the
Promised Land; some of these rules relate to the management of domestic
affairs.

Swift to take chances that end in **the dollar**,
Yet open **of hand** when the dollar is made,
Maintaining the "meetin'," exalting the scholar,
But a little **too** anxious about a good trade ;
This is young Jonathan,[1] son of old John,[2]
Positive, peaceable, firm **in the** right,
Saxon men all of us, may **we be** one,
Steady for freedom and **strong in her might**.

Then, slow and sure, as the **oaks have** grown
From the acorns that fell on that autumn day,
So this new manhood in city and town,
To **a** nobler stature will grow alway ;
Winning by inches, holding **by** clinches,
Slow to contention, and slo**wer to** quit,
Now and then failing, never once quailing,
Let us thank God for the Saxon grit.

ROBERT COLLYER.

(Read at the New England dinner in commemoration of the
Landing of the Pilgrims, Dec. 22, 1879.)

[1] **Jonathan**: *i.e.* "Brother Jonathan." During the early part of the **Revolutionary War** General Washington placed great reliance in the good judgment of Governor Jonathan Trumbull of Connecticut. In emergencies he was often heard to say, half humorously, "We must consult Brother Jonathan." From this fact some authorities suppose the name of "Jonathan" came, in time, to designate the American people.

Others think it was derived from Captain Jonathan Carver, an American traveller among **the** Indians before the Revolution, whom the aborigines were accustomed to call "Our dear brother Jonathan."

[2] **John**: *i.e.* "John Bull"; a nickname occurring first in Arbuthnot's satirical **"History of John Bull,"** 1713. He applied it in ridicule to the **famous Duke of Marlborough; later,** it came to designate the English nation.

DECORATION.[1]

" Manibus date lilia plenis." [2]

'MID the flower-wreathed tombs I stand,
Bearing lilies in my hand.
Comrades! in what soldier-grave
Sleeps the **bravest of the brave**?

Is **it he who sank to rest**
With **his colors round his** breast?
Friendship makes his **tomb a shrine**,
Garlands veil it; **ask** not mine.

One low grave, yon trees beneath,
Bears **no** roses, wears no wreath;
Yet **no** heart more high and **warm**
Ever dared the battle-storm.

Never gleamed a **prouder eye**
In the front of **victory**;
Never **foot had firmer tread**
On the field **where hope lay dead,**

Than are hid within **this tomb**,
Where the untended grasses **bloom**;
And no stone with feigned **distress,**
Mocks **the** sacred loneliness.

---

[1] Compare Bryant's fine poem " The Conqueror's Grave."
[2] Strew lilies with generous hands.

Youth and beauty, dauntless will,
Dreams that life could ne'er fulfil
Here lie buried, — here in peace
Wrongs and woes have found release.

Turning from my comrades' eyes,
Kneeling where a woman lies,
I strew lilies on the grave
Of the bravest of the brave.

T. W. HIGGINSON.

SACRIFICE.

THOUGH love repine, and reason chafe,
There came a voice without reply, —
" 'Tis man's perdition to be safe,
When for the truth he ought to die."

R. W. EMERSON.

INDEX TO NOTES.

312 INDEX TO NOTES.

Wode, 159.
Woman's voice, 91.
Word, 70.
Wot, 239.

Wrekin, 57.

Xerxes, 73.

Yeomen, 44, 52.

Yew, 168.
Young plants of grace, 172.

INDEX TO AUTHORS.

ELEMENTARY ENGLISH.

Stickney's Readers.

Introductory to Classics for Children. By J. H. STICKNEY, author of *The Child's Book of Language*, *Letters and Lessons in Language*, *English Grammar*, etc. Introduction Prices: **First Reader**, 24 cents; **Second Reader**, 32 cents; **Third Reader**, 40 cents; **Fourth Reader**, 50 cents; exchange allowances respectively of 5 cents, 8 cents, 10 cents, and 10 cents. **Auxiliary Books** Stickney & Peabody's *First Weeks at School*, 12 cents; Stickney's *Classic Primer*, 20 cents.

THESE are distinctively reading-books. Their object is to help the pupil to a mastery of the rudiments of reading in the shortest possible time and at the least expense of effort, and to provide an ample quantity of the reading-matter that will be best for practice, for implanting a literary taste, and for personal culture. In principles, methods, appliances, and material, these readers are believed to be a marked advance.

1. They are based on the right idea of what a reading-book should be.

2. They secure the best results at the least expense of time and effort.

3. Brightness of style and vivacity of expression render the selections invaluable in inculcating a love of reading and in training the language faculties.

4. Having been prepared by a teacher of long and successful experience, they are, in the fullest sense, practical, containing nothing which will not stand the test of school-room use.

5. They contain an unusually large amount of interesting material for sight and test reading, and so do not involve the expense of a supplementary series. They are therefore cheaper than other reading-books.

6. They have been indorsed by leading educators, and adopted by such cities as New York, Philadelphia, Boston, Chicago, Washington, Brooklyn, Cambridge (Mass.), and hundreds of other cities and towns. Where once tried, even as supplementary, they make their own way.

March's A-B-C Book.

By F. A. MARCH, LL.D., Professor of the English Language and Comparative Philology, Lafayette College, Pa. 12mo. Boards. 40 pages. Mailing Price, 22 cents; Introduction Price, 20 cents.

Primer and First Reader.

By ELIZABETH A. TURNER. 12mo. Boards. 122 pages. Mailing Price, 24 cents; Introduction, 20 cents; Allowance for an old book, 6 cents.

SHORT sentences, careful grading, judicious introduction of new words, and interesting matter, render the book exceedingly practical and successful.

Stories for Young Children.

By ELIZABETH A. TURNER. 12mo. Boards. 92 pages. Mailing Price, 24 cents; Introduction, 20 cents; Allowance for an old book, 6 cents.

SUFFICIENTLY interesting to hold the attention of a class, and at the same time, in thought and language, simple enough to be easily read and comprehended by children from six to eight years of age.

Stories for Kindergartens and Primary Schools.

By SARA E. WILTSE. Square 12mo. iv + 80 pages. Illustrated. Boards: Mailing Price, 30 cents; for introduction, 25 cents. Cloth: 40 and 35 cents.

THESE stories have been told to children; in truth, they are a Kindergarten growth. They charm without exciting fear, and delight without a suggestion of the immoral side of life.

Twilight Thoughts.

Stories for Children and Child Lovers. By MARY S. CLAUDE. Edited by MARY L. AVERY, with a Preface by MATTHEW ARNOLD. 12mo. Cloth. 104 pages. Mailing Price, 50 cents; for introduction, 40 cents.

THE Preface by Matthew Arnold is an ample indorsement of this book.

Memory Gems in Prose and Verse.

Selected by W. H. LAMBERT. 12mo. Boards. 160 pages. Mailing Price, 35 cents; Introduction, 30 cents.

THIS book contains three hundred and forty-six "Gems," selected from more than one hundred and fifty authors.

CLASSICS FOR CHILDREN.

In forming the mind and taste of the young, is it not better to use authors who have already lived long enough to afford some guaranty that they may survive the next twenty years?

"Children derive impulses of a wonderful and important kind from hearing things that they cannot entirely comprehend." — Sir Walter Scott.

IT is now some six or seven years since we began publishing the Classics for Children, and the enterprise, which at first seemed a novel one, may fairly be said to have passed the stage of experiment.

It has been the aim to present the best and most suitable literature in our language in as complete a form as possible; and in most cases but few omissions have been found necessary. Whether judged from the literary, the ethical, or the educational standpoint, each of the books has attained the rank of a masterpiece.

The series places within reach of all schools an abundant supply of supplementary reading-matter. This is its most obvious merit.

It is reading-matter, too, which, by the force of its own interest and excellence, will do much, when fairly set in competition, to displace the trashy and even harmful literature so widely current.

It is believed also that constant dwelling upon such models of simple, pure, idiomatic English is the easiest and on all accounts the best way for children to acquire a mastery of their mother-tongue.

A large portion of the course has been devoted to history and biography, as it has seemed specially desirable to supplement the brief, unsatisfactory outlines of history with full and life-like readings.

The annotation has been done with modesty and reserve, the editors having aimed to let the readers come into direct acquaintance with the author.

The books are all printed on good paper, and are durably and attractively bound in 12mo. A distinctive feature is the large, clear type. Illustrations have been freely used when thought desirable. The prices are as low as possible. It has been felt that nothing would be gained by making the books a little cheaper at the expense of crowding the page with fine type and issuing them in a style that would neither attract nor last.

The best proof of the need of such a course is the universal approbation with which it has been received.

Æsop's Fables.

Edited by J. H. STICKNEY, with a Life of Æsop, and a Supplement containing fables from La Fontaine and Krilof. xvii + 204 pages. Illustrated. Boards: Mailing Price, 40 cents; for introduction, 35 cents. Cloth: 60 and 50 cents.

Hans Andersen's Fairy Tales.

Edited, for school and home use, by J. H. STICKNEY.
FIRST SERIES: Supplementary to the Third Reader, for children from eight to twelve years of age. viii + 280 pages. Illustrated. Mailing Prices: Cloth, 55 cents; Boards, 45 cents. For introduction: Cloth, 50 cents; Boards, 40 cents.
SECOND SERIES: Supplementary to the Fourth Reader, for children from ten to fourteen years of age. 352 pages. Illustrated. Mailing Prices: Cloth, 55 cents; Boards, 45 cents. For introduction: Cloth, 50 cents; Boards, 40 cents.

Kingsley's Water-Babies.

Edited by J. H. STICKNEY. 200 pages. Illustrated. Boards: Mailing Price, 40 cents; for introduction, 35 cents. Cloth: 60 and 50 cents.

The King of the Golden River; or, The Black Brothers.

By JOHN RUSKIN. A legend of Stiria. 54 pages. Illustrated. Boards: Mailing Price, 24 cents; for introduction, 20 cents. Cloth: 30 and 25 cents.

The Swiss Family Robinson.

Edited by J. H. STICKNEY. viii + 364 pages. Illustrated. Boards: Mailing Price, 50 cents; for introduction, 40 cents. Cloth, 60 and 50 cents.

Robinson Crusoe.

The famous English Classic. Edited for Supplementary Reading in Schools, by W. H. LAMBERT. 263 pages. Boards: Mailing Price, 40 cents; for introduction, 35 cents. Cloth: 60 and 50 cents.

Kingsley's Greek Heroes.

Edited by JOHN TETLOW, Head Master of the Girls' High and Latin Schools, Boston. 185 pages. Illustrated. Boards: Mailing Price, 40 cents; for introduction, 35 cents. Cloth: 55 and 50 cents.

Lamb's Tales from Shakespeare.

Measure for Measure has been omitted. 320 pages. Boards: Mailing Price, 50 cents; for introduction, 40 cents. Cloth: 60 and 50 cents.

Scott's Tales of a Grandfather.

Being the history of Scotland from the earliest period to the close of the reign of James the Fifth. Abridged by EDWIN GINN. vi + 286 pages. Boards: Mailing Price, 50 cents; for introduction, 40 cents. Cloth: 60 and 50 cents.

The Peasant and the Prince.

By HARRIET MARTINEAU. viii + 212 pages. Illustrated. Boards: Mailing Price, 40 cents; for introduction, 35 cents. Cloth Mailing Price, 55 cents; for introduction, 50 cents.

Scott's Lady of the Lake.

Edited by EDWIN GINN. 268 pages. Boards: Mailing Price, 40 cents; for introduction, 35 cents. Cloth: 60 and 50 cents. Canto I., 5 cents.

Scott's Lay of the Last Minstrel.

With map. Edited by MARGARET ANDREWS ALLEN. 150 pages. Boards: Mailing Price, 35 cents; for introduction, 30 cents. Cloth: 45 and 40 cents.

Adventures of Ulysses.

By CHARLES LAMB. vii + 109 pages. Boards: Mailing Price, 30 cents; for introduction, 25 cents. Cloth: Mailing Price, 40 cents; for introduction, 35 cents.

Stories of the Old World.

Prepared expressly for this Series by the Rev. ALFRED J. CHURCH, M.A., author of *Stories from Homer, Livy, Virgil*, etc. 354 pages. Boards: Mailing Price, 50 cents; for introduction, 40 cents. Cloth: 60 and 50 cents.

Plutarch's Lives.

From Clough's Translation. Edited by EDWIN GINN, with Historical Introductions by W. F. ALLEN. xvi + 333 pages. Illustrated. Boards: Mailing Price, 50 cents; for introduction, 40 cents. Cloth: Mailing Price, 60 cents; for introduction, 50 cents.

Scott's Talisman.

Edited by DWIGHT HOLBROOK, Principal of Morgan School, Clinton, Conn., with an Introduction by Miss CHARLOTTE M. YONGE. xii + 454 pages. Boards: Mailing Price, 60 cents; for introduction, 50 cents. Cloth: 70 and 60 cents.

Scott's Quentin Durward.

Edited for this Series, with an Historical Introduction, by CHARLOTTE M. YONGE, of England. 312 pages. Boards: Mailing Price, 50 cents; for introduction, 40 cents. Cloth: 60 and 50 cents.

Irving's Sketch Book.

With full Notes, Questions, etc., for **Home** and School Use. By HOMER B. SPRAGUE, Ph.D., and M. E. SCATES, formerly of the Girls' High School, Boston. 126 pages. Boards. Mailing Price, 30 cents; for introduction, 25 cents. Cloth: Mailing Price, 40 cents; for introduction, 35 cents.

Shakespeare's Merchant of Venice.

HUDSON and LAMB. 115 pages. Boards: Mailing Price, 30 cents; for introduction, 25 cents. Cloth: 45 and 40 cents.

The Arabian Nights.

Selections, edited by Rev. EDWARD EVERETT HALE, D.D. Illustrated 376 pages. Boards: Mailing Price, 50 cents; for introduction, 40 cents. Cloth: 60 and 50 cents.

The Vicar of Wakefield.

Edited with Notes, for use in Schools. 238 pages. Boards: Mailing Price, 35 cents; for introduction, 30 cents. Cloth: 55 and 50 cents.

Scott's Guy Mannering.

Edited with Notes, and a Historical Introduction by Miss CHARLOTTE M. YONGE. 525 pages. Boards: Mailing Price, 70 cents; for introduction, 60 cents. Cloth: Mailing Price, 85 cents; for introduction, 75 cents.

Scott's Ivanhoe.

Edited with Notes, and a Historical Introduction by Miss CHARLOTTE M. YONGE. 554 pages. Boards: Mailing Price, 70 cents; for introduction, 60 cents. Cloth: Mailing Price, 85 cents; for introduction, 75 cents.

Scott's Rob Roy.

Edited with Notes, and a Historical Introduction by Miss CHARLOTTE M. YONGE. viii + 507 pages. Boards: Mailing Price, 70 cents; for introduction, 60 cents. Cloth: 85 and 75 cents.

Tom Brown at Rugby.

By THOMAS HUGHES. Edited by CLARA WEAVER ROBINSON, with a Sketch of the Author's Life by D. H. MONTGOMERY. xiii + 387 pages. Boards: Mailing Price, 60 cents; for introduction, 50 cents. Cloth: Mailing Price, 70 cents; for introduction, 60 cents.

Benjamin Franklin.

His Autobiography, with Notes, and a continuation of his Life compiled chiefly from his own writings. By D. H. MONTGOMERY. Illustrated. viii + 311 pages. Boards: Mailing Price, 50 cents; for introduction, 40 cents. Cloth: Mailing Price, 60 cents; for introduction, 50 cents.

Gulliver's Travels.

The Voyage to Lilliput and the Voyage to Brobdingnag. By DEAN SWIFT. ix + 162 pages. Boards: Mailing Price, 35 cents; for introduction, 30 cents. Cloth: Mailing Price, 45 cents; for introduction, 40 cents.

Rasselas, Prince of Abyssinia.

By Dr. SAMUEL JOHNSON, with a Sketch of the Author. viii + 157 pages. Boards: Mailing Price, 35 cents; for introduction, 30 cents. Cloth: Mailing Price, 45 cents; for introduction, 40 cents.

Selections from Ruskin.

Edited by EDWIN GINN, with Notes and a Sketch of Ruskin's Life by D. H. MONTGOMERY. xxv + 148 pages. Boards: Mailing Price, 35 cents; for introduction, 30 cents. Cloth: Mailing Price, 45 cents; for introduction, 40 cents.

The Two Great Retreats of History:

I. The Retreat of the Ten Thousand, taken from Grote's "History of Greece"; II. Napoleon's Retreat from Moscow, an abridgment of Count Ségur's narrative. With Introductions, Notes, and Pronouncing Index, by D. H. MONTGOMERY. xv + 318 pages and two maps. Boards: Mailing Price, 50 cents; for introduction, 40 cents. Cloth: Mailing Price, 60 cents; for introduction, 50 cents.

Heroic Ballads,

With Poems of War and Patriotism. Edited with Notes by D. H. MONTGOMERY. pages. Boards: Mailing Price, cents; for introduction, cents. Cloth: Mailing Price, cents; for introduction, cents.

OTHER BOOKS FOR SUPPLEMENTARY READING.

Washington and His Country. See description under *History.*
Pilgrims and Puritans. See description under *History.*
English History Reader. See description under *History.*
Footprints of Travel. See description under *Geography.*
Our World Reader, No. 1. See description under *Geography.*

THE SERIES OF CLASSICS FOR CHILDREN

HAS been most cordially approved by the press and the critics, and endorsed by teachers, superintendents, and school boards. The books are in wide use (1) as regular readers, (2) as supplementary readers, and (3) in school and home libraries. Out of hundreds of testimonials we can present but a very few : —

The Critic, *New York:* A capital series.

Education, *Boston:* These books are remarkably cheap, well printed, well edited, and should have an extended use.

William H. Payne, *Pres. of Peabody Normal College, Nashville, Tenn.:* I think too much cannot be said in favor of this list of publications, destined, I believe, to create a correct taste for reading, and to displace much that is now working injury to the mental and moral habits of the young.

J. H. Vincent, *Supt. of Instruction, Chautauqua Assembly:* I desire to express my great satisfaction with the taste, skill, and wisdom of the work. I wish it abundant success.

Mellen Chamberlain, *Librarian, Boston Public Library:* These publications seem to me to be of great value, whether regarded as home reading or for use in public school.

H. O. Wheeler, *Supt. of Schools, Burlington, Vt.:* These books form an admirable series for reading in the home as well as in the school.

F. Louis Soldan, *Prin. of Normal School, St. Louis, Mo.:* The idea underlying these books is meritorious in itself, and its execution admirable.

W. M. Crow, *Supt. of Schools, Galveston, Tex.:* Permit me to say that I regard your series of Classics for Children as the best literature in the best form that has ever been presented to the young people of our country.

B. B. Snow, *Supt. of Schools, Auburn, N.Y.:* As to results, I venture to say, from our experience, that no one who undertakes the method [of dispensing with regular " readers "] will willingly abandon it. Our reading exercise is the most interesting exercise of the day. The pupils look forward to it eagerly, the interest is absorbing, and the exercise is reluctantly discontinued. I may add that the teachers are as much interested as the pupils.

Hazen's Complete Speller.

EDITIONS AND PRICES. — Part I., Primary: 12mo. Boards. 54 pages. Introduction, 10 cents ; allowed for old book, 3 cents. Parts II. and III., Intermediate and Grammar, and Test Speller: 12mo. Boards. 148 pages. Introduction, 20 cents ; allowed for old book, 6 cents. Complete (Parts I., II., and III.): 12mo. Boards. 194 pages. Introduction, 25 cents; allowed for old book, 8 cents.

IN this book spelling is taught on a rational plan, by the aid of intelligence as well as memory. It has many features of special merit that practical teachers have been prompt to recognize.

W. T. Harris, *formerly Supt. of Schools, St. Louis:* It gives evidence of long experience on the part of the author in the matter of teaching spelling.

www.ingramcontent.com/pod-product-compliance
Lightning Source LLC
Chambersburg PA
CBHW031336070726

47496CB00017B/1132